OBSIDIAN PRINCE

PAIGE E. EWING

CITY OWL
PRESS

This book is a work of fiction. Names, characters, places, and incidents either are products of the author's imagination or are used fictitiously. Any resemblance to actual events or locales or persons, living or dead, is entirely coincidental and not intended by the author.

OBSIDIAN PRINCE
Liliana and the Fae of Fayetteville, Book 3

CITY OWL PRESS
www.cityowlpress.com

Cover Design by MiblArt. All stock photos licensed appropriately.

Edited by Lisa Green.

For information on subsidiary rights, please contact the publisher at info@cityowlpress.com.

Print Edition ISBN: 978-1-64898-504-1

Digital Edition ISBN: 978-1-64898-503-4

Printed in the United States of America

PRAISE FOR PAIGE E. EWING

"Paige Ewing has written a romp of a book in Precise Oaths. Liliana is an engaging, sympathetic heroine with a striking view of the world. One of the things I enjoyed was the way it made me look at being neurodivergent in a new way without once being preachy. What's more, Precise Oaths is tremendous fun. Liliana's quirky worldview is mixed with pure determination and ingenuity, along with a strong moral core. The writing is clean and flowing, with a host of terrific characters and great worldbuilding. It's hard to write a thought-provoking book that's also fun to read, but Paige pulled it off in spades." — *Angela Knight, New York Times Bestselling author*

"Liliana may not always know how to act with humans, but she has deep knowledge of the ways of the Fae and the Others. Some unlikely alliances and Liliana's abilities give us a rollicking adventure and set the stage for more stories to come. It's a lovely book and I look forward to reading the sequels. I need to know what happens next!" — *Nancy Jane Moore, author of The Weave*

"A delightful paranormal fantasy with romantic elements. *Precise Oaths* takes place in the not-so-distant future, when fae, shifters, and normals coexist in an uneasy reality. Liliana is spider-kin—a neurodivergent loner who tells fortunes and longs for connection with others. Thrust into a murder investigation, she ends up having to work with unexpected allies to find the real killers and keep her new-found friends safe. Liliana is strong and intelligent, but she's not good at peopling. Which makes sense, because she's not human. But she is kind, loyal, and determined to make things right. I was rooting for her right from the start. This is an excellent beginning to a new series by paranormal fantasy author Paige Ewing. Fans will adore Liliana!" — *Patrice Sarath, author of The Sisters Mederos*

To my favorite nephew, Ethan, who was smart, handsome, funny, and a very good friend. He only lived sixteen years, but during that time, he saved one life, helped save another, and shared his home with a friend who would have been homeless. He also got expelled from school for figuring out how to alter the urinals so they sprayed everyone who used them, putting that on Tic Tok, and getting over a million views.

Also to my favorite niece, Lyla, who is smart, pretty, fun, and the real reader in her generation, although she also loves living in video game worlds. She got caught as a kid reading a book with a flashlight under the covers. I felt like a real author for the first time when my brother told me she was sneaking to read a book I wrote. You're an awesome young lady, and I look forward to seeing the amazing life you build for yourself.

Dramatis Personae

Liliana: spider-kin fortune-teller with many eyes, webbing, and arm blades, aka Lilly.

Dr. Peter Teague: Celtic wolf-kin, Lilly's best friend, civilian forensics bio-scientist for Fort Liberty.

Dr. Nudd: goblin doctor with healing magic, Siobhan's best friend, Pete's mentor.

Col. Alexander Bennett: Sidhe Fae prince, half human, commander of the Special Enemies and Tactics (SET) unit made up mostly of Other soldiers, created to combat enemy Others.

Det. Shonda Jackson: normal human Fayetteville police detective who knows about Others.

Lt. John Runningwolf: badger-kin soldier with cybernetic legs and nanite strength and healing enhancement. Col. Bennett's second in command.

Siobhan: Fae flower sprite with a business customizing firearms, cybernetic arm and eye.

Janice Willoughby: Liliana's best customer for many years. Rabbit-kin homemaker.

Dr. Andrew Periclum: lion-kin cyberneticist, king of the lion-kin pride of North Carolina. Created Siobhan's and Runningwolf's cybernetics.

Tray Bradley: Periclum's right hand, lion-kin enforcer, dome champion.

Daniel Magoro: lion-kin CEO of a construction company, past dome champion, now in his early 60's.

Arel Magoro: lion-kin wife of Daniel, matriarch of the pride.

Kazi Magoro: Daniel and Arel's grown daughter, past bouncer at the Mirror club.

Marilyn Bradley: Tray Bradley's estranged lion-kin wife. Mother of his toddler son, Simon.

Ben Harper: Science teacher at the middle school Janice's children attend. Pete's beloved. Normal human who doesn't know about Others, including not knowing his boyfriend is a werewolf.

William Eliot III: Wizard, part Sidhe water Fae with powerful magical abilities. Lover of Col. Bennett.

CHAPTER 1

DECISION

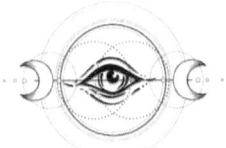

WHEN COLONEL ALEXANDER BENNETT OPENED HIS front door, Liliana the spider-kin seer noted that he didn't have to unlock it. He probably thought it was pointless to lock his door in the middle of Fort Liberty surrounded by security drones, cameras, and soldiers. A skilled assassin could walk right through all that. Like she had.

The lamplight behind the handsome Fae lit the scars on one side of his dark-skinned face as if they still burned. He looked down at her petite form from his towering height, dark brows furrowed in puzzlement. "Liliana." He looked behind her at the quiet neighborhood for officer and family housing to see if anyone else accompanied her. The light from a streetlamp on the corner lit the yard, making it clear she was alone. "How did you get on base?"

"I walked in through the front gate. You gave me permission, remember?" He'd given her a base pass with her name on it the last time they spoke.

"I never forget when someone saves my life."

"I was saving my friends. You were just in the same room that would have exploded."

He huffed, not quite a laugh, but an amused quirk touched the edges of his lips. "So, what brings you here?"

As she'd told him, if his future path continued, he would be murdered soon. What she hadn't told him was that more than once, she considered not waiting for fate to end his life and simply killing him herself. A landed Fae prince here in Fayetteville, North Carolina would draw a lot of danger to her new friends. Liliana had been alone a long time. Now that she had friends, she would not allow anyone to hurt them. "I need to know whether I should save your life."

"Still trying to make up your mind?"

"Yes."

"Well, come in then." Colonel Bennett opened the door and stepped aside. He held his custom-made wide-barreled pistol casually down behind his leg. He probably thought she wouldn't notice. She'd already seen it with her fourth eyes before she closed them outside the door. "I apologize for not being properly dressed," he said. "The gate guards didn't tell me you were coming."

"I didn't want to talk to them. They would have made me go through the scanners and stand still to let the cameras see me." The cameras would have documented her face for authorities whose notice she'd been careful to avoid.

He raised his eyebrows. "You walked in through the front gate, but avoided the gate guards, the cameras, and scanners?"

"That's OK, though. I like the way you're dressed." His sweats and t-shirt looked comfortable. The short sleeves showed off the rich dark mahogany of his well-defined arms.

"I'm glad to hear it." He chuckled. "I'm wondering if I should come down hard on the guards for being lax or put you on the payroll as a security consultant."

Liliana shrugged. "It's not their fault. I am good at getting past guards. I am content with my current profession, though. Thank you." She enjoyed her fortune telling business, guiding people away from danger and toward happiness.

She looked around. The entryway was a small, tiled area with a bench, side table, and mirror. Shiny black dress shoes and matte green combat boots were lined up in a neat row under the bench. A camo jacket hung on a coat hook on one end of the bench above the combat boots. A deep blue jacket brightened by an array of colorful ribbon bars hung from the other end above the shiny dress shoes. Keys, a wrist phone, and a wallet lay in a bowl on the small table next to the bench.

"Can I offer you anything?" he asked.

"You don't have any tea."

He chuckled. "No, I'm afraid I don't."

"That's okay. I'm not thirsty." Liliana stepped into the large open living room, trying to think of something complimentary to say as social rules required. His house was furnished like a picture in a magazine. A sleek modern room-bot dusted the baseboards. There was no indication anyone lived here but the cleaning bot. Aside from the insistence on order, there were very few clues to the personality of the Fae prince in his living space. "I like your back door." It was good to have an alternative exit in any home in case, for instance, someone walked in one door and accused you of murder. You could escape out the other one.

Colonel Bennett glanced at the curtains that were pulled nearly shut across the sliding glass door on the other side of the big living room, hiding the view from human eyes. "The back yard is one of my favorite places. Would you like to see it?"

"Yes." Liliana opened her fourth eyes since he had invited her to. The cat-slanted swirly lavender and teal eyes above her eyebrows focused through the curtains. She could see any time or place with her fourth eyes, so this was a simple matter. The yard was dark, so she refocused to see it in tomorrow morning's sunlight. "It's very pretty."

Colonel Bennett chuckled. "I meant, would you like to walk out in the back yard and see it with me? There's something I don't get to share with many people that I think you can appreciate."

"Oh." He was offering to share something of himself to help make her decision. That was exactly why she came. "Okay."

He opened the curtains, then slid the glass door aside for her. The back door wasn't locked either. The small back patio formed an island of natural flagstone surrounded by a sea of green and a riot of blooms, even in the dark of the late spring evening. The cool air smelled rich and alive. The stars seemed somehow brighter, their subtle colors visible even to her human first eyes, but she opened her second eyes anyway so she could see the beautiful place more clearly. The metallic green domed eyes on her temples brought nearly a full circle into view, lit with the unnamed colors of wider spectrums that made night as bright as day.

The Fae prince slid the door closed behind her.

Without turning around, she watched him with her second eyes. The gun was still in his hand down by his thigh. "Are you afraid of me?" she asked him, still looking out at the garden with her human first eyes. She breathed deep, drinking in the heady richness of night-blooming jasmine.

"Why do you ask?" He stepped up beside her, the breeze didn't so much as ruffle his high and tight buzzed black hair. Alexander Bennett seemed like a perfectly adapted piece of the night. His army green t-shirt and grey sweatpants managed to look regal on him. She suspected with his proud bearing, he would look like a king even if he wore dirty rags. "Should I be afraid?" His deep voice blended with the richness of the jasmine on the breeze.

"The danger to your life is still not from me." The same light wind that danced around Bennett without seeming to touch him tugged at Liliana's skirt. It tossed her thick dark hair behind her, baring her face. She ducked a bit, looking down at the prince's bare toes. That curtain of hair usually shielded her, protecting her from stares. She felt a little brazen without it.

The prince stepped out into the grass. He reached for her hand to guide her on the uneven flagstone path he walked beside. She didn't need help, but she took his hand. He had taken hers when she offered it before, even though he had not needed it. Taking his when offered seemed proper.

His fingers were incredibly long. He could probably encircle her waist with his hands. The dark tone of his skin made her own dusky olive seem pale in comparison.

"What makes you think I'm afraid?" He sounded mildly insulted, although it also sounded a little like he might be playing with her. She wished she could open her third eyes to see his mind and soul. She wanted to know what he meant, but he didn't like for her to look inside him.

He turned in front of her, waiting for an answer.

She stopped walking, but he was already very close. Their height difference meant that she found herself staring at his chest. He had an excellent chest, with broad shoulders above the top of her head. Pronounced lines of muscle were visible through the thin t-shirt. He smelled like soap from a recent shower. It took her a few moments to remember that he asked her a question.

Maybe Liliana misinterpreted his actions. She tilted her head and considered. No, the pistol in his hand made no sense unless he feared her. "You don't carry a gun when everyone comes to visit, do you?"

He held up the gun as if to show her. His teeth flashed in what seemed like a self-deprecating smile, which rang false to her. There was nothing self-effacing about this man. "Let's just say I'm a little cautious. I've heard some things about spider seers that make it seem prudent."

Liliana thought about that, then nodded. "If it makes you more comfortable, I understand."

He chuckled low. "Very generous of you." He turned, his hand in hers, guiding her further down the twisting stone path.

The spider-kin shrugged. "I could cut off your hand before you could shoot me in any case." The hard skins of rock Fae were impervious to many things. However, Liliana's first mother had not mentioned mineral Fae skins when listing the things she would not be able to cut with her arm blades. Solifu had mentioned widow spider armor in that list, but it hadn't helped much when Liliana was forced to fight them or die. In any case, the prince was in his human form, so he would be as easy to kill as anyone.

Colonel Bennett's body shifted with his next step, weight more forward on the balls of his feet, his knees bent. "Are you sure of that?" His free hand with the gun came forward more.

It was a good fighting position without appearing aggressive. The prince outweighed her by a hundred pounds of solid muscle. Liliana smiled and admitted, "Not entirely sure." She liked that she wasn't certain she could beat him in a physical fight. Added to that, he ruled both earth and fire in Fort Liberty as his bonded domain. He also knew well how to use his native Sidhe ability to control plants to deadly effect.

She was on his home ground, literally. His magic could turn even the grass against her. Yet, she wasn't afraid of him. Neither was she comfortable with the tower of raw strength walking at her side. His presence was like the cool wind in her hair. Exhilarating.

Here was a man who had been properly trained to fight. He kept his body strong despite fighting most of his battles behind a desk, and others with a wave of his hand. Her father would have respected this prince. Simon of Nemea might have named the man an enemy and killed him, but he would have respected him.

"I saved your life twice," she said. "I might one day soon save your life again. There is no advantage for you to gain in killing me, so ..." she shrugged. "It doesn't matter. You will not use the weapon."

"What does advantage have to do with murder?" he asked. She again got the impression he was playing with her, a verbal sparring game. His dark eyes studying her unshielded face felt a little unsafe, a little exciting.

"Advantage, hate, rage, or fear," Liliana said. "Or to protect themselves or someone else. Those are the usual reasons why sane people kill." His hand held hers all the time they talked of murdering each other, warm and strong, but not too tight. She could pull free at any moment if she wished. "You only threatened me in the car because you were afraid. You are not afraid now. There is no advantage to you in my death. I do not threaten you." She shrugged again. "You are not angry and have no reason to hate me, so the gun simply helps you feel more in control. I accept that. I am always armed, myself. You being armed puts us on even ground."

Her second eyes caught the corner of his mouth crooking for a moment before his features went back to the pleasant, unreadable blank expression he seemed to cultivate. His body relaxed a little. His weight shifted back to the center of his bare feet. "Well, since I have your approval to keep my weapon, maybe you could tell me what you came here to ask."

How was she supposed to decide whether he was a man whose life was worth fighting for? "I'm not sure," Liliana said. "Usually, other people ask me questions."

Colonel Bennett nodded. "That works out well. I'm used to being the one asking the questions. Maybe you could start by telling me what sort of danger I'm supposed to be in."

"Okay. We should go back inside, though. Your feet will get cold." The path had gone much further than she thought possible in an ordinary back yard, twisting and doubling back on itself. The winding path had to cross a yard far larger than those of the houses near him. Distance was deceptive with tall bushes, trees and vines on trellises turning the back yard into a beautiful maze with little benches. His house backed up against one of the patches of forest that dotted the huge Army base so without seeing the fence, she couldn't tell where his yard ended.

He barked a quick laugh. A smile stayed behind as he looked around at the rich greenery. "I never feel cold here." That smile softened his whole face. It was perhaps the first heartfelt smile she'd seen on him. It warmed her.

She looked down at his feet in the lush grass where he walked next to her. The grass seemed to caress his bare skin. All the plants in his garden faced inward, turning subtly as they passed, as if the Fae prince were the sun. As much as the inside of the house had been bare of personality, the garden path was filled with it. Here, Alexander Bennett was truly at home.

That one real smile magnified the attraction Liliana had felt since the first moment she met him. She would mourn if this extraordinary man died. She wasn't sure if she would fight for his life at the risk of her own, but she did not wish him any ill.

"You are going to be murdered in your house soon," she warned him. "You should lock your door."

They circled around a tiny artificial pond, no bigger than a cookpot. Startled frogs splashed into it, hiding under the water plants, despite how early in the year it was. A waterfall as wide as her hand, splashed over rocks making a pleasant sound. It masked any trace of traffic noise from the street. They finally reached the wooden back fence. An arched gate covered with moonflower and wisteria vines led out to the forest beyond.

"Is there any way I can avoid this danger?" He sounded unconcerned, bored even, while they discussed his near certain death.

"You ask very good questions," Liliana told him. "Most people don't." She stopped still in front of the gate, opening her fourth eyes.

Will locking his front door keep him from getting murdered?

But she saw nothing different. With the overbright coloring of a future vison, she saw him in the kitchen bending over to get something out of the refrigerator. She wasn't sure when, but it was late at night. He looked tired. He sighed as he stood up with a bottle of orange juice in his hand.

A bullet of some kind effective against Fae fired from a high caliber handgun penetrated his forehead.

Liliana controlled her instinctive shudder as she watched him die again.

She couldn't see the killer. Death was so hard to see around. The hand holding the gun wore black leather gloves. It was angled up. The murderer would be someone considerably shorter than he was with small hands, a woman possibly. Death was immediate as his blood and brains splattered the immaculate kitchen. The orange juice bottle shattered on the tile.

Liliana closed her fourth eyes and swallowed hard. Sudden death featured in so many of her visions lately that she had become inured to the shock, but she still hated it. Even if he lived, she could not unsee. His death would feature in her ugliest dreams. Either the prince would ignore her advice, or locking his door would not keep the murderer out.

Alexander Bennett released her hand. He waved his in front of her face to bring her attention back to the moment. "I would like an answer to that question."

"No. And please don't do that. It's annoying." People who thought her feebleminded because of her different way of thinking had done that to her when she was younger. "You can touch my arm or the back of my hand to get my attention, or just speak to me."

The prince's eyebrows went up. His grip on the gun became less relaxed. "You're not going to answer me?"

"No. That is the answer." Liliana forced herself to glance up at his face for a moment with her human eyes. "I am sorry. As far as I can tell, without having a high probability of making matters worse, there is no way for you to avoid the series of events that will lead to your death."

He scoffed as if he found the situation amusing. "Not sure how I could make the situation any worse." No one was that unbothered by discussions of their own death. His bland face and voice must hide his true emotions. His face was like the mirror surface of his thoughts that had been protected against her third eyes' vision with magic when they'd spoken before in his car.

Liliana held up her hand with one finger raised. "In my current vision, you die quickly. If you change things, there is a high probability that you will die slowly in agony." She added another finger. "Sometimes I see other people dying with you." She brought up a third finger. "Sometimes I see an explosion in your house. Several houses around yours catch fire with people screaming and dying inside them." She added a fourth finger. "In a few, flickery, unlikely possibilities, I see a bomb falling. Where this block is now, there will be a massive smoking crater." She held up another finger.

He showed teeth in a grimace, holding up a hand to stop her. "I understand now. There are worse things than me dying." He opened the gate. Holding it for her, he took her hand again on the other side. There were no flagstones outside his yard. Instead, soft herbs crushed under Liliana's ballet slippers releasing a sweet minty scent.

Alexander Bennett walked beside her. "If my death is unavoidable, then what can you do about it?" He looked down at her as they walked in a tunnel of vividly alive but increasingly untamed land.. Tall trees held the weight of wild grape vines and Virginia creeper. The white star flowers of blackberry brambles dotted the tangled flora around them, months early. The ground beneath her feet stayed soft and clear as if welcoming her and the tall man who walked beside her.

"I can fight your murderer to protect you." She glanced up at him, meeting his eyes for the brief moment she could comfortably tolerate.

His handsome, scarred face gave nothing away, his eyes just deeper bits of shadow in the night.

She wished again that he would allow her to open her third eyes.

"If you can fight off this attacker, why couldn't I?" his deep melodious voice asked the question as if chatting about the weather, with a bit of flirting thrown in.

She knew that smooth voice covered his emotions but was frustrated that she couldn't find out what they were. She found herself falling a little under the soothing spell of the secluded woodland location, the starry night, and the cool breeze. Some quality of his deep voice hit her in the belly like an intimate caress. It was very distracting.

The path ended in a circle of tangled rose bushes with a small carved wood bench in the middle. Climbing pink roses covered an arched trellis above the bench. Their scent filled her lungs like a caress. The bushes blocked the wind, making the little garden circle in the wild forest feel sheltered and warm.

The prince sat on the bench. He guided her to sit beside him by the hand he still held.

"The one who would take your life will catch you by surprise.

You will have no chance to fight back." She looked down at her knees, letting her hair fall to cover her face.

The big warm hand that held hers let her go. Alexander Bennett pushed her hair back behind her ear, baring one of the iridescent green second eyes on her temple so she saw him clearly painted in colors with no names. His fingers lingered in the strands. "But you can defeat this killer?"

Liliana glanced up at him with her human eyes, shifting the colors of his face back to the normal spectrums of shadowed brown. "I cannot see your murderer's face. But I would not be caught by surprise." In this starlit garden, rich with the scent of roses, she felt more comfortable meeting his gaze. "I have seen myself fighting. Sometimes I win. Sometimes I die."

She swallowed. His scars were thick along his cheek and temple, but the burns marred only his skin. They hadn't altered the beauty of the structure of his face. The moonlight made a shimmer that highlighted the high cheekbone on the unmarred side and put glitter in his eyes. Just then, she had no desire to look away from something so fascinating. "I cannot save your life without risking my own."

"Why would you do that?" He focused on her, his attention so sharp she had to look away again. It was too much.

Looking down at her knees, she fiddled with the satin edge of her quilted cape. Her hair fell back into a shielding curtain. "My friends admire you," Liliana told him. "But I don't know you. I don't have any reason to fight for you. That's why I'm here." Her human eyes were still on her knees, but she peeked at him through the curtain of her hair with her second eyes.

"Then it seems I am doomed to die." In a broad smile, the prince's teeth flashed dark in her second vision contrasting with his warm, bright skin, as if his words were a joke.

The smile was handsome, charming, and never reached his eyes.

"Unless, that is, I give you a reason to defend me." He tucked her thick hair back behind her ear, again baring the iridescent green dome of the eye on her temple. He leaned in close, unbothered by her inhuman eyes, and whispered into her ear, "Should I give you a reason?"

His warm breath on her ear made Liliana shiver. She wondered why he was whispering. There was no one else there to hear. She looked up at him with her first eyes to shift the colors of his face back to normal and tilted her head. "Yes, please. A reason to save you is what I'm looking for."

He closed the short distance between them until his lips touched hers.

CHAPTER 2

LAND BONDS

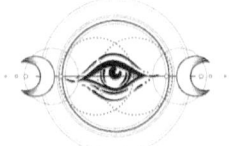

Liliana made a small, surprised sound, but did not pull away. Alexander kissing her seemed like an excellent idea. She just hadn't been expecting it.

His big hand cupped her cheek as he pushed gently against her lips until she opened them for him. He licked into her mouth as his long fingers buried themselves in her hair.

Holding a handful of her thick hair at the base of her neck, he tilted her head back a bit more so he could kiss her even more thoroughly.

Alexander Bennett is very good at kissing.

Liliana wasn't sure what to do. She never kissed people with her third eyes closed, but the prince had threatened to shoot her once when she looked into him with her third eyes. His eyes were closed, so if she opened hers, he wouldn't know. Technically, she had not given him her word that she would never look into him, only that she would stop doing it at the time.

She opened her third eyes, the smallest ones, like black pearl tears, so she could see the rich overlapping colors of his multi-layered soul.

He liked kissing her. The warm glow of pleasure overlaid all, but that enjoyment was just the surface. A complex web of different motivations lay underneath. There was a growing tinge of acid green fear, not of her, though. While he doubted his danger before, he was beginning to believe her. Gaining her as an ally seemed to be his primary motive for kissing her, a cold calculated ice blue logic that was at odds with the rest of his emotions. Firework sparkles told her he found her amusing. The image of her in his mind emphasized grace and intriguing mystery. The image was sexy and dangerous. Her fierce nature appealed to him just as his did to her. But in that view of her, she saw him recognize her value as an ally. She saw a willingness in him to bed her for that reason alone. Using seduction, he could gain what he wanted from her.

Liliana closed her third eyes as she pulled away from him. He was quite exceptional at kissing, but she did not like many of his reasons for kissing her.

He raised an eyebrow at her in question as she pulled away.

"I had three parents," she said. She knew that the statement was a leap from one part of her divided brain to another that he wouldn't be able to follow but didn't know how to build the bridge verbally.

He chuckled at the seeming non sequitur. "How did that work?"

"My mothers both loved my father and each other. They were happy for a long time."

"I see." Alexander sat up straight. "You're aware of my affair with William Eliot, then?"

She nodded, pleased that his agile mind built the bridge for her.

"Does me being involved with another man disturb you?"

Liliana shrugged. "I had three parents. Unlike my mothers, I only want men. I could want two men. But I don't like lying."

"Ah, you are uncomfortable with me pursuing my interest in you without his knowledge." Alexander put a hand to his heart and bowed slightly in respect. "No lies involved. Our relationship isn't exclusive. He sees others as well."

She knew that. While that should have been reassuring, William

Eliot's relationship with her best friend Pete's frequent work partner, Sergeant Giovanni, did not look like a good one.

Liliana stood up abruptly. She walked to one of the rose bushes, the biggest of all, on the edge of the clear, low herb circle, across from the bench. It was robustly healthy and covered in blossoms. She inhaled the rich fragrance from a large multi-colored bloom. From a creamy white center, the petals edged to scarlet as if each flower had been dipped in fresh blood. Double delight was one of her favorite rose varieties, but a pampered hybrid like that required great care to thrive. "Did you plant these?"

He walked up very close beside her, stroking one of the swollen buds with the tip of one long finger. The flower opened slightly for him, although it stayed a bud, not yet fully developed, the barest promise of a flower to come. The stem twined around his fingers. He plucked it, parting the stem without effort. The bud gave itself to him, rather than being torn from the parent plant. "When I first came here, I found the roses already here, struggling to live, choking under creeper and brambles. It must have been a garden, but it had been abandoned by whoever lived here before. It took a year of work to get everything blooming again."

"Why didn't you use your magic? You could have made the flowers bloom in a day."

He shrugged. "Gardening is relaxing. I dig in the dirt and, with some cooperation from nature, I make something beautiful with my own hands. It feels right, good. Maybe it's in my blood. My father's ancestors were sharecroppers and enslaved farmhands before that. Bennetts have been coaxing the earth to grow good things in North Carolina for four generations." He pressed the flower's stem into her palm. It uncoiled from around his wrist and coiled around hers instead. Though thorny, the long stem didn't hurt her.

She looked down, embarrassed by the simple gift. "You are a prince descended from slaves."

His chuckle was bitter. "My mother's people, especially my half-sister, Aurore, never let me forget that. My mother could care less about my ancestry in general, but I also inherited mortality from my human father. To Queen Titania, mortality is an unforgivable flaw."

Liliana inhaled the delicate fragrance of the rosebud as she looked around with her second eyes. The vivid aliveness of this place made it seem almost like a third presence. She tilted her head to one side.

On impulse she opened her third eyes, the ones that saw minds and souls. Everywhere Liliana had ever gone, rivers of green life energy ran just below the earth's surface, like blood vessels in a living body. In some places she had been, the rivers in the earth were thin, the pale Green sluggish. In the Fayetteville area, the rivers were particularly strong. In the last decade, they had pulsed even brighter with glowing health.

In the ground beneath her feet, the earth was filled to bursting with brilliant Green living power. It flowed in a gushing stream away from this point as if she stood at the center of a great spring. If the Green rivers were blood vessels, then Liliana stood on the beating heart of the world.

"The land chose you here," she whispered. She closed her third eyes before glancing up at him.

He looked impressed. "I wondered if you would be able to tell. There aren't many people who would understand."

"How did it happen?"

His eyes looked somewhere far away.

Liliana opened her fourth eyes to follow him as best she could.

"One night, I couldn't sleep, so I came out here to relax. I pulled weeds for a bit. The moon was full, so it was easy to see what I was doing, but I still managed to cut my hand on a thorn from this bush. When the blood fell on the ground, I ..." Alexander shrugged after a moment.

With her fourth vision, Liliana saw him on his knees on that night a decade past. Green rivers flowed up into him, lifting him until he floated free. His mouth opened in a silent scream of agony or ecstasy. Green flowed through his veins like blood, glowing through his human skin until his obsidian Fae form burst free. The

Green fountained from his translucent stone form back into the deep earth.

"I can't describe it really, but you wanted to know me. This place is as much a part of me now as my hands or feet."

Looking up at the face of the Fae prince, his face filled with peace and contentment, silvered on the edges by moonlight, and surrounded by the warm, sheltered garden with the rich scent of roses, Liliana had a horrible thought. The land was part of the prince. The prince was part of the land. "What will happen to the land if you die?"

"I honestly don't know. Nudd has been trying to teach me, but he isn't Sidhe, so his knowledge is spotty." He made that bitter chuckle again. "No one among the Sidhe in Europe saw any reason to teach me about land bonding. The mortal descendant of slaves wasn't supposed to ever be chosen." He put a hand in her hair, leaning down as if he wanted to kiss her again.

She needed to think. Alexander kissing her made that very difficult.

Liliana strode back up the path.

After a moment, he caught up to her. He opened the gate for her. They walked in silence side by side back up the twisting path to his back door.

While he closed the sliding glass doors behind her, she looked down at the flower in her hand in the full light of his living room lamps. It was an ivory-colored barely open bud with traces of red at the edges of the petals.

Lovely, delicate, and new. She would have to take care not to damage it. "I saw you kill Andrew Periclum."

He didn't try to get close to her again. He stayed behind her at the back door.

Her second eyes let her watch him without turning around. The broad spectrums of her second sight made him look otherworldly, like a demon from a nightmare, his warmth glowing in colors that were not red against the cooler not-blues of the curtains behind him

"Killing the king of the North Carolina lion-kin pride,"

Alexander told her, his deep voice expressionless, "would be politically unwise."

"True," Liliana said. "But Andrew Periclum broke his word to you, killed soldiers under your command with his experiments. He tried to kill Doctor Nudd who was sworn to your service. You couldn't honorably allow that. You used your bond to earth and fire to end his life without physically acting against him."

"Who do you intend to tell about that?" His gun no longer pointed at the ground. It was aimed at her back.

Liliana sighed, exasperated, and shook her head.

"What?" he asked.

She turned to face him so she could see him in normal colors. "You keep pointing guns at me. It's making it very hard for me to like you."

The corners of his mouth quirked.

Liliana realized something then. That tiny twitch of lips was a genuine amused smile. The broad smile he gave her just before he kissed her was for show, a politician's charm. But that tiny twitch, the one her comments kept putting on his face, was as real as the warmth she'd seen when he stood in his garden.

As that subtle smile touched his face, the tip of the gun barrel dipped half an inch. "I suppose that does make it difficult," he said, with more amusement in his deep voice.

He was not going to shoot her. She didn't need her third or fourth eyes to be certain of that. "You like me," she said, surprised.

"I did kiss you," Alexander pointed out.

"You kissed me because you calculated that it was to your advantage."

"And because I like you."

"Why?" She tilted her head to one side. She understood her value as an ally, but she did not see why a Fae prince or a US Army Colonel would enjoy the company of a socially inept spider seer.

"You say exactly what you mean. Everything out of your mouth is the absolute unvarnished truth. I'm not used to that. It's ... refreshing."

"I like you, too."

"Why?" His lips quirked in that genuine smile as he turned the tables on her.

"My father was lion-kin. Andrew Periclum was an unworthy king of lions. Simon of Nemea would have cheered to see him get blown into bits. I wanted to cheer, too. He hurt my friends."

She tilted her head to the other side. There was a lot more to it than that. She wasn't certain when her opinion of the prince had shifted. The kiss hadn't hurt. It was very nice. But there was more. "I was raised to respect men of honor. You keep your word. You honor your obligations, even when it isn't easy or pleasant. You protect my best friend, Pete, even though you worry he might treat you as an enemy if he knew what you were. You made Siobhan a court guardian to make her happy, even though other seelie Fae have treated you badly. And you look good with your shirt off."

He barked a startled, genuine laugh.

Liliana thought about what she said that might be funny. "I shouldn't have said that last part out loud."

"I'm not offended, Liliana." The way he said her name was a caress, filled with the genuine smile he refused to show. He set his gun down on the little table by the door next to the bowl that held his wallet, phone, and keys, and stepped close to her.

He didn't call her Madam Anna like her customers did, nor Lilly like her friends did. He made his own unique category that included only himself, neither friend nor client.

Both of his huge hands pushed her hair back from her face. He put his thumb under her chin to gently coax her face up.

Liliana looked at him with her human eyes, seeing the handsome surface, beginning to know the complex layered soul that lay beneath, even without her third vision to help. His eyes were not pure shining blue like Pete, her favorite wolf-kin. The deep brown in his eyes mixed with flecks of gold and streaks of black held far more fascination for her. They were complex eyes that could change with the light or the time of day, or the mood of the man behind them. "You put the gun down."

"You made your decision."

Liliana nodded slightly without dislodging his hands from her face. She liked them there. "I will fight for you."

He bent down, his eyes starting to close.

"I have already decided. You don't have to kiss me again to convince me."

"But I want to kiss you again."

"If you kiss me, I will look into you," she warned him. "I always look when kissing. I like to see into people when they kiss me, so I can see their feelings and share their pleasure. I stopped kissing you before because I didn't like some of your reasons for kissing me."

He stopped, body curved down to reach her much shorter stature. The subtle smile disappeared. "I told you to stay out of my head." His touch on her face was no longer gentle.

"I apologize for not asking permission first, but I did not expect you to kiss me. You surprised me."

"Apology accepted. You won't do it again." His hard voice made it sound like an order.

But Liliana did not like kissing when she couldn't properly see the person doing it. "I give you my word," she swore precisely, "that I will never look into your mind without your permission, except when we are kissing."

His jaws tightened. He stood to his full height, his hands dropping away from her face and hair. "Then I think we're done here."

Liliana nodded. "I will go home now."

His reaction to her warning was what she expected from him. She should not feel disappointed.

But she did.

She wanted him to kiss her again. She just wanted him to do it for the right reasons.

The spider seer sighed and left.

Her decision was made. That was what she came for, wasn't it?

CHAPTER 3

DIFFERENT KIND OF SHOVEL SPEECH

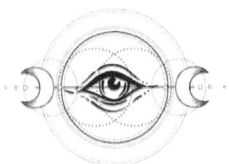

LILIANA'S SLEPT FITFULLY WITH STRANGE DREAMS THAT she couldn't remember. She had the oddest feeling that the Fae prince was at the heart of much of her turmoil. He might, in many ways, be the solution as well.

A warm, tingly feeling lingered on her lips, as if Alexander had kissed her just before she opened her eyes. The faint scent of roses disoriented her for a moment until she saw the bud he gave her last night sitting in a vase on her dresser. The hints of red on the petal edges had spread overnight as the bud began to open.

Her father, Simon of Nemea, would have respected Colonel Alexander Bennet. He was the first man she desired that she could say that about, aside from her former crush on Pete.

She wished her father could meet Alexander.

The spider-kin smiled a little at the bittersweet thought. Her lion-kin father would have growled at the Fae colonel. He'd have threatened to rip him apart and eat his liver if he hurt her. Even so, he might have considered the land-bonded Sidhe prince to be one of the few men on earth good enough for his baby girl.

Ah, that would be a shovel speech!

Ben Harper, the Normal teacher Pete loved, taught her the term. Thinking of her formidable father being all growly at a man she desired made her chuckle. Now, she understood. Her father had loved her, so he would not permit any man to hurt her. A shovel speech was an expression of caring.

Her blood-fire time was coming in a few years when she must mate whether she wished to or not. She had to choose someone to father her daughter when spider-kin biology forced her hand. Alexander might be a good choice for that time, even if he wouldn't make a good life mate since he didn't love her.

Pete had advised her to give their relationship time and patience, though. Back when Alexander had kissed nothing but her hand, Pete said men often kissed women they didn't love. But love could grow and develop, bloom into something far more beautiful in time, like the rosebud in the tall vase on her dresser. It was an intoxicating dream, that she might claim a man like that for life. An unlikely dream, but a heady one nonetheless.

Liliana touched her lips where the handsome Fae kissed her the night before. She wanted that to happen again, possibly she wanted it more than was safe for her heart.

There was one big complicating factor with the Fae colonel, though, even beyond the complicated prince himself. Alexander was involved with another man already. Her first suspicion had been that his relationship with the other man was the real relationship in his life and he'd kissed her only to manipulate her using seduction.

But that wasn't true. She'd seen into his heart and soul. Alexander wanted her. He said he liked her. She believed him. He had proven before that he had the innate honesty of most Sidhe, but he also had the Fae ability to shade the truth to his best advantage. He was not pretending to want her just to gain her as an ally, but that was still a central motivation for pursuing her.

For now.

If she wanted him to be more motivated by desire and affection, she would have to give the relationship some time and have some patience. She wrinkled her nose. That course of action was no more appealing to her than it had been to Pete when she gave him the same advice regarding his relationship with Ben Harper.

She would also have to decide how she felt about the third person in their triangle. William Eliot III was handsome and charming on the surface. All she knew about the man, though, was that he owned a very big old plantation house just outside of town. He had a powerful azrai grandmother, a Sidhe water Fae who had long ago been bonded both to Elliot River in Scotland and to the Laird of the nearby town.

That and William Eliot was also involved with Pete's friend, Sergeant Zoe Giovanni, in a way that was manipulative, not romantic and sweet. That part bothered her a lot.

Liliana pulled a long green velvet scarf from one of her drawers. When laid across her head with the ends twisted, she could make it into a turban. It would hide her fourth eyes while she checked on Sergeant Giovanni and William Eliot.

It would also look rather nice with that little green lace-up vest, and the pink chiffon bare midriff shirt under it with wide three-quarter sleeves. She matched the top with a skirt made of purple, pink, and fuscia scarves. A beaded belt embroidered with a green rose leaf pattern and pink rosebuds pulled it all together. She was delighted by her brightly-colored reflection in the mirror, twirling to let the skirt fly out. This would make a wonderful dancing outfit the next time her friends had a party.

She made breakfast, some oatmeal with cinnamon, walnuts, and blueberries paired with fragrant pear ginger tea. While she sat on her back porch swing, rocked, and ate her breakfast, Liliana opened her fourth eyes. A question would help her focus her sight.

How is William Eliot treating Sergeant Giovanni? Is he making her happy?

Sergeant Giovanni sat behind her desk on base. A fancy thin gold box full of confections sat on her desk, open. She offered Pete one of the little chocolate-covered candies inside. "They're amazing," Giovanni said.

Pete grabbed one at random and popped it into his mouth. Nodding, he said, "Can't argue with the guy's taste in chocolate.

Or, women, for that matter." He winked at his friend. "I'm happy for you, Zoe."

"Who are you, and what have you done with Dr. Peter Teague?" Zoe said, her face scrunched suspiciously. "I know you don't like William."

"I said to go slower. Check the guy out a little more. He shifts from being all business with logistics and spending all his time with the Colonel to suddenly wanting to take you out. It just didn't feel right."

"But now, he's okay because...chocolate."

Pete chuckled. "Well, chocolate never hurts." He stole another confection and popped it in his mouth, making happy sounds about the melting goodness on his tongue.

"Hey, watch it." Giovanni swatted at his hand. "That's a small box and it's already half gone. The rest are mine. Tell your boyfriend to buy you your own chocolate." Her face split in a very wide grin as she looked past Pete's shoulder to the door of her office. "William!"

A handsome, dark-haired young man who wore sunglasses even inside leaned in the doorway, a bouquet of flowers in his hands. "Hello, there, lovely lady. Any chance I could steal you away to get some dinner?"

"I'd be delighted. Perfect timing." She grabbed her uniform hat and strolled out of the building arm in arm with the handsome wizard.

Pete watched them go, his face unhappy now that Giovanni wasn't looking.

The vision was barely shaded as past. It probably happened just yesterday, maybe at the same time that she and Alexander Bennett were walking hand in hand behind his house.

Liliana wondered if anything more had happened. She worried about the bespelled locket she'd seen in previous visions.

When will the wizard give her the locket?

She saw a fancy dinner with even less past shading. A delighted smile lit Sergeant Giovanni's face as William Eliot fastened the locket chain around her neck.

Ah, he gave it to her last night. What happened next?

Giovanni blinked for a moment, as if confused, then smiled at William Eliot with an even greater warmth. "Thank you." Her fingertips touched the gold hesitantly. "It's ..." she blinked, as if fighting tears. "I don't think anyone has ever given me anything so wonderful."

William Eliot popped a fried mushroom in his mouth at the fancy restaurant. "Well, it should make things a lot easier."

"Easier?" she asked, voice dreamy.

"Yeah. For me, at least." He waved down a waitress. "Can I get the check?"

When the waitress came and left again, he wiped his lips with a cloth napkin, then asked, "What do you know about Pete's sword?"

"Pete's sword?" Giovanni's brows knit in confusion. "I don't understand."

William snapped his fingers under her nose. "Just give me the details on his sword. That's what I want. You want to make me happy, don't you?"

"Of course I do." Giovanni took his hand and laid her cheek against it. "I'll make you so happy."

William Eliot pulled his hand away with a disgusted look. "Well, I'm not very happy now because you haven't told me what I asked."

"Oh, I'm so sorry." She seemed on the edge of tears.

"I'll be a lot happier when you tell me everything you know about Pete's sword."

Giovanni brightened only a little, looking worried. "I don't know much about Pete's sword, though. Just that his mother gave it to him before she died when he was a kid. It's ancient. Is that enough?"

"Where does he keep it?"

"It's usually in his van somewhere, but oh! I remember. Ben mentioned that someone stole it. Is that what you were wondering about? I mean, his sword isn't something Pete and I discuss a lot." Giovanni's brows knit as if concentrating on pulling something from the depths of memory. "Why do you want to know so much about Pete's sword?"

"Just because I do, and you're not going to tell anyone I asked about it."

Giovanni shook her head as if to clear her vision. "I'm not?"

The wizard answered, "I wouldn't like that."

Giovanni's knitted brows smoothed back to a look of besotted joy. "Of course. I would never do anything you wouldn't like."

"No, you wouldn't." He stole a grape off her plate.

She pushed the whole plate over to him with a smile.

"Now, do you know anything about Alexander that he doesn't want anyone else to know?"

"You mean Colonel Bennett?"

Liliana knew Giovanni was fiercely loyal to her commanding officer. She would never answer that question.

The military police sergeant scrunched her eyebrows in deep thought. "Well, you know his dad was murdered when he was a teenager. At first, the authorities thought he did it."

Liliana pressed her lips together in anger. That was an ugly spell. And William Eliot wasn't just using it to get information on Pete's sword like Alexander asked him to. He was using it to dig up any dirt he could on Alexander himself.

I hope Pete gets the locket away from Sergeant Giovanni soon.

A vision flashed into life with the vividness of current time. Right this moment, Pete held up a frosty cup to a moon-eyed Giovanni at her desk. The locket was prominently displayed on its short chain, even though visible jewelry wasn't acceptable for an MP in uniform.

"It's not candy, but this milkshake is deliciously rich chocolate." He had two cups with lids and paper straws. Pete took a long draw from one straw, expression blissful. "You know you want it."

Sergeant Giovanni eyed the cup greedily. "Yeah, yeah, you know my chocolate weakness. Now, shut up and hand over the cup."

Pete held out the cup. "Here, now we're square."

"It's no big deal. I told you. I'm sure William will buy me many more—ah, ah! That's cold!"

The lid popped off the cup just as Pete held it toward Giovanni, spilling sludgy brown icy mess on the front of her uniform.

"Zoe! Oh, no, I got it on your new locket, too. Here, let me clean it off. You run some water on your uniform before it stains." Pete ducked behind Giovanni. He unhooked the locket before she could protest.

"But, I ... I promised I'd never take it off."

"Not a problem. You didn't take it off. I did." Pete ran down the hall to the nearest bathroom while Giovanni still seemed to be considering if that counted. He dumped the necklace in the sink like he thought it might bite him and turned the water on full blast.

He opened the locket under the water as Liliana had advised him to, rinsing out a bit of crusty brown inside, probably the wizard's dried blood, odd bits of hair, and a tiny color pic of his face. Pete left the water on for a few minutes washing every trace of anything but metal away.

Liliana checked on Sergeant Giovanni.

For a moment, the military police sergeant looked lost, wandering after Pete, one arm raised as if to stop him or call him back. Then she stopped, blinking as if just waking up. She looked down at the mess of chocolate ice cream on her shirt, and ran back into her office.

She dug out a spare uniform blouse from a bottom desk drawer before running to another bathroom, unbuttoning as she went.

By the time Pete satisfied himself that the locket was clean and emerged from one bathroom, Giovanni had long since come out of the other one wearing a clean, dry uniform blouse. She held the rinsed blouse in her other hand.

When Pete emerged, she held out a hand imperiously, her foot tapping. "Give."

Pete placed the locket back in her hand. "Um, you can have my milkshake?" he offered, sheepishly.

"Oh, that's not going to cut it, buddy. You owe me big time for that mess." She hooked the chain around her own neck while she spoke, the locket settling back in place. She tucked it under her uniform blouse. "When I get off duty, you owe me pie."

Pete grinned. "Pie it is. Never let it be said I don't pay my debts."

She punched him in the shoulder playfully. "Jerk. I have no idea if this stain will come out."

Liliana let out a sigh of relief. She stirred honey in her now perfectly brewed tea. Sergeant Giovanni was out of danger. Again.

The spider seer sat back and looked around her garden, enjoying the faint scent of rosemary from the bushes by her back sidewalk. A neighbor child bounced a basketball in their driveway. Liliana loved her little house in her quiet neighborhood. Having fought to keep it made home feel all the more precious.

I wonder how this will affect William Eliot's plans?

Her fourth vision shaded into a slight touch of the overbright future, probably later today. Pete and Giovanni shared dinner at a dining facility on base, laughing. Pete, with great ceremony presented her with a huge slice of chocolate cream pie with plenty of whipped cream on top. "Apology pie."

She dipped a spoon in with delight. "Apology pie is pretty good. Not as good as fancy chocolates, but it'll do."

Pete reached for a fry on her plate. She smacked his knuckles with the spoon she'd used on her cream pie. "My food. Eat your own fries."

Pete chuckled, licking whipped cream off his knuckles.

Sergeant Giovanni kept looking down at her wrist as multiple text message notifications flashed on her wrist phone. Her expression twisted in annoyance.

"Eliot?" Pete asked.

"Yeah. I'm not sure what bee got in his bonnet, either. He's acting weird. Said he's coming here. But not for dinner, just to pick me up. He won't even say where he's taking me." She grabbed her cover and got up with a sigh. "I'll have to see what's up with him. Maybe something bad happened."

"I'll pay up. You can meet him out back."

The sleek electric sports car with a silvery metal rose hood ornament pulled up in the parking lot behind the dining facility, away from the prying eyes of most of the people there.

Wiliam Eliot got out. He stalked toward Giovanni. "Get in the car."

"Why?" she asked. "Did something happen?"

"Because I said so." He grabbed her arm. "You wouldn't want to make me unhappy, would you?"

"Seriously? What's going on with you?" Giovanni asked, not budging.

William Eliot looked confused for a moment, then looked at her throat. "I told you not to take off the locket."

Giovanni pulled the chain to reveal the locket that had been tucked under her uniform blouse. "I didn't. What does your gift have to do with you acting so weird?"

"Get in the car, you simpering cow. I told you my behavior is perfectly normal." He yanked her arm hard enough that she stumbled forward.

As Pete stepped out into the parking lot, Giovanni twisted her arm out of William Eliot's hand, yanked off the locket, and threw it in the wizard's face. "How about you get in the car, asshole. Keep right on driving." She turned on her heel. "Men," she grumbled as she stalked back across base toward her own car.

William Eliot stood next to his fancy sportscar, holding the locket, looking dumbfounded.

Pete said, "Huh, strange that she wouldn't put up with you being an ass to her, even after you gave her that bespelled piece of jewelry."

Eliot's hand clenched around the locket. Even with the dark glasses he always wore, his glare at Pete could wither plants. "You did this."

Pete showed Eliot a lot of teeth. "I won't bother with the 'if you hurt her,' part, because I know what you tried to do. So, let's get straight to *stay the hell away from Zoe, or I'll bury you so deep, no one will find the body."*

Oh.

Liliana recognized that this was a shovel speech. But she did not think everything Pete said was figurative. He might be genuinely threatening to kill Eliot.

"I don't have any idea what you're talking about." William Eliot sneered at the wolf-kin. "I gave my girlfriend a gift. That's hardly a crime."

Pete's vicious smile gained sharper canines. "Hell, if I rip you apart, I can bury you in pieces. I won't have to dig as big a hole." The wolf-kin stalked towards the wizard. Pete stayed in human form, but his muscles were loose and his attention focused, all predator even in his pale human skin.

"Fine. Let's do this." William Eliot tossed the locket into the open window of his car. He pulled an amulet out from under his shirt. "You don't scare me."

Liliana bit her lip, her knuckles white on her teacup. Pete did not have his legendary sword with him and the wizard had serious power. Asrais were not creatures she would want to tangle with. The wizard was only one quarter asrai, but that was enough to give him considerable power.

The two men moved more behind the building by silent accord, out of the sight of passersby in a blind spot of the base surveillance cameras.

William Eliot touched his amulet with one hand. He held the other up toward Pete as if asking him to stop. He snarled a word in a language Liliana didn't recognize. An odd distortion of light appeared in a large disk about six feet across, protecting the wizard from attack.

He pulled a small flask from his pocket, poured a tiny amount of clear liquid, probably water, into his hand, and pulled it up like taffy into a long, clear blade. He shifted to a low fencer's stance, smiling back with the same hunger, if fewer teeth. He beckoned Pete closer. "Come on, wolf. I thought you wanted to play."

Pete looked a little non-plussed. He circled William Eliot, hesitating. He tried to find a way around the magical shield, but it shifted as the wizard turned to keep the red wolf in front of him.

Liliana wondered if Pete had ever fought a wizard before.

The red wolf picked up a piece of gravel from the pavement. He tossed it at the shield. It bounced off with a rippling shimmer like the surface of a pond. Eliot's smile widened under his dark glasses. He also moved like he knew what he was doing with a sword.

He lunged toward Pete.

The red wolf slipped to the side, far faster than a human could have. Pete's leg shot out, under the wizard's shield. The wolf-kin swept across his ankle while most of the man's weight was on his front leg.

Liliana smiled. She'd taught Pete that foot-sweep technique.

Eliot fell, but rolled back to his feet, the shield covering him so Pete had no way to take advantage.

Pete circled again, looking for a way past the wizard's defense.

As Eliot rolled to his feet, he slashed at Pete. His sword of water passed through the distortion of the shield without resistance and cut a slash across Pete's sleeve as he brought his arm up in an instinctive defense. If he'd had a shield, it would have been a good counter. Without a shield, it might have gotten his arm sliced open to the bone if the cut had been an inch or two closer.

Pete growled low, looking at the slice in his shirt, then leaped on the wizard without warning.

The wizard held up his hand with confidence.

Pete ignored it.

He landed on the wizard, hands and feet passing through the visual distortion of the shield without resistance, tackling him onto his back.

The look of shock on William Eliot's face was comical.

Pete looked just as surprised as William Eliot to land on the wizard instead of the shield.

The wolf-kin held William's wrist down, so he couldn't use the water sword while he punched him in the nose hard enough to smash his dark glasses. The shimmer of the shield vanished as Pete's fist went right through it.

The red wolf bared teeth that were far sharper than possible for a human. He grabbed Eliot's collar. "Stay. Away. From. Zoe!" He punctuated each word with a hard shake.

Slamming Eliot's hand against the pavement made the water sword dissolve into a puddle.

Liliana let out her breath in relief, returning her mind to the fine morning where she sat rocking on her porch swing. Her vision of the future reassured her. Pete would be fine when he fought the wizard that evening. There was no need for her to intervene in any way.

She went to take a sip of her tea, discovering the cup was empty. She had appointments coming up, but she still needed more information. Now that the young wizard was no longer a threat to the sergeant or to Pete, she could focus on learning what sort of man he was.

The relationship between him and Sergeant Giovanni had been unpleasant, but William Eliot did not initiate it for any reason of his own. His behavior when he believed her bespelled told Liliana that Eliot didn't have any real interest in Sergeant Giovanni at all.

Colonel Alexander Bennett instigated the ugly situation by asking the wizard to retrieve information on Pete's sword or retrieve the sword itself.

What will happen when William Eliot tells Alexander about the fight?

Her fourth vision shifted, a few hours further into the future, later that same evening. The sun was set, the sky filled with stars and swiftly blowing clouds. The wizard stumbled to Colonel Bennett's home, limping on one ankle. He held one bloody scraped elbow. He let himself in through the back fence gate and the glass patio sliding door, neither of which were locked.

Colonel Bennett sat on his couch reading an actual solid, paper book. Liliana thought she was the only one who still read paper books. As his patio door opened, the prince placed a satin marker between the old yellow pages and stood.

Liliana couldn't resist tilting her fourth vision to get a look at the book title. Ursula Le Guin's *The Left Hand of Darkness*. An excellent story. For some reason, even relaxing in his home, Liliana expected to see the Colonel reading something like Sun Tsu's *Art of War* or going over mission reports. It took some mental gymnastics to think of Colonel Alexander Bennett not at least thinking about his job.

Eliot stumbled into the prince's embrace. "He nearly killed me." Tears were thick in the wizard's voice, though none fell.

The prince put gentle hands on the younger man's face, studying his injuries. He had a split lip. Blood crusted around his swollen nose where it had stopped bleeding, but a dark stain of drips showed on his synth silk shirt. "I think you'll live," he said with an affectionately amused tic on the corner of one lip.

Alexander wrapped his arms around the younger man, stroking his back.

"My magic didn't work on him," the wizard whined, sounding like he had a bad head cold. "I've spent most of my life honing my magic. It just rolled over him like rain on an umbrella. He punched me in the nose right through my shield."

"Who did this?" Alexander asked. "Not many have that level of magical immunity."

"That damn dog of yours," Eliot wrinkled his swollen nose. "Teague." He said the name like it tasted bad.

The hand stroking Eliot's back stopped. The Colonel's jaw tightened. "Celtic wolves are immune to many forms of magic. I told you to get the sword without getting Pete involved. What happened?"

"Don't worry, I didn't hurt your precious red wolf. He broke the spell I had on his sergeant friend, though, somehow. I'll have to spell his pretty boyfriend instead to get more information."

"I see." No trace of emotion leaked through the prince's voice or face. "Did you get the sword?"

Eliot shook his head against the prince's broad shoulder. "No, before that damn red wolf messed up my spell, Giovanni said it was gone, stolen." He squeezed a little tighter into the prince's embrace. "Damn it. I won't fail you. I think there are a few other angles to pursue. I won't give up, I promise."

The prince hugged him, but Liliana saw the Colonel's eye roll at Eliot's histrionics. Then, he pushed the younger man to arm's length so he could study his face. "This spell you used on my sergeant, and intend to use on Pete's boyfriend, what are the effects?"

The wizard shrugged. "It makes them think they're crazy in love with me, do anything I tell them to."

Alexander's brows knit. "I can see where that would be a useful strategy, especially with Giovanni. She seems to fall in and out of love every other week. But don't use it on Ben. Pete and Ben are too close. It could cause serious repercussions."

Eliot waved a hand. "Oh, don't worry. When they've done what I need, I'll just tell them I don't want them anymore, and they'll kill themselves. With them dead, no one will ever have a chance to tie anything back to us."

"That's not how I do things and you know it." Anger hardened Alexander's square jaw. His hands dropped away from the other man.

The young wizard chuckled. He snuggled up to Alexander's broad, unyielding chest again. "I know you'd rather keep things civilized, but those spells only affect Normals. It wouldn't hurt anyone important."

Alexander's arms did not lift to embrace the young man again. Instead, he twisted his body out of Eliot's arms, disengaging. His voice went blank and bored as he turned his back to the wizard. "You said the spell on my sergeant is broken. You haven't put it on anyone else yet. Correct?"

William Eliot nodded. "Yeah, but I will." He straightened his back. "I swear I will at least get the details of what happened to the sword. I'll get it for you if at all possible. If Aurore wants it bad enough to send her pet assassins, it must be important. Just leave it to me."

He turned a cold stare on William Eliot. "I think you've done enough." The ice in his voice could cause frostbite. "Despite your failure, I will arrange for the payment we agreed on to be sent to you."

Liliana shivered as all emotion leeched from the Fae prince's previous warm reassurance. She would hate to be in the wizard's shoes. Gone from warmth and welcome to ice and rejection in a moment.

"I will no longer be needing your services, in any capacity," Alexander turned his back again on the handsome, wounded man whose eyes filled with genuine tears this time.

"I don't care about the money. I just..." Eliot wrapped his arms around himself.

Liliana recognized the look on the man's face. He had no reason to seduce Sgt. Giovanni, hurt Ben Harper, or fight Pete. Eliot had done all the cruel things he did for only one reason, for love of Alexander Bennett. He had tried so hard to impress the prince. Liliana suspected he genuinely didn't understand what he'd done wrong.

"I'll inform my superiors that your services are no longer needed." Alexander sat down. He picked up the book he had been reading, opening it to the marked page as if Eliot were already gone.

Liliana was appalled. There was no sympathy, no gentleness to the end of a relationship that had seemed well established just moments before. She had seen how calculating Alexander could be, but had no idea he could be so deliberately cruel.

"But we're the same, you and I, a mix of royal Fae and human. I thought we were forever." A tear rolled down, streaking the dirt on the wizard's cheek. "You said ..." He stumbled to a stop.

Alexander Bennett looked up from his book, his face devoid of any emotion. He looked bored, as if breaking someone's heart was a routine task for him. "What did I ever say that led you to the conclusion our arrangement was permanent?"

"I just ... I thought you loved ..." Another tear dripped down the wizard's face. It ran over his sharp cheekbone and dripped off his jaw.

Alexander gave him a blank, bored look, one eyebrow raised as if wondering why the man was still standing in his living room.

"I see." Eliot nodded, took a deep breath, and straightened his shoulders. "I was wrong." He limped out the same way he'd come in.

As Eliot left, the pain on his face quickly transformed into fury. His puffy, tear-filled eyes flashed red like hot coals without his dark glasses to hide them.

The spider-kin snapped the handle off the cup she had been drinking tea from.

Liliana despised Eliot. The more she saw of William Eliot III, the less she wanted to have anything to do with him. But at that moment, she felt heartsick for the handsome young wizard.

She had begun to consider the Fae prince as a potential life mate. Now, she wondered if she should reconsider her previous decision, and let Alexander Bennett die. His heart was as cold as the obsidian stone of his Fae form.

Anyone who loved the unseelie prince would be setting themselves up for heartbreak the moment they made a mistake.

CHAPTER 4

THREE LIONESSES

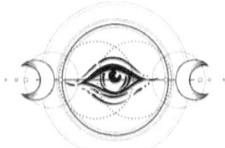

IN AN EFFORT TO DO SOMETHING WITH HER DAY MORE useful than being furious at Alexander Bennett, Liliana spent every spare moment that she wasn't in appointments searching for options to help Ben find his way into their world. Pete and Ben deserved to be happy. They were obviously a far better match than she and Colonel Bennett were. But Ben would never marry Pete, not until he truly knew the wolf-kin—not just the public part of his life, that he was a bio-scientist forensics consultant for Fort Liberty's CID—but the more secret aspects of his life as a red Celtic werewolf. That would require the science teacher to accept the hidden world of magic and creatures that most Normals believed to be mythological.

Every time Liliana tried to focus, though, she kept bumping into images of Alexander Bennett that would not leave her alone. She ignored the flashes of the prince's handsome face that continually appeared whenever she didn't focus hard on something else. She couldn't get her unruly mind to stop thinking about him, but she could make sure it no longer affected her life.

The one thing she would never do was allow herself to love someone who broke hearts without a second thought. She wasn't an idiot. Alexander Bennett was a cold-hearted pig. She would have to get over her interest in him.

She would focus on finding a good path for Ben and Pete. Her own love life would have to wait until she met someone new.

There seemed to be a hint of something that might help Ben and Pete in the direction of her favorite client, Janice Willoughby, and her rabbit-kin children, some of whom were Ben Harper's students. The possibility didn't seem very solid, though. Given time, Liliana hoped a better solution would come into existence as probabilities shifted.

A more immediate problem had to be dealt with, in any case. The day when four assassins of the Order of the Wolfhound would come to kill her favorite red wolf was almost here.

For the next few weeks, when they met in the woods for training, Liliana encouraged Pete to use combat practice to work out some of his sadness from Ben turning down his marriage proposal. He took her advice to heart. He fought as if a demon lived inside him.

Combat practice was good therapy. The spider-kin knew that from long experience.

Pete sparred with his friends so intensely that he injured Doctor Nudd. A broken ulna was nothing that the goblin's own medicines and magic and a few days' rest wouldn't cure, though. There were still a few days until the Wolfhounds would come. Doctor Nudd had time to repair the damage.

Pete was mortified that he hurt his mentor, but Liliana was delighted. She was even more delighted that he might have injured her if she hadn't foreseen it. The Celtic wolf had become a far more formidable opponent since that first day they met when Pete tried to kill her. If their one-on-one battle took place now instead of back then, Pete might even defeat her.

The red wolf's death, that Liliana had seen as certainty a few months before, now was a tiny flicker of unlikely possibility. In combat, nothing was ever certain, but as long as he had his sword on the night in question, Pete's survival was now as close to certain as such things ever were. Pete would live, Lou Willoughby, Janice's husband, would live, Doctor Nudd would live, and the assassins from the Order of the Wolfhound would die.

Liliana still hoped to be there, herself, to fight at the side of her favorite red wolf, but none of the future visions she saw included her. She did not know why, yet, but it made her glad that Pete would be able to hold his own, even against four trained killers.

In the meantime, she had neglected her business by taking time off. Several customers had been put off for weeks. She had to make up for it. Liliana spoke with as many as five or six customers a day, where normally, she limited herself to a maximum of four. That many social interactions and that much exploration into their lives with her fourth eyes could be exhausting. She welcomed the distraction, though. As long as she searched the lives of her customers for the best paths toward happiness, she avoided thinking about the handsome Fae prince who had no heart.

One day, a brand-new customer called to make an appointment. Liliana's phone number was on her sign so that happened sometimes. She knew nothing about the woman except her name, Arel Magoro. Her name wasn't enough to let Liliana find the woman with her fourth eyes. She had to know what she looked like. The prospect of seeing a new customer made her nervous but provided an excellent distraction.

She looked around her business space. Every mystic knick knack was clean of dust and placed for optimum visual impact on her new customer. Brightly colored scarves hung to decorate every surface. Her clocks were polished clean and ticking merrily. The little shop that she'd created from the dining room of her house looked exactly as it should. She gave the crystal ball a last quick polish with her sleeve to remove a smudge. According to her clocks, it was 9:58. Her new customer was due at 10:00.

Liliana sat in her chair at the small round table with the crystal ball in the exact center and three chairs waiting to be filled by customers on the other side. At precisely 10:00 AM and about thirty seconds, just after the clocks all stopped chiming, someone knocked on the door. The spider seer smiled. She liked punctual customers.

She opened the door. There were three women. Only one woman had spoken to her on the phone. No more than two customers had ever come to see her at the same time, except when she met Pete, Sergeant Giovanni, and Detective Shonda Jackson. They accused her of murder and Pete tried to kill her. The similarity sent a frisson of nervousness up her spine.

There were three chairs on the client side of the table, but the third was just meant to be a place for people to set their things that was not on her table.

The new clients were tall athletic women. The one who appeared to lead was past fifty, but more fit than most twenty-year-olds. She was a lovely woman with skin as dark as burnt oak, high round cheeks, and a shading of iron gray threaded through her braided black hair. Another of the women looked enough like the oldest that she must be her daughter. Her hair was in shoulder-length dreadlocks. The third had dark brown hair and dark olive skin, about the same shade as Liliana's from her Greek and Egyptian heritage. She held herself a lot like Liliana did when lots of people looked at her, as if the air around her were heavy.

Liliana bowed them into her workspace with the usual dramatic flourish of graceful arms and flowing sleeves. "Welcome. Madame Anna sees all. Only the truth of what is, what was, and what might be." She used the proper customer voice with the singsong intonation. She wanted to make a good impression on her new customers in spite of the uncomfortable feeling they gave her.

She sat down in her wooden chair on one side of the little round table and gestured a graceful invitation to her new customers to sit in the other chairs. Rather than sit in the third chair, the daughter stood behind her mother with muscular arms crossed in a way that made Liliana think "bodyguard." She had a good stance, solid, grounded, and balanced, with knees bent and weight shifted forward. If Liliana tried to harm either of the other two women, she had no doubt that the daughter would react in time to protect them.

Liliana approved. It told her that the women were wary of her, but if they knew anything about her nature, that would be sensible.

Looking into their faces for so long overwhelmed her. Fighting the instinctive desire to retreat into a corner, she looked into her crystal ball instead. People expected her to look at the ball, so it had the benefit of making both her and her customers more comfortable.

She started her routine with a gesture to the curtained windowsill. The decorated box with a slot on top that people put money in sat there. Few merchants still dealt in cash, or the modern equivalent, transferrable pay cards, but she did. She had no interest in digital banking or setting up accounts, even in the anonymous computer currencies. Liliana did not own a computer or have much clue what to do with one. Neither did she have a birth certificate or any other form of official identification that she could use to set up an account in person at a bank. The increasing dependency on digital forms of payment made things tricky for her for a time, until the pay cards came along. There were many times when people didn't want all the information about what they purchased, where, and when to be recorded. Pay cards were untraceable. Only the amount deducted from people's banks and put into the card was tracked. Once in, the card could pass from hand to hand indefinitely, until it was used to purchase something. Then, the money passed back into another bank's accounting system.

"Pay me what you feel is fair for truth that cannot be seen by other eyes," she intoned. "I see what is, what has been, and what might be. Ask and the truth shall be yours."

This was when customers asked her questions. Liliana waited.

The three women looked at each other.

"My daughter worked security at The Mirror club in Raleigh," the elder woman ventured. The woman's voice was a melodious alto, the voice on the other side of the phone that had set up the appointment, Arel Magoro.

"Oh." Liliana licked her lips. She fiddled with her sleeves under the table. "I am sorry about your employer," she said to the standing woman.

The daughter snorted. "I doubt that."

Liliana glanced up. It had been a long time since anyone doubted her word.

Arel Magoro gave her an apologetic smile. "My daughter came to work early that morning. She saw the security footage before the military confiscated it."

"Oh." The spider seer took a breath. She leaned to the front of her seat, weight partially on her feet, so she could spring up to run at any moment if needed. "I had no quarrel with Lady Daphne and her nest until they tried to kill my best friend. I am sorry things happened as they did."

The three women glanced at each other.

"The Celtic wolf is your best friend? Or the Army sergeant?" Arel asked, still without any sign of aggression or disturbance.

Liliana tilted her head, wondering. "The red wolf is my best friend. I like Sergeant Giovanni, but she does not trust Others, so she keeps her distance from me." Were these women also widow spiders like the Mirror club owner, Lady Daphne, and her nest sisters? Were they looking for revenge? She brought up her hands to rub her eyebrows as if her head pained her. Between her fingers, she risked a glance with her third eyes at the three women to see if they were human or Other.

Their auras held the feral shine of beast-kin. She sneaked a glance from a single, barely open fourth eye to see their Other faces. She saw tawny fur, long canines, and large golden eyes.

"Oh! You are lions!" she exclaimed. "I am a lion's daughter. I lost touch with the pride when my brothers moved away. It is good to meet you."

The three lionesses all wore identical expressions of confusion.

Arel Magoro spoke for the group. "We thought you were spider-kin."

"I am spider-kin like my first mother, but my father was Simon, son of Simeon, cousin of Lycurgis, the last king of the lions of Nemea."

The daughter snorted again. "You are a lousy liar. That isn't even possible."

Liliana sat up to her full height. She looked up into the sneering face of the young lioness, chin high with pride. "I am not a liar. I tell only the truth, always." Her shoulders sagged a little. It was hard to be proud of her honesty when she didn't choose to be truthful all the time. Liliana just did not know how to lie, any more than she knew how to write computer code. "I tell the truth, even when it would be better if I didn't."

Arel Magoro gave her daughter a look over her shoulder that made the younger woman shrink a bit. "Forgive Kazi, seer. You must know, of course, that the lions of Nemea have been extinct for centuries. They are little more than a legend now."

"My father ..." Liliana had not talked about her father much with anyone since her brothers moved away to the coast. "Simon of Nemea left his pride so that his younger cousin could be king. He felt he would be a better leader, but my father knew he would defeat his cousin in the Challenge. A few decades later, he heard that his pride had been defeated in battle when he was far away in Egypt with my mother. The Nemean lions were considered too dangerous to be left alive by their enemies. They slaughtered the entire pride, to the last child."

Arel nodded. "We know the legend. The downfall of the greatest pride to ever be is a tale told often among lions." She glanced fondly over her shoulder. "To teach our children that even the strongest can fail."

"My father did not fail his pride. He was not there. If he had been there to fight, maybe things would have been different," Liliana said. Simon of Nemea had been a legend, at least in her eyes.

Arel chuckled low at that. "The story goes that they were

outnumbered a hundred to one, and their enemies were led by
Heracles, a granite Sidhe Fae with impossible strength. I don't see
how one lion, no matter how formidable, could have made a
difference."

The spider seer looked down at her hands, blinking to hold back
tears. She wasn't even certain what she mourned. Her illusions of
her father's invincibility had shattered a long time ago when she saw
him ripped apart by a dozen red wolves. "Simon of Nemea is dead,
but he was not the last Nemean lion. I had four brothers. Two died
fighting beside our mother and father, but two came to America
with me and my second mother. The descendants of my brothers,
Jason and Petros, still live in North Carolina, I think. I have lost
track of them over time, but it is possible that you have some of the
blood of the lions of Nemea yourselves. We could even be related."

When Liliana said that last bit, the younger lioness, Kazi, rolled
her eyes. "Right."

The lioness with the dark brown hair and olive skin looked
thoughtful.

"Oh." Liliana said. "You do not understand. My father was over
eighteen hundred years old when he died ninety-three years ago."
These women did not know about the long-term effects of spider
seer venom. It was less well known now that most people thought
her kind were extinct. "The fate of a spider seer's mate is tied to hers.
My father lived for many centuries because my mother did. They
died on the same day, fighting side by side."

For the first time, the brown-haired woman spoke up. "I heard
that spider-kin live forever. I didn't know about their mates living so
long. If your father died ninety-three years ago, then how old are you?"

"I am one hundred forty-six. I will be one hundred forty-seven
years old..." Liliana considered the date on the calendar with the
pictures of butterflies that she kept on her kitchen wall. She hadn't
realized what day it was. "Oh. I will be one hundred forty-seven
years old in three days."

Arel chuckled, showing a gap between her top front two teeth, in a bright smile that matched the laugh lines around her eyes. "And I thought I was getting on in years."

Liliana looked at her with all eight eyes for a moment, now that she knew she didn't need to hide what she was. "You appear to be in excellent health." She looked forward in time to see how far death was from this beautiful older woman. Liliana barely flinched as she saw the woman die. "You have many more robust years to live, assuming you and your daughter escape being murdered within the next week."

It was an unfortunate aspect of watching over her favorite red wolf that she had become less affected by visions of sudden horrific death. She expected it these days.

She looked into the crystal ball focusing her fourth eyes. Now, she knew why these three lionesses had come to her. Arel Magoro wished to avoid her death. Anticipating the questions, Liliana searched for the source of danger and a moment when it could be side-stepped.

The lioness with the smile lines around her eyes would be ripped apart by a group of men in full lion form. In Liliana's visions, Arel and her daughter both fought valiantly. They took several of their enemies down with them, but in the end, they were pulled down by sheer numbers.

It was all too similar to the way Liliana's parents had died. Her stomach twisted in horror despite her increased resistance to the sight of bloody death. Liliana shuddered. "You must leave Fayetteville very soon or you will be torn apart by more lions than you and your daughter can fight."

"That's not what we wanted to talk to you about," the elder lioness said. "At least, not exactly."

"You do not wish to know how to avoid your own death and the death of your only child?" The spider seer had never been more astonished by any words spoken in her life.

"Well, we already know about that." Arel Magoro's voice was rich with sadness. "That's why we need your help, seer."

"Ask. I will give you only the truth, but I cannot guarantee that it will be what you want to hear."

The woman nodded. "The pride-king of North Carolina died recently."

"Andrew Periclum was an unworthy king of lions," Liliana said, lips tight with anger.

Kazi Magoro chuckled. She sounded so much like her mother in that moment. "That's the first thing you said that I wholeheartedly believe and agree with."

Arel sighed. "Periclum was our king, worthy or not. Now that he's dead, a successor must be chosen. There is some disagreement as to who will be the next king since he had no sons."

"Some disagreement," the brown-haired woman repeated with a derisive laugh that sounded almost like a sob. "Arel, the pride is tearing itself apart."

From what Liliana had seen in her vision, that was literally true.

Andrew Periclum had been a cruel, lying, arrogant cur, but his father had been pride-king, and his father before him. The stable continuity of a smooth succession held the pride together. His death had implications that Alexander Bennett didn't consider when he killed the lion-kin with his magic.

To be fair, this was not Alexander Bennett's fault, as much as a part of her would have welcomed another reason to be mad at him. Liliana would have killed Andrew Periclum herself if the prince had not. That mangey, parasite-ridden garbage eater tried to kill her friends.

"I am very sorry," Liliana said, tightening her lips. She was not even a little sorry Andrew Periclum was dead, but she was sorry his death might cause theirs. "There must be a Challenge to choose the new king. You know this." Somewhere in the pride of North Carolina were the grandsons and granddaughters of her brothers. This was a problem that would affect Liliana's own family. "I do not know how, but I will help in any way I can."

"Can you tell us who will win the challenge? Who will become the next king?" the brown-haired woman asked.

The spider seer nodded. That was simple enough. She focused her fourth eyes on the results of the ritual combat that would choose the new pride-king. Liliana saw a lot of death. Street violence had already begun to erupt between factions who backed different potential kings. Not just lions. The king of the pride was the arbitrator of all beast-kin disputes, the unofficial leader of all beast-kin. An abandoned hanger on the north edge of Fort Liberty had been put to use as a place for the Challenge. A domed cage made of steel beams welded into triangles was being constructed, as was traditional.

The Challenge had been sacred for centuries before Simon of Nemea was born. It might be older than written history itself. Once, the Challenge had been fought in open arenas, but the dome of triangles had been the place for such things for as long as Liliana could remember. Unlike an arena, the dome could be constructed wherever it was needed. Inside a dome, young lions often fought contests of courage and skill to gain rank within the pride. It was meant to be a place where a lion's strength could be honed and tested.

"I see a huge lion-kin with a claw scar over one side of his face that pulls his upper lip into a permanent sneer. Oh." Liliana recognized the man who drove the car that nearly ran over Alexander Bennett. Tray Bradley had also witnessed his king's death, but Alexander Bennett's subterfuge made it look like a simple accident. "It is Bradley."

"Tray Bradley," Kazi's jaw tightened.

The brown-haired woman sank in on herself, as if Liliana had placed a huge rock on her. "Not Tray."

"I am sorry," Liliana said. "If the paths of the future do not change, this man, Tray Bradley, will rule the lions of North Carolina."

Arel rubbed circles into the brown-haired woman's back. "We'll find a way to fix this, Marilyn. Don't give up."

Liliana looked for a connection between the disheartened woman and the lion-kin who would soon become king of the North

Carolina pride. She saw Tray Bradley beating the woman, Marilyn, with his fists until she would have had to go to the hospital or die if she were human. Again and again. The woman never left her abusive husband until she had a baby. For a time, Bradley had been gentle with his wife and new baby. But the boy had barely been toddling when his father aimed a casual kick at him for some annoyance.

Emotionally charged events always stood out sharpest in Liliana's fourth vision. She saw the moment when the cowed expression on Marilyn's face changed as she held her crying baby. She went from terrified to a cold rage. Underneath the battered wife, there was still a lioness.

As Liliana watched, Arel Magoro bundled the brown-haired woman and her tiny son in a coat. They rushed in the rain to her car.

Tray Bradley chased them with a shotgun, shouting threats.

Kazi drove the car. She and her mother helped to get the woman and her baby away from the abusive man.

Liliana nodded in satisfaction. That was how it should be. The pride took care of its own.

"Tray is your ex-husband." Liliana assumed the woman had the good sense to divorce such a horrible man.

Marilyn shook her head in denial. "He wouldn't sign the papers. I was too scared to push it as long as he left us alone. Now ..." She put her face in her hands.

Liliana did not have any wish to see Marilyn's fate if her abusive husband became king. She had already seen what would happen to the two women who helped her get away from him.

"This is not acceptable," Liliana said. "Tray Bradley is even more unworthy than Andrew Periclum was. These are not pride-kings. These men would not know honor if it bit them on the leg."

Arel smiled warmly at her. "Spoken like the daughter of a lion-kin prince."

"Are there no better candidates?" Liliana asked them. "If you could choose the next king, who would you choose?"

"I wish someone like Daniel could become king," Marilyn Bradley said wistfully.

The scowl that seemed permanent on Kazi's face faded into a smile as warm as her mother's. Her aura brightened with gold and creamy white; pride and love. "Daddy would make a great king."

Arel shook her head, face tightening with what looked like anger, but her soul shaded acid green with fear. "That's silly talk. Your father is too old. He could never beat Tray in the dome. He'd get himself killed if he tried."

Liliana tilted her head, considering. She looked into Arel Magoro's past. She saw a huge lion-kin with skin as dark as midnight and muscles on his muscles. The man had been a champion of the dome games in his youth. When young lions of his generation tested their skills against each other to impress the lionesses and gain rank within the pride, he had been the best.

Andrew Periclum lied when he told Doctor Nudd he earned his title. He became king because he was born a prince. The dome challenge was intended to prevent large scale battles when a king died without a clear heir, or a fair portion of the pride did not think the heir was a worthy successor.

Honorable lions throughout the pride supported Andrew Periclum back then because he was the old king's only son. Liliana remembered one stocky stranger had challenged, but there had been others in the pride who supported that man's claim. They must have known he had a legitimate reason to question Periclum's fitness to rule. With the mess Periclum made of the pride's reputation, that one man brave enough to stand against him seemed heroic in hindsight. Foolish, but heroic.

Daniel Magoro did not call challenge that day. He helped build the dome instead. Back then, he had no way to know that Andrew Periclum would become an unworthy king. If he had challenged then in his prime, many things might have been different. That assumed that Kazi, Marilyn, and Arel's faith in Daniel Magoro was well-placed.

"If you believe that Daniel would be a good king, then choose a

champion who can defeat Tray Bradley to fight for him." The
spider-kin wondered why the three women hadn't already done
that.

"A champion?" Kazi said, confusion on her face.

"It's one of our oldest traditions," Arel told her daughter. "A
champion can fight for someone else that they feel would make a
better king. The champion answers any Challenges, but the king
rules."

Kazi said, "Like how Tray beat the crap out of anyone who
dared to question Periclum?"

"Like that, only more civilized," Arel said. "Disputes are
settled in the dome with the whole pride as witness, not with
broken kneecaps in back alleys." She turned to Liliana. "It's not a
tradition many people have followed. My grandfather told me
about it. But if someone wins the challenge now, they want to
rule themselves. People think that being a strong fighter makes
them good kings."

Marilyn shook her head, face dark. "It doesn't matter. No one
can beat Tray."

Looking into the past and the future, Liliana followed Tray
Bradley in several fights, from barroom brawls through dome bouts
and occasional leg-breaking enforcement for Andrew Periclum. The
big lion was a formidable fighter. He was also heavy on his feet and
led with his right too often. "I could beat him," Liliana said.

All three women laughed at her.

The spider seer's ears flushed hot. She hated being laughed at.
She studied the three women with her third eyes, wondering what
she said that was so funny.

Oh.

They were not laughing at her. They thought she was joking.

"I defeated a Celtic wolf in single combat."

They stopped laughing.

"The wolf became my ally, then my friend. With his aid, I
defeated four widow spiders."

Kazi nodded. "I saw the footage of you and the Celtic werewolf killing Lady Fairchilde. What happened to the others? Kristen, Margaret, Stella?"

"The red wolf killed Margaret."

"You're saying you killed Kristen and Stella by yourself?" Kazi looked down her nose at the petite spider seer. "Kristen wasn't a fighter, but Stella was the best. She trained all the security personnel. I saw you on the dining room camera get thrown through a glass door. Stella went after you but didn't come back. Did you trick her somehow?"

Liliana looked into Kazi's dark eyes with her own third eyes for a moment, then looked down. What Kazi did not say was that Stella had been someone she admired. "I am truly sorry for both deaths, but they were necessary. Kristen was pregnant. The nest was murdering people to feed her unborn children. She was in the process of killing Pete so I had no choice." The spider seer didn't dare look into the past or she would cry. "Stella fought with honor, courage, and great skill. I tried to let her walk away peacefully, but her beloved would not go." Liliana closed all her eyes for a moment in regret, but she couldn't have done anything else. She touched her shoulder where her spider-kin nature had faded even the scar from Stella's worst attack to unblemished skin. "Stella would have killed me if I had not killed her first."

Kazi's nostrils flared for a moment, then she looked down as well. "Was that what you said to her? There was no sound on the video. You held the red wolf back, let her leave without a fight." She swallowed, then looked back up at the spider-kin. "I also saw that red wolf fight. I've never seen strength like that, even in a bear-kin."

"He is even better now. I trained him," Liliana said with pride. "I taught him what my father taught me."

"Your father, a prince of the Nemean lions," Kazi said, like she was asking if Liliana was going to stick with that unlikely story.

Liliana nodded. Her father was who he was. Their belief or disbelief made no difference.

Arel asked, "Seer, since this red wolf is your friend, could you ask him to be Daniel's champion?"

"I could." Liliana looked into Pete's future and saw a problem. The assassins from the Order of the Wolfhound were coming for Lou Willoughby in three nights. The Challenge was also in three nights. Pete could not be in two places at once. He needed to be there to protect the defenseless rabbit-kin mechanic.

Arel saw her hesitation but misinterpreted it. "I know Celtic wolves only defend Normals and seelie Fae, but we've put some money together, donations from a bunch of us. We can pay the red wolf. Tell him that if Tray Bradley becomes king, the whole Other community in North Carolina will suffer. There could be a pride war. Normals are bound to get caught in the crossfire."

"Pete is a very unusual red wolf. He will not fight for money. He would be insulted if you offered. He protects whoever is in danger, Normal or any kind of Other, including Fae of either court. His oldest friend is an oak goblin."

All three lionesses had identical expressions of shock and disbelief. "But goblins are unseelie Fae!" Marilyn said.

The spider seer shrugged. "Pete loves him like a favorite uncle. He is a very unusual Celtic wolf. Pete would be honored to aid you because it is right, but ..." She trailed off.

Liliana had warned Janice Willoughby. The rabbit-kin intended to take her children and flee to New Jersey in two days, ostensibly to visit her mother. The spider seer gave her word to her most loyal customer that her husband, Lou, would be safe. The Celtic wolf would protect him. "I will not ask him. The red wolf has other business that night. People will die if he is not where he should be."

"People will die if Tray becomes the pride-king," Marilyn Bradley pointed out.

Liliana nodded. "I agree this is not an acceptable outcome. But Pete cannot be Daniel's champion in three nights, so we will find another way." She said it with confidence, even though she had not yet decided how to make that happen. Liliana was a lion's daughter. This was her pride, too. She would not permit another unworthy king to be chosen.

She had to be careful, though. It was far too easy to make things worse. If Daniel Magoro was not the man these women believed him to be, then she might be responsible for the evil done by the next unworthy king.

The spider seer dove into visions of Daniel Magoro in the past. Solid visions of him in the future did not exist, only vague impressions, flickery with improbability. Those brief images did seem to be good, though. Arel and Kazi smiling. Marilyn raising her son in peace.

Liliana foresaw that if Daniel did become king, since Daniel had no sons of his own, Marilyn and Tray Bradley's son would be the next king. The boy would grow into his father's brute strength, but it would be tempered by honor and compassion that his pride family would teach him.

From the fleeting glimpses the spider-kin could see, Daniel would be a good king. But she had to be sure. Power could change people. "Mrs. Magoro, I need you to answer a question for me, now." Normally, she didn't ask clients questions, but this was a special case. If anyone knew this lion-kin, it would be his wife.

"What is it?" The elder lioness gave Liliana her full attention.

The spider seer returned that attention with all eight eyes at once. "Is it simply that he is your husband and you love him, or do you believe that Daniel Magoro would make a good king? Is he a man of honor who keeps his word always? Would he rule with a strong will, tempered with a good balance of justice and mercy?"

"Yes." Arel answered without hesitation. There was no trace of doubt anywhere in her mind. She not only loved her husband, she admired him.

Liliana didn't bother looking into the mind of Kazi, Daniel's daughter. With few exceptions, all men were heroes in the eyes of their daughters.

She looked into Marilyn Bradley's mind instead. "Do you believe that Daniel Magoro is the best possible lion to become pride-king?"

"Daniel would be a better king than any I've ever known." There was little hope in the woman's heart. She did not believe that Daniel

Magoro could become king. But there was a great deal of longing. Marilyn, the woman whose trust had been repeatedly betrayed by a man who should have protected her, believed in Daniel Magoro. The elder lion had no reason to protect her and her child. He had taken Marilyn and her son in, sheltered them, treated them like family even though it put his own family in danger, because it was the right thing to do. That was the kind of man Daniel Magoro was.

"I will meet Daniel Magoro. I will come to your house tomorrow afternoon, after my last appointment. If he is the man that you all believe he is, I will be his champion."

CHAPTER 5

PRIDE AND ANGER

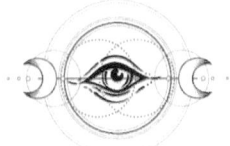

THE THREE LIONESSES HAD A BLUE SUV THAT SEATED
eight people comfortably. Arel drove Liliana to the Magoro home
the evening after they'd first spoken. She gave Liliana the shotgun
front seat. The other two lionesses sat behind her. Liliana felt like a
child inside the giant vehicle. It was meant for much larger people.

The Magoro home was at the back of a suburban
neighborhood, the only house on the end of a cul de sac. It had a
small, neat lawn in front, stood two stories tall and looked like it
could house a hundred. Since the land was wedge shaped, she
suspected the back yard was far larger than the front. All around it
the forest still stood. It appeared to have been made from the logs of
the trees that used to stand where the lawn was now. A peaked metal
roof sheltered , polished and sealed natural logs that framed huge
windows.

Daniel Magoro, a massive man with very dark skin and iron-grey
hair cut short, opened one half of the double front door big enough
to drive the SUV through. A small, fluffy black and tan dog also met
her at the door, barking furiously.

Arel gestured to her. "This is Madame Anna, the seer I told you
about that Kazi saw on the surveillance video defeating her old
bosses. She wanted to meet you."

Liliana looked up at the Magoro patriarch, who picked up the dog with the piercing bark, quieting it. "Andrew Periclum was not a worthy king of lions. Tray Bradley will be worse. My father was lion-kin. I am a pride-child. I am not going to permit the pride to have another unworthy king."

Daniel nodded. "Arel said you might shed some light on what we could do about the situation."

"You should invite me in, first."

The big man huffed a deep chuckle. "So I should. Come on in, Madame Anna."

"I am Liliana. My friends call me Lilly. I might die for you, so, you and your family can call me Lilly, even though Kazi is not my friend. She hates me."

Daniel looked at his daughter.

She shrugged, lips tight, not denying it.

Marilyn Bradley bid them good night, even though it was early evening. She went straight upstairs as soon as they entered the house. Liliana glanced after her with her fourth eyes. Marilyn was packing. She intended to get herself and her son out of North Carolina before the Challenge. She did not believe that Liliana could win.

The spider seer approved. Regardless of whether she won or lost the fight in two nights, Marilyn Bradley and her son would be safe. The spider seer had already saved two lives and she hadn't even fought the battle yet. Liliana's decision to fight for a worthy pride-king was a good one. If she died, then it was an excellent death. If her father were here, he would be bursting with pride.

Of course, if her father were here, she would not have to fight in the dome against a big lion. He would do it instead. Liliana missed him desperately, but she could not wallow in old grief now.

She walked into the cavernous central great room of the Magoro home and marveled. As beautiful as the house had been from the outside, the exposed beams, the high roof with light pouring in from giant windows edged in beveled glass on either end of the massive central room—made her stop for a moment and stare.

For once, she didn't have to search for something nice to say. "Your house is beautiful."

Daniel Magoro spread his arms wide in the middle of the great room, smiling. As large as he was, he fit comfortably into the big open space with plenty of room to spare. "This was one of the first things I built once my business took off. I always hoped we'd have a big family to fill it up." He shrugged. "Best laid plans. It's been good to have Marilyn and her boy making it feel more lived in."

"You are in the business of building things?" Liliana asked.

"I own Magoro construction. I'm up to more than sixty employees these days."

Liliana opened her fourth eyes. She looked into the past.

Daniel Magoro began a business with one big pickup full of tools. He'd paid for the downpayment from his savings doing yard work as a teen. At first, he did smaller construction jobs, but they rapidly grew. Many lion-kin worked for him now, as well as the jackal-kin and hyena-kin who seemed to always live on the fringe of any pride. Beast-kin of a dozen other species, including some of mixed heritage like her. There were some in the beast-kin world who looked down on those who made children with mates outside their own race. Daniel Magoro was clearly not one of them.

The spider seer sat on a giant leather couch that left her feet dangling like a girl's while she watched Daniel Magoro of the past with her fourth eyes. The huge lion directed his employees with authority and fairness as his business flourished.

His company built this whole suburban sub-division. He claimed a big piece of un-developed property at the back as his own. Not just the house and yard were his, but the entire cul de sac.

She saw him hold his wife's hand through the difficult birth that nearly took her life. Doctor Nudd managed to save both mother and child but advised them against having more. Liliana watched Daniel playing in the newly landscaped backyard with his young daughter. As she grew, Daniel taught Kazi fighting skills, just as Liliana's father taught her.

Liliana smiled, feeling a strange mix of joy and melancholy.

Daniel Magoro reminded her of her own father so strongly. They looked nothing alike, but under the skin, Daniel Magoro and Simon of Nemea could be brothers. Since her brothers Petros and Jason's grandchildren and great-grandchildren might still live in North Carolina, it was even possible there was a blood relationship between them.

They were similar kinds of men. Good men. Strong men to whom strength meant the ability to help and protect others, not the ability to force others to do their bidding. While Arel and Kazi went to the kitchen to fetch tea for her—she had no idea why that took two people—Liliana told Daniel why she was there. "All three lionesses who came to me for help believe that you would be a better pride-king by far than Tray Bradley."

Daniel, sitting in a huge reclining armchair that fit his mass well, huffed another deep chuckle. "Tuffy would be a better pride-king than Tray Bradley."

Liliana looked at the tiny, fierce ball of dark fluff in Daniel Magoro's lap. "Tuffy?"

He winced, and pet the fluffball, who immediately jumped down. "Kazi was still a child when she named him."

The dog sniffed Liliana's ballet slipper. She pulled her dangling feet up, folding them under her. Dogs were somewhat unpredictable about how they reacted to spider-kin.

The dog jumped onto the sofa, sniffed her skirt while she held very still, then laid down next to her, seeming to decide she wasn't dangerous.

Liliana was not quite as certain about the little dog.

"He doesn't bite," Daniel Magoro commented. "He just barks a lot."

"Okay." Liliana petted the dog's thick fur warily. When her caress appeared to be acceptable to the little beast, she looked at the man she came to meet. "Your family believes you would be a good pride-king, but that you cannot beat Tray Bradley in the dome."

Daniel Magoro sighed. "In my youth, I could have showed that excuse for a man the error of his ways." He rotated his right shoulder making an audible cracking noise. "Don't ever get old."

"I would prefer to get old than not."

Daniel huffed that deep chuckle again. "No argument there."

As a final confirmation, she looked into him with her third eyes as she sipped the tea Arel Magoro gave her before returning to the kitchen with her daughter, leaving her alone with Daniel.

Bleah.

Made from concentrate. The tea tasted like overbrewed black tea that had been left on the counter for a week. She knew the social rule about not showing her displeasure, so she took a polite pretend sip and set the cup on the end table next to the couch.

Her third eyes told her what she expected to find. Daniel Magoro was, in fact, the man that his wife, daughter, and friend believed him to be. She saw a strong will, a lot of stubbornness, but also compassion, deep love for his family, and loyalty to his pride.

She also saw something else.

She saw a vision of a likely future with him fighting Tray Bradley, to challenge for the right to be the new king. The big lion was past sixty. Tray Bradley was a dome champion two decades younger. But Daniel's honor demanded that he at least try, even if it meant his death.

That is a problem.

Liliana stood up, dislodging the fluffy dog that had settled with its head in her lap. She faced Daniel in his big chair. Suspecting his intention was not something he'd want his wife or daughter to know, she said quietly, "You cannot fight Tray Bradley, Daniel Magoro."

He stood from the chair to face her. "I can and I will." He also kept his voice low.

Liliana felt very tiny standing in front of the patriarch of the Magoro family but didn't relent under the big man's glare. "There is no possibility that you will win. Tray Bradley is not fighting to first blood." Her voice had started to rise. He held up a big hand with a glance toward the kitchen, asking her to keep the argument quieter. She whispered, "He will kill you."

The old lion crossed his giant arms over his impressive chest. "Maybe I'll take my chances."

Liliana sighed in frustration. Deciding whether or not to fight for him was why she came, rather like she had done with the Fae colonel. She hadn't anticipated having to convince a former champion of lion-kin dome fighting that a petite spider-kin girl should fight in his place.

"It is not just your own chances that you take, Daniel Magoro, but the chances of every member of the pride of North Carolina." The spider-kin stepped closer to the lion whose arms were as big around as her waist. She pointed at his chest with her finger, scolding him like her first mother used to scold her. "I am a lion's daughter. This is my pride, too. If Tray Bradley becomes the pride-king, the lions, jackals, hyenas, cheetahs, the pride families of North Carolina, all beast-kin in the area, will once again be ruled by a man who knows nothing of honor or justice."

"You're just giving me even more reasons I should challenge."

There was no way she could win this argument with words, the least effective weapons in her personal arsenal.

"There is only one way to settle this." Liliana walked out the front door. The fluffy little dog trailed behind her.

Daniel Magoro followed. His wife and daughter who heard the door open followed them out.

Once they were outside, Liliana found a good clear place in the lawn and lifted her fists. She would not use her arm blades on the man she was supposed to be fighting FOR. "Fight me."

Daniel stopped a few feet in front of her, his quizzical expression turning to laughter. He threw his head back, patting his knee. He thought she was joking.

Liliana's lips twisted in annoyance. She hated being laughed at. For once, she could do something about it. While he was off balance, she foot-swept the huge lion-kin onto his butt on the grass.

He stopped laughing when he hit the ground. With some

groaning and popping of knees, he got back up. He brushed his hands off and shifted his weight into a good stance. "Fine, let's do this. If I can't beat a pint-sized girl, you're right. I've got no business going into the dome." He threw a carefully pulled swing at the spider-kin.

In one motion, Liliana ducked the blow, stepped diagonally, and shoved on the back of Daniel's shoulder at full extension while hooking her ankle in front of his.

The big lion went face first onto the grass this time, with a grunt of pain, as his elbow on the side with his bad shoulder smacked down hard enough to scrape. He rolled over and sat up, holding his elbow. "Okay, I see your point." The big man sighed. "It just doesn't seem right, though. The dome is supposed to be the test for kings."

"I am good at fighting. I am not a leader. I am not even lion-kin. No one in the pride would follow me." Liliana held her hand out to him, the polite thing to do. It was also an apology to the man who she hoped would soon be her king. "You have already earned my loyalty and I just met you. You will be a good king."

Daniel accepted her hand. "I'm glad one of is sure of that."

"I must pass this test for you. Once you are king, then your test will begin. The pride has not had a worthy leader in decades. They will not be easy to lead."

Kazi, who had watched the exchange, bristled with anger. "Just because you can beat up an old man doesn't mean you can defeat a dome champion in his prime."

Liliana sighed. She'd just defeated Kazi's magnificent father in front of her. She had already thrown her mentor off a building. The only way it could be worse would be if Liliana stabbed her fluffy dog. "I have the best chance of anyone available."

"Tray will turn you into a bloody smear." She clenched her hands at her side. "Why are you even here?" She let out a gusty sigh. "Get that Celtic werewolf. That's who we need."

"Pete is already busy that night, fighting four assassins protected by powerful magic, protecting an innocent Other from being torn apart, and keeping the fabric of reality from being destroyed by an evil Fae princess." Liliana used the hands throwing in the air gesture she'd seen Siobhan use. It fit her feelings. "Believe it or not, your problems are not the worst that need dealing with just now."

Kazi blinked, then her scowl returned. "Right. And your dad was a Nemean lion."

Liliana sighed. She suspected something was going on that she didn't understand. She opened her third eyes to look into Kazi. *Oh.* "If someone has to win the dome battle for your father to be king, you wish it were anyone but me. But most of all, you wish it were you."

Kazi scowled even harder.

The spider-kin wondered if her face would be lined by bitterness when she was her mother's age, rather than laughter.

"Daddy taught me how to fight. So did Stella. I'd have a better chance than you."

"I defeated both Stella and your father." Liliana dropped into a fighting crouch holding up one finger.

"What is that supposed to mean?"

"My finger is a knife. You are left-handed. Your left arm from elbow to wrist is a short sword. We will fight as if this yard were the dome. If I kill you with my knife, I will fight as your father's champion. If you kill me with your sword, you will fight for him."

Kazi's scowl flattened to a grim line as her lips tightened together. "Deal," she said, holding up her arm with hand flat like a blade.

Without further warning, she drove the flattened fingers toward Liliana's face.

Liliana dropped to one knee, removing the support of her legs so gravity pulled her down faster.

Kazi's hand skimmed the top of Liliana's hair as the spider seer's knees hit the lawn grass.

Liliana poked the tall girl in the belly with her finger.

Kazi looked down. Her deep frown returned. "That wouldn't be fatal."

Liliana shrugged and stood again with her weight on her toes.

When Kazi swung the "sword" toward her neck in a feint, spun with a foot-sweep and finished with a slashing blow to the body, Liliana stepped in close to her opponent. The feint would have missed so she ignored it. Liliana skipped over the foot-sweep and trailed her finger along Kazi's neck as she spun, deflecting the final blow with her wrist to the taller woman's elbow.

"GRRR!" Kazi growled and started to shift.

Her father's hand closed on her shoulder. "So, my daughter is a sore loser. Is that what I see?"

Kazi froze. Her shift reversed before her dark skin had finished growing tawny fur. "She cheated! She only won because she's small. I can beat her in my other form."

"She will still be small in the dome," Daniel Magoro said. "She's been careful not to hurt either one of us. That alone should make it obvious she's better than either you or I. It's a lot harder to defeat without harm than to hurt someone to win. You taught me that."

Kazi blinked tears. "Stella taught us that when she was training us to use minimal force as a bouncer."

Liliana closed her first eyes and opened her fourth. She watched Stella teaching angry young women with chips on their shoulders, Kazi among them. They were all angry for multiple reasons but being strong women in a world that encouraged strength only in men contributed to the rage in them all. Stella taught them to channel it, to control it, to turn that rage into an advantage.

And Kazi loved her for it. Liliana could see the admiration radiating from her young face as she looked at Stella in an unguarded moment in the past.

When Liliana opened her human eyes, a tear streamed down her cheek. "I am so sorry." But she knew there were not enough apologies in the world to ever make this right. "I cannot bring Stella back. You may not believe me, but I would if I could."

There was only one way she could atone. A life for a life. "Your father will die in three days if I do nothing. He intends to challenge Tray Bradley, himself."

Kazi looked up at her big father in horror. "Daddy, is that true?"

Arel, who had been watching up until then, shook her head in exasperation. "We talked about this."

Daniel shrugged. "The man is going to target my family. Plus, I couldn't just stand by and do nothing this time."

Arel put a hand on his massive arm. "You had no way of knowing Periclum would be such a terrible king."

"Maybe not," Daniel growled. "But I know now. I won't let it happen again."

Liliana cut into what looked to become a heated family argument. "It no longer matters. I will face Tray Bradley. If I live, Daniel may not believe he can be a great king, but he will be a better king than Tuffy."

Daniel huffed his surprised chuckle breaking the tension. Even Kazi was surprised into cracking a half smile.

Liliana turned her full attention to the young woman again. "I will give you a life in exchange for the life I took. Either my life or your father's. If I die in the dome, my life is given. If I win, then your father's life is given, since I will keep him from dying in the ring."

Kazi crossed her arms. "What are you talking about?"

Arel put an arm around Kazi's shoulders. "There is a very old custom. Life price is paid in gold or something valuable to the surviving loved ones, but another life is considered the true price to pay for a wrongful death. Usually, the life of the murderer is forfeit."

She looked at her mother. "She's offering to pay me for killing Stella by either dying or keeping Daddy from dying?"

"Exactly."

Kazi's watery eyes looked down at Liliana, then away. "I saw the footage. All the footage on a backup system the military cops didn't know about." She shrugged. "Stella was about to chop up a friend of yours with a meat cleaver. Instead of attacking her, you tried to talk her into leaving. She tried to kill you anyway."

Liliana nodded. That was true.

"You don't." Kazi stopped and cleared her throat. "You don't owe me anything. I'd have done what you did in your position. Stella just wasn't who I thought she was."

"She was loyal and in love," Liliana said. "Maybe you would have done the same in my position, but I think I would have done the same in hers."

Liliana turned to Arel, wiping tears from her own eyes. "I will go home now. The day after tomorrow, come pick me up at my house and take me to the dome. I will be Daniel's champion."

Arel Magoro drove her home in the giant navy-blue SUV. Marilyn and Kazi rode in the seat behind them. The three lionesses seemed to go everywhere as a set.

"Do you really think you can win?" Arel asked when she pulled into Liliana's driveway.

Liliana looked forward in time with her fourth eyes to see if she would win in the dome against Tray Bradley. Possibilities flickered. Some of those possibilities showed her own brutal death. Some involved his. Neither seemed more likely than the other. She might win. She might not.

"It is possible, yes. If I do not, and you do not leave North Carolina right away, then you will die. Your daughter will die." She turned to look at Marilyn. "If you stay, you will die, and your son will be raised to become a cruel bully, just like his father."

Marilyn shifted, tawny hair crawling over her skin in a moment, filling the SUV's huge back seat, her rounded ears brushing the roof of the big car. She growled a lion's deep warning. "I won't let my son become like Tray."

Liliana looked. "You and your son will survive if you leave the state before the challenge, but without a pride, I do not see an easy future for a lone lioness with a little child." They would survive, but they would not thrive.

All of the lionesses looked grim.

"There is another possibility, though," she offered them.

There was little hope in the three faces, two dark and human, one tawny, large-eyed, with a wrinkled nose and lifted upper lip showing fang tips.

"I could win," Liliana said. "This is of equal probability to the other outcome. If I win, Daniel will become king. And your son, Marilyn, would be king after him, a good king like the man who helped raise him."

Marilyn's split demi-lion lips covered her teeth, her half snarl fading away. She looked down. "What will you want from us in return?" she rumbled, wariness in her tone.

Liliana blinked all her eyes. "I want a worthy pride-king."

"Why would you risk your life for us?" Kazi challenged. "You're not even lion-kin."

"I am a lion's daughter."

CHAPTER 6

BUNNIES AND BEN

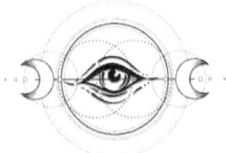

SINCE THERE WAS A FAIR CHANCE THAT LILIANA WOULD not survive her attempt to help an honorable man become the new king of the North Carolina pride in a few days, there were a few things she needed to take care of. She had promised her best friend, Pete, that given time and patience, his beloved Ben Harper would come to understand the world held more than the laws of science admitted. Once he accepted that the world was wider, he would be more receptive to learning his boyfriend was a werewolf, rather than thinking that one of them must be insane. If Pete just flat told him, or worse, showed him, Liliana saw a lot of restraining orders in Pete's possible future paths.

But Ben was no closer today to accepting the existence of Others than he was when Liliana said those words to Pete. The futures she had seen were many and varied, but none of them led in the right direction.

She needed to set Ben on a path more likely to lead to a good outcome for him and Pete, even if they got married after Lilly was dead. Her dearest friend deserved happiness. It also disturbed Ben Harper how little he knew of his boyfriend's life. Both men's paths would be better ones if Ben could be coaxed into accepting the hidden world.

Being confronted with something with big teeth out of a nightmare or Liliana's disturbing eyes as his first experience did not lead to good outcomes. Liliana needed to find a gentler way.

Ben taught science at the middle school on base at Fort Liberty. Janice Willoughby's eleven-year-old son, Sam, was one of his students. But Liliana didn't see any path where Janice could coax Ben in the right direction. The spider seer would have to intervene directly in some way.

So, Liliana sat on the back side of the roof of Janice's house, hidden under the sheltering shade of the big old oak that stretched its long limbs clear over the peak of the roof. The spider seer leaned against the chimney, watching as Janice's children played in the backyard, the tree's twigs screening her from their view.

Janice had five children, but the other three had gone to a sports game with their father. The eleven-year-old, Sam, opted to stay home with Janice and play with his baby brother. The sixth grader didn't seem interested in sports, despite having boundless energy.

In North Carolina, basketball was the game most revered. Liliana imagined all the people staring, the all-important ball moving unpredictably, the constant need to focus attention when a thousand other things demanded it. She shuddered.

In Liliana's opinion, Sam was the only Willoughby child with good sense. Playing basketball on a school team seemed worse than combat with a werelion.

While Liliana watched from her hidden perch, Sam ran around from the bottom of the playscape's slide to the ladder repeatedly. He swung on the swings, climbed on the rope bridge, and swung from the monkey bars.

Janice's youngest, the toddler, Kayden, circled the yard. His bright red tricycle following a trail worn into the grass.

Their shaggy golden retriever mix followed dutifully behind him.

Sam spotted a butterfly. He chased it from flowering bush to bush, trying to get it to land on his hand, panting from all the running and climbing he'd done. The fluttering painted lady didn't seem interested in leaving the yard which was surrounded by lilac bushes just inside the privacy fence despite the determined little boy chasing it from flower to flower.

The Willoughby family had gone to a great deal of trouble with the eight-foot privacy fence and the bushes to make certain their back yard was concealed from outside eyes. The reason became obvious a moment later.

As little Kayden zoomed by on his well-worn circuit, followed by the dog, Sam shifted to rabbit form. He bounced up on the dog. His rabbit feet splayed over her furry back as he rested.

The dog seemed quite accustomed to the children becoming four-footed and furry. It bent its neck to the side until muzzle met rabbit paw, gave one quick sniff, and went back to trotting behind the tricycle. The three of them made a cute little parade.

Anyone outside the family seeing the children become lop-eared brown rabbits could be dangerous. Good that they were well-screened. But ...

If Liliana peeked around the chimney, she could see Ben in the next yard over, sitting in the gazebo while he graded assignments from Sam's science class.

If only he could see his student turn into a lop-eared bunny. That would convince him animal-kin were real in a non-threatening way. But not if they did it in front of him on purpose. Then, he'd think it was a stage magic trick, put on for his benefit.

Is there some way that Ben Harper could see into the Willoughby's backyard at a crucial moment?

Liliana's fourth eyes showed her a flicker of a possibility, an image of Ben peeking through a knothole in the fence, a tiny breach in the privacy armor that she hadn't known existed until then. She sat up straight.

I need Janice's help.

The spider seer scrambled down to the eaves of the house. She dropped her upper body over the edge, leaving her legs on the shingles. This angle made her long curly hair dangle a fair distance past her head. She had an urge to swing her head to feel her hair move.

Janice Willoughby was sitting on her back porch sipping an iced drink. She was absorbed in a scrolled out electronic book reader while her children played.

"Hello," Liliana said, considering Janice from upside down.

Janice yelped in surprise and threw half her drink into the air.

For a moment, Liliana wondered why she was so startled. *Oh.* The spider-kin broke a social rule. She knew this one. "I'm sorry. I should have gone to the front door."

Janice laughed as she stood, brushing liquid off the arm of her lawn chair. "That would be appreciated." She shook her hand, flinging drops off of it.

"Okay," Liliana got her full self back up on the roof.

"No, wait, not now," Janice said. "Do that next time. Just tell me why you're here now."

Liliana dropped her upper body back over the lip of the roof, swinging her hair a little extra just for the interesting sensation. "I have an idea of how we can gently introduce Ben Harper to the hidden peoples."

"Oh! That would be great. I've been sort of hinting around at things, but he just looks at me like I'm nuttier than a squirrel turd."

"I saw Sam play with your dog while in full rabbit form. The dog doesn't threaten them?"

"Never." She patted her leg.

The shaggy golden dog lay down on the grass, unburdening itself of a half-grown rabbit that started nibbling on the lawn. Then the dog trotted over to Janice.

"Wendy has the gentlest nature. She plays with them like they're her own puppies." She rubbed the dog's head affectionately.

"Does she ever play chase with them?" Liliana asked.

"Sure," Janice bent a little sideways, trying to look at Liliana's face more straight on. "Why do you ask?"

"I have an idea. There's this knothole in the fence over there." Liliana told Janice what she had in mind.

"Have you foreseen this working?"

In her excitement at the idea, Liliana had forgotten to look. She opened her fourth eyes, looking right then while she hung there. None of the new futures branching from this moment were bad, but some succeeded in sending Ben along a path toward expanded understanding of the world, and some did not. There were many possibilities branching forward. Ben's own curiosity would be the determining factor. "There is a chance that it will work, but it is uncertain."

"Worth a shot, then." Janice waved the two children up to her. After Sam shifted back to boy form, she explained in a soft voice for telling secrets what she wanted him to do.

The smaller child, Kayden, rocked his tricycle back and forth as he listened, but Liliana wasn't certain how much he understood until he said, "Me!"

Sam grinned. "Mr. Harper would be less likely to suspect a trick if Kayden did it."

Janice smiled. "Are you sure, Kay?"

The toddler nodded vigorously. "Me."

Liliana ducked back under the oak's heavy branches on the roof to watch as Janice put her plan into action.

The fence that the two houses shared had twin gates facing the street side by side. Janice left through her gate. A spring shut it behind her. She knocked on Ben's gate. "Hey, Ben, you back there?"

Ben opened the gate for her, and she went into his yard. "Hi, Janice. What's up?"

"I'm sorry to bug you, but I was about to make an apple crumble pie and discovered I'm out of cinnamon. Any chance you could help me out?"

"I think I could be persuaded, especially if I get a piece of that pie."

"Deal."

Ben went inside his house. When he returned, he handed Janice a small spice jar.

"Great, you're a lifesaver," she said. "I've got a bunch of apples that are about to go bad if I don't use them."

While they talked, Sam and his baby brother had both turned into rabbits. They started a game of chase with Wendy in the grass. The dog ran away from the baby rabbits as if they were terrifying. Then, she turned the tables and chased them, causing joyful bounces in two directions. The smallest of the Willoughby children, a handful of fur and cuteness, rolled onto his back, squealing like he was in terrible distress, his tiny, furry legs kicking in the air.

Janice made a convincing expression of alarm and ran to the fence. She looked through the knothole to see her toddler on the ground, kicking and squealing in rabbit form like he was being killed.

The concerned dog had its nose buried in the child's furry belly trying to determine what distressed him. It looked a bit like the dog was eating the baby bunny.

"Oh, no!" Janice said, in a somewhat less convincing way. Her hand over her mouth covered her attempts to smother a grin. She ran out of Ben's yard and back through her gate simulating panic. Liliana thought her performance had convinced Ben.

"Are you all right?" she asked loud enough that Ben, just a few feet away on the other side of the fence, could hear. "Come back to human form so I can see if you're hurt."

The baby bunny shifted back to a toddler without difficulty.

Liliana was impressed by the level of shape control in one so young. By the time he was an adult, Kayden would have the kind of control she'd only seen in Pete. He'd be able to change just his ears to hear something, or just his legs to leap amazing distances while still mostly in human form.

Janice scooped him up and hugged him. "Don't scare me like that. From all that noise, I thought Wendy hurt you. Were you afraid?"

The little one grinning in her arms, nodded enthusiastically.

Janice couldn't suppress a snort. She continued to fuss over her youngest, glancing occasionally at Liliana where she perched on top of the house, peeking around the chimney. She could see Ben Harper standing in his own backyard, confused and a bit worried about what just happened.

He could hear Janice fussing over her toddler. He had to be wondering about the "human form" remark.

Liliana held her breath, waiting and hoping. All it would take to change everything would be for Ben's curiosity to overcome his polite nature.

From the corner of her eye, Janice watched Liliana, waiting for a signal.

Ben looked at the knothole, a tiny aperture into the never-glimpsed backyard right next to his. It would be rude to look, breaking a strict social rule. But Janice's quick glance through that knothole told him he could see. It was right there if he wanted to look.

The teacher looked around, making sure no one else would see him breaking that social rule.

Liliana ducked behind the chimney, continuing to watch him with her fourth eyes.

This was the moment. From here, all of Ben and Pete's futures branched. If Ben's polite, do-as-I'm-supposed-to, believe-what I've-been-taught nature was stronger than his curious, find-out, learn-something-new nature was, then Pete might as well walk away, and when his broken heart began to heal, find someone new.

Ben bent over to put his eye to the hole.

With a broad grin, Liliana punched the sky where Janice could see.

Janice smothered a triumphant grin. "Sam, why don't you play chase with Wendy a little in rabbit form so Kayden can see she isn't dangerous."

But the kid was ahead of her. As soon as Sam saw Liliana's signal, he ran around the yard once on his four bunny legs.

The dog chased him, her tail wagging.

Then, he shifted form. The long bunny ears vanished into a

blonde head. Limbs lengthened and fur vanished leaving a normal-looking little boy. "See, no problem," Sam said to his baby brother.

Ben rubbed his eyes. "But ..." He stood there for another long moment staring through the hole at the perfectly normal child that he knew well... who had been a rabbit a moment before.

Kayden squirmed out of his mother's lap. Standing next to his big brother, he said, "Safe?"

Sam patted him on the back. "It's fine. Wendy won't hurt you."

Kayden shifted to his tiny, fluffy bunny form, standing on hind legs to look at the now huge in comparison dog.

Wendy bent down and touched noses with the baby rabbit.

Sam scratched the dog behind the ears. "See, Kay. She won't hurt you." He got a messy lick in the face as a reward.

Kayden shifted back to human form. "Safe!" he said, loudly.

Janice handed the boys back their shorts that had been abandoned in the grass earlier.

They pulled them on.

She gave Kayden a quick hug, whispering, "That ought to do it," in his ear. "Let's go inside and make a pie, boys. I'll let Kayden stir the crumble topping. Sam, you can roll out the dough. What do you say?"

Both boys cheered and followed their mother into the house. Wendy followed, wagging her shaggy blonde tail.

"How ..." Ben stopped as if uncertain how to finish. He stood up from the hunched posture he'd needed to see through the knothole. Jaw slack, he stared into space.

After a long moment, he said, "I need coffee." He tripped on his back steps on the way into the house. "Or maybe something stronger." His tablet and stylus lay abandoned on the picnic table.

Liliana looked into Ben and Pete's future. She smiled as many of the former paths disappeared, fading into better paths. In one strong possibility, she saw the two men dressed in tuxedoes saying vows while surrounded by flowers.

She nodded in satisfaction. She'd done what she could for Pete's future.

Ben Harper's curiosity would do the rest.

CHAPTER 7

THE OPPOSITE OF DYING

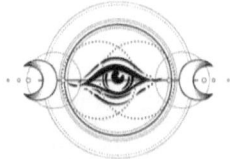

THE NEXT EVENING AFTER WORK, LILIANA CLIMBED ONTO her own roof.

She jumped onto the tall pine that grew next to her house and climbed as high as she could. The trunk thinned, wobbling under her weight. She popped out an arm blade, reaching up to cut the webbing that held Pete's sword to the slender trunk.

She scrambled down a silk line. The spider-kin dropped to her toes in the light of the headlights just as Pete's van pulled into her driveway to pick her up.

The Celtic wolf exclaimed with delight. "My sword! You found it!"

"It was not lost," Liliana told him. "I stole it."

Pete gave her a puzzled look. "Why would you steal my sword?"

"So that no one else would steal it." She handed the old sword to him, wiping away a stray strand of her webbing stuck to the worn leather scabbard.

"Ookaay." Pete accepted the sword. "Thanks for giving that back...I guess... since you were the one who stole it in the first place."

"Your van will break tomorrow." Liliana walked over to the vehicle. "You will leave it with Lou Willoughby for repairs. Assassins of the Order of the Wolfhound who serve the house of the unseelie

Queen of Air and Darkness will come tomorrow night while Lou is working late on the van. They will be looking for your sword, and they will kill Lou Willoughby if you are not there to protect him." Liliana poked Pete in the chest with her finger. She did her best to make her voice sound like her first mother's. "If you do not use your sword, they will kill you, too. Use your sword. Your gun and knives will not work."

Pete got a sheepish expression on his face, looking down at his too-large boots. He hadn't listened to her when she told him to shoot the stone giant in the right hand, her only weak point. Liliana paid the price that time in bruises and blood. Pete would pay the price this time if he didn't heed her warning. "I'm listening this time, Lilly. Promise. I'll use the sword."

Liliana nodded. "Good. Also, call Doctor Nudd to go with you so that he can help you fight the four assassins. His cudgel will not pierce their protective magic to do them damage, but the sheer force of it will help keep them off you both, and off Lou Willoughby."

Pete got an odd look on his face. He put a proprietary hand on the old vehicle. "What's wrong with my van?"

Liliana shrugged. "I have no idea." She looked at the big green panel van as if it came from another planet. "I do not understand why this machine runs in the first place."

Pete snorted. "Well, maybe you could give me a clue from what you saw."

"It will make a funny noise tomorrow, but it will work fine tonight." Liliana got in on the passenger side, stepping up, and settling on the worn seat. "You can still take me to the party. I am going to dance."

"Oh, that's class. I've got my drums in the back. Siobhan and Doc are ready to make some music, too. I'm looking forward to it."

Liliana smiled. "I am also."

Pete put his sword in the hidden compartment in the back of the van, under the small couch that could double as a bed. The back of Pete's large van had all the amenities of a tiny apartment. He'd told Liliana that he lived in that van when he was younger, when he was a young orphan in the college work-study program.

He started up the engine which sounded normal, shrugged, and started driving toward Doctor Nudd's house.

"You must not tell anyone that you have the sword back," Liliana told him as they moved through the busy after work traffic. "Not even your beloved."

Pete's brows furrowed. "What's wrong with telling Ben?"

"You can tell him afterward." Liliana smiled to herself. "In fact, telling him will help him come closer to our world."

"How?"

"He and I agreed to an experiment to show him that I could see the future. He would put the sword where I could steal it. If I was wrong about the future danger to you, then I would return it in a year." She smiled to herself, fangs peeking out, foreseeing the consternation on Ben Harper's face. "Tell him our experiment was a success, and I returned the sword to you when you needed it so you didn't die. You can tell him about the assassins and Lou."

"He knew about this?"

"I convinced him to help me steal the sword by telling him that if I could truly see the future, then letting me steal the sword and give it to you at the right time would save your life."

Pete looked down at the sword, frowning.

"He did not believe I could see the future but was willing to let me steal it anyway. Your life was more valuable to him than his belief in the world as he sees it." It was the best comfort she knew how to offer her friend.

Pete smiled at her, wanly, as the auto-drive kept them moving through the traffic. "Maybe there's some hope for us after all."

"Give him time and patience. There is hope." Liliana smiled to herself, seeing in her fourth vision the moment when Ben sat on the couch, spiked coffee in his hand, the shock on his face turning to thoughtfulness as he considered the ramifications of children who could become rabbits. "There is progress, even. I made sure of that."

Pete reached an arm across, leaned over, and hugged her sideways. "I'm really glad I met you, Lilly."

She turned toward him, hugged him back, and smiled at his chest. "I would have preferred that you had not tried to kill me when we met, but ..." She shrugged. "I am really glad I met you, too, Pete."

Pete asked. "Are you going to fight with me when the Wolfhound assassins come after Lou tomorrow night?

"No, I will not. I must be somewhere else. But you will do fine without me. Doctor Nudd will help you instead."

Pete nodded, watching the traffic go by, face pensive. "This is what you've been training me for, right?"

"Yes. You are ready, now."

"Where will you be?"

"Hopefully, not dying, although that is a strong possibility."

"Oookay, then." Pete shook his head. "You know, I would feel a lot better if I thought you were kidding or exaggerating."

Liliana smiled. "Don't die, Pete. Make your enemies die instead."

The red wolf grinned back at her, bright and fierce. "You, too, Lilly."

Siobhan and Nudd were already sitting on the wooden double rocking chair on the big back porch of Nudd's rambling house with grass on the roof. They made merry music with their mismatched instruments, a bass guitar for Siobhan and a violin for Nudd. It echoed through the forest with no neighbors near enough to complain.

Liliana jumped from the vehicle almost before it stopped. She ran to the backyard, leaping into the low branches of the trees that grew from the surrounding forest right up to shade the back porch her friends made music on.

She bounced to the music as she swung from branch to branch as if they were the swings of a trapeze. She left behind long lines of silk that trailed down to the green grass in the small clearing behind the porch.

It had been so long since she'd had the joy of dancing with long silken sashes, woven from her first mother's silk dyed bright colors, hanging from the old circus tent's tall superstructure. She missed that desperately. The only part she didn't miss was that she used to have to dance in front of hundreds of staring strangers who paid for the privilege.

Now, only her friends shared in her expression of the sheer joy of living in a world filled with music. It was so much better. Knowing that she might die the next night gave her dance an extra edge. Tonight, she was in every muscle and drop of blood, from her hair to her toes, alive.

Pete added a hand drum beat to the music after a time. It wasn't long until another friend arrived. Detective Jackson's acoustic guitar joined along with her voice in a wordless song, as if her voice were another instrument, harmony one moment, and a soaring melody the next.

Doctor Nudd's home-brewed mead flowed. Everyone's auras showed bright sunny yellow happiness to her third vision.

Another car stopped and more people came, but Liliana was lost to the music and the dance by then. She would see what friends had come later. For now, her mind filled with motion and joy as she swung and spun and leaped in time to the music.

Her foot touched grass, twisting and spinning in a pirouette that made her wide red satin skirt spin out into a circle. In one hand, she caught a trailing silk line as she pushed off into the air, arms wide, back arching, as if she flew, up and up, the long wing-like sleeves of her bare midriff red blouse adding to the illusion. She released the line at the top of the arc, and flipped twice as the music did a hard double-beat.

Her ankle hooked a line, winding it around so that her dive shifted and she swung upside down, one leg, bare of tights today, stagged up. She rolled out of the embrace of the silk on her leg flying free for a moment, the full moon making it easy to see the branches and silk and grass that was her stage.

The cool wind tossed her long hair and the flowers from her garden intertwined with the tresses. The evening air played in her hair like fingers as she flew. Her feet fell on a slender branch that she let bend under her weight. When it started to spring back up, she used the momentum to flip before dropping her toes back to the grass just as the music reached a crescendo.

A final flourish as the musicians reached a mutually agreed ending had Liliana make one last leap flipping into a twisting layout so she landed in front of her friends, bending her knees to absorb her weight into a flourish and bow, like she would if they were a paying audience back in her youth.

Her chest heaved as she panted with the exertion. Sweat coated her skin. She laughed for the sheer joy of being.

Her friends all set down instruments so they could applaud each other as much as her. She joined in, delighted to have such wonderful music to dance to and such wonderful friends to dance for.

When she looked up from the bow, she saw the two latecomers.

Lieutenant Runningwolf stood to one side, a small smile on his face, wearing jeans and a concert t-shirt. She'd never seen him out of uniform, but she barely noticed him.

Beside him stood the Fae prince, Colonel Alexander Bennett, in charcoal gray slacks and a synth silk black shirt like a living shadow amidst all her brightly dressed, happy friends.

She shut all but her human eyes. She'd given him her word not to look past his skin without his permission. Or if he kissed her, although that was unlikely to happen again.

She didn't want to talk to the handsome Fae prince. He was cold, cruel, and hurt people who loved him. But she liked that dumbfounded look on his face. It gave her a feeling of power.

Pete said, "Hi, Colonel, John. What brings you two by?"

"Uh," Alexander Bennett said. "I, um ..." He cleared his throat. He tore his gaze off Liliana finally, looking over to Pete. "Sorry. I came to let you know there's been another murder, a corporal on my SET team, a hyena-kin. No one remembers him deciding to camp in that area, but his body was found there torn apart like the others."

Pointedly ignoring Alexander Bennett while he spoke with Pete and Detective Jackson, Liliana faced John Runningwolf. "You are looking well despite the dangerous experiment Andrew Periclum did on you."

The stocky badger-kin smiled. "Doc Nudd's been clearing my system of toxins every week or so with his magic. It seems to work. I'm getting the benefits of the nanites like Doc Periclum wanted, but none of the bad side effects."

"Dying is a very bad side effect. I am glad that you are not dying."

"Yeah," He chuckled. "I'm pretty happy about not dying, too."

Liliana grinned up at him. "This party is the opposite of dying."

John's face turned wistful. "I can see that. I wish I'd brought my keyboards." He sighed. "We'll have to go investigate that latest murder, anyway. With the victims all being literally torn apart, it's obviously an Other doing it."

"I think my friends would welcome you to add your music to theirs. I will ask them to invite you next time. Bring your instrument. I like having many harmonies to dance to."

"Was that what you call dancing? That was incredible. Made quite an impression on the Colonel."

Liliana's smile faded to a scowl. "He can be impressed all he wants. I do not care."

John's eyebrows climbed. "Mmm. I see. You don't care at all about the Colonel being impressed with you." He glanced at Bennett, who was still talking to Pete but kept stealing glances at them.

Liliana tilted her head to one side, wondering why what John Runningwolf said sounded odd even though it seemed to be a simple statement of truth. "Right," she said, then shrugged. "I will go home now. My friends will not make any more music. They'll have to go investigate the new death."

She walked around the sprawling house.

Behind her, she heard running footsteps. "Liliana, wait." It was Alexander Bennett's voice.

Liliana kept walking, ignoring him.

His long strides caught up to her as she reached Doctor Nudd's driveway.

"Don't you have a killer to hunt?" Liliana asked.

"Maybe you can help with that."

Liliana did not look. She had no wish to aid Alexander Bennett just then. "You have clues, a detective, and a smart forensic biologist. You do not need me to help."

A self-driving cab pulled up. Liliana had told it before she left her house what time to come get her. She opened the door to get in.

"Have I done something wrong?" Alexander asked.

"I see many things, even when I do not look into you."

"What did you see that has you giving me the cold shoulder?"

Liliana's shoulders were not cold. She was still hot from her exertion, in fact. And she wouldn't give Alexander Bennett the time of day right then, much less one of her body parts. "I have no idea what you're talking about. I just don't want to talk to someone who is cruel to his lovers."

He winced a little. 'You saw me and William part ways."

"You mean, I saw you coldly dismiss someone who loved you. You have made a very dangerous enemy."

He sighed. "It couldn't be helped."

Liliana snorted and got in the car. She told the polite voice of the computer her address, but Alexander Bennett held the door open so she couldn't leave.

"He wouldn't have believed any less callous rejection. Too sure of himself."

"I don't care." She popped out one arm blade, hooked it around the edge of the door, and yanked it out of the prince's hand.

As soon as the door closed, the auto-cab drove away, leaving Alexander Bennett standing alone in Doctor Nudd's driveway. Liliana watched with her fourth eyes without turning around.

She considered the possibility that saying she didn't care was one thing Liliana had never done before.

It was a lie.

CHAPTER 8

CHAMPION

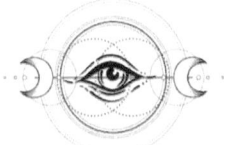

THE NEXT NIGHT, A LION-KIN IN A CORPORAL'S UNIFORM waved them in through a small seldom-used entrance to Fort Liberty. The entire Magoro family drove on base in their big SUV with Liliana in the shotgun seat. They didn't even request Liliana's base pass, or anything from the Magoros. All the cameras, camera drones, and other base security precautions were turned off for this one entrance. Officially, it was closed. There was a big sign that said so.

Every adult lion in the two-hundred miles or so surrounding Fayetteville gathered together at an abandoned hangar on a part of the base far from most everything else. The parking lot was full. There were even more beast-kin than Liliana remembered the last time she witnessed a pride-king's succession. There had been more time since the death of Andrew Periclum for everyone to gather. Even out in the parking lot, she could hear the echoes of growling, shouting, and occasional roars coming from inside the big metal building next to a small disused airstrip.

Liliana and Daniel Magoro walked side-by-side across the parking lot, toward the building full of angry lions and other beast-kin. Arel and Kazi fell into step on either side of them, small smiles on their faces as if they had already won. The fifty-fifty fighting chance that Liliana offered was far better odds than they'd had before they met her.

Daniel paused in front of the door, waving his wife and daughter inside ahead of them. He squeezed Liliana's shoulder with a massive hand to stop her for a moment outside the door. "Thank you for this, but I have to wonder why you're risking your life for us. Are you expecting something in return?"

Liliana smiled at his belt buckle. "If I die, leave this state immediately with your wife and daughter. Maybe try Canada?"

Daniel grumbled low in his throat, a lion's growl in human form. "I'm not inclined to run."

"I know. But if you do not run, your family will die." Liliana held onto Daniel's tree trunk arm whispering urgently to him. "This is what I want in return. Survive. Save your family. Start over somewhere else. Give me your word."

The old lion looked down at her, a muscle on the side of his jaw jumping as it clenched and unclenched. "All right. It's not that much to ask, I guess."

"Promise," Liliana said. A pride-king's word was law. If this lion would be king, then he would keep his word scrupulously.

Daniel nodded. "You have my word that if you don't win, I'll leave the state right after the challenge with Arel, Kazi, Marilyn and her son."

Liliana did not look into the future to see if the Magoro family would survive. She believed Daniel would keep his word. He would at least try to escape. If the spider-kin died tonight, she would die believing she had bought a few more good lives with her blood. She patted the old lion's arm. "Don't worry about Marilyn and her son, they left North Carolina this morning. You will have to call them back if I win."

"Huh. Guess she doesn't have much faith in you."

Liliana shrugged. "Faith is not what drives Marilyn Bradley. Protecting her son is what drives her actions."

"Good for her," Daniel commented.

Daniel pulled the door open. Arel and Kazi waited for them just inside. A wave of noise swept over them—shouts, growls, and hundreds of voices, all charged with anger, anxiety, fear, and excitement.

Liliana cringed. She grabbed the lion-kin's arm. "Daniel."

"What else do you want?" Daniel's voice was wary, as if he expected her to extort something else from him now that it was too late to change his mind.

"I am not good with crowds. Just get me to the dome, put a sword in my hand. I will be fine after that."

Arel Magoro leaned down to look in Liliana's face. "What do you mean, you're not good with crowds?"

Lilliana avoided the lioness's eyes. "You'll see." She hunched in on herself as if she were walking into the winds of a hurricane. Her petite form hid behind the broad wall of Daniel's body. Arel and Kazi closed ranks on either side of her, a half step behind the big patriarch.

They waded together into the crowd. There was a lot of passionate arguing punctuated with growls around them. Minor skirmishes here and there as arguments turned to quick spats with giant clawed demi-lion hands. There were a few of the other large predator-kin, too, bear-kin, and some of the other big cats, plus a few varieties of wolf-kin and some creatures that Liliana didn't try to identify. The future of the beast-kin of North Carolina would be decided here, and everyone wanted to have a say. She noticed there weren't any rabbit-kin or any other prey species. They might want a say in their leaders, but knew better than to get in the middle of this crowd of teeth and claws.

Daniel's big body got even bigger as he shifted. Tawny fur flowed over his massive muscles before she closed her eyes again. He roared as if to terrify a huge herd of gazelles. Everyone fell silent. Even the scuffles of minor fistfights or claw fights stopped.

Liliana huddled behind him, trying to be as small and inconspicuous as possible, hoping no one would notice her.

"I am the king of lions!" Daniel roared. "Who here would follow me?"

Arel and Kazi shifted to demi-lion form. They roared in one voice from either side of Liliana, "I will!"

Other lions' voices declared themselves for Daniel in the crowd. Liliana was surprised to hear so many. They had to know that Daniel couldn't win, but they supported his claim nonetheless. It spoke volumes for the respect the old lion had earned.

There was a commotion in the crowd, a great deal of shouting and growling.

Liliana tried to shrink even further into herself. All of her eyes were tightly closed. She held onto the back of Daniel's belt as a guide so she wouldn't get lost in the crowd. She would not be able to stop her mind from shutting down if she opened her third eyes. The overwhelming emotions in the room would assault her. Seeing so many strangers so close to her would make her shut down if she opened even her first eyes. She hunched her shoulders and trusted Daniel to guide her, blind, through a crowd of angry lions.

"I am the king of lions!" another deep male voice roared from the crowd. "Who follows me?"

A chorus of roars of support so loud it vibrated the floor beneath her feet followed. Tray Bradley had many followers. The majority of lions in the vast echoing hangar, though, kept silent, voicing their support neither for Daniel, nor for Tray. Since Tray Bradley's victory had to seem almost certain, their silence said that they did not support him, but were too afraid to oppose him. The jackal-kin, hyena-kin, and other beast-kin hovered around the edges of the hanger, or sat in the rafters, observing, but not voicing support of either side. Everyone followed the pride-king, but non-lions rarely had any real say in who that would be.

After several seconds, when the noise level fell to where he could be heard, Daniel shouted, "There are members of the pride who would follow me. I challenge you for the right to lead." There was another roar, this time from many throats, even those who had remained silent before. When that roar died down, Daniel's reverberating voice rang out again. "Tray Bradley, you must face my champion in the dome."

Uh oh.

There was a swell of confusion, rather than support after that statement. Most of the older members of the pride knew the tradition of champions. Many of the younger ones did not. Some questioned, some explained, some argued. The crowd devolved toward chaos.

The same loud voice as before, which Liliana assumed must belong to Tray Bradley, roared, "Enough!" The voice was much closer now. Bradley must have worked his way to them through the crowd.

"You will not face me yourself, old man? What are you, a lion, or a chicken?" Bradley's voice now spoke directly in front of Daniel. "Bawk, bawk, bawk!" he crowed. The lions around him snickered.

Liliana cracked one human eye to look up. All she could see was shaggy black mane covering the back of Daniel's head and shoulders in a long V that ended halfway down the massive back in front of her. In demi-lion form, Daniel was even more tremendous than he was in human form. The spider-kin could see nothing of the lion-kin she would have to fight around the giant furry back, but Bradley's voice had come from further up than Daniel's, as if Tray Bradley looked down at the gigantic lion-kin.

Daniel chuckled, low. "I'm a little old to be baited into foolishness like a boy on a playground. I care enough to choose what is best for the whole pride, not just for my personal pride."

Grumbles of approval came from behind Liliana. She was still flanked by Kazi and Arel, a Magoro lion on every side. But around them, the voices that had spoken for Daniel had worked their way through the crowd until they stood with the Magoros. Liliana stood in the center of a small island of supporters in a sea of enemies and those too cowed to take sides.

"Who would be dumb enough to fight me, but not want the crown for himself?" Tray asked.

"The daughter of a lion," Daniel answered. "She has no claim to the crown, but she and a single ally defeated an entire nest of widow spiders in Raleigh. She will fight as my champion."

Technically, that was not true. Liliana and Pete had not defeated the widow spiders alone. They also had help from Siobhan's machine gun and useful battle intelligence from Doctor Nudd, but she didn't think now was a good time to try to correct the mistake.

Daniel reached a furry arm behind himself, put it around Liliana's shoulders, and brought her forward.

The spider-kin hugged herself tight. She snapped her single open eye closed again. She knew everyone in the room was trying to get a look at her, which was probably difficult through the crowd of much bigger lions. As long as she didn't see them looking at her, she could hold on.

She heard a confused muttering, then a boom of laughter from Tray Bradley. That started off a chain reaction of nervous laughter from the lions around him, his staunchest supporters, no doubt.

Daniel's massive paws rested on Liliana's shoulders. He squeezed, claws well-sheathed. She was grateful. The contact anchored her in the here and now, keeping her mind from going away.

When the nervous titters died down, Daniel said, "I have the right to choose any champion willing to fight for me. Madame Anna volunteered to put her life on the line to support my claim." The lions at their backs, Daniel's supporters, made sounds of surprise.

"You can't be serious?" Tray Bradley said, a laugh still in his loud voice. "I'll slaughter that little girl."

"Challenge has been fairly issued. You must face Anna in the arena or forfeit your claim." Daniel's dignity quieted the unruly crowd. He added with a smile in his own voice, "Unless you're afraid to fight her?"

Bradley's answer was a growl that turned away, fading into the crowd.

Everyone, on either side, erupted in raucous cheers. No matter who won or lost, lion-kin always enjoyed ritual combat. Joyous yips and howls joined the roars. Most other predatory beast-kin enjoyed watching a good fight, too.

Daniel guided a functionally blind Liliana toward the dome. From the sounds of voices going up toward the high ceiling, some sort of bleachers for spectators had been erected. Around them, hundreds of lions, jackals, hyenas, bears, wolves, and who knew what, found places from which to watch the fight.

The lions who supported Daniel stayed around the Magoros until they reached the dome itself. The spider-kin risked opening one human eye a crack to peek at the dome. Her father often spoke fondly of testing himself against another lion in such a place, a thousand years before she was born. She wondered how different the domes were now from then.

She risked a peek. It stood perhaps 15 feet high in the center and 50 feet across, a solid steel cage of tilted triangles like some playground equipment she had seen, but on a larger scale. On either side was a double-door like an airlock with a space between the doors in the form of a smaller dome, like a rounded cage filled with weapons.

Lilliana hated cages.

The bleachers went up to her right and left, filled with excited beast-kin watching eagerly. The spider-kin shivered inside, reminded of the stares of the crowd back in her circus days.

Liliana hated being stared at.

She closed her eye again to shut out the staring faces, even as Daniel opened the first cage door. He had to duck to get through the opening.

"Are you sure about this?" Daniel whispered to her. Kazi closed the outer door behind them. Daniel's supporters stayed by it, guarding.

Liliana nodded. It was all she could manage.

Daniel placed a sword hilt in her right hand. He buckled a heavy shield onto her left arm. That felt right. It felt ... natural ... good.

Her parents had always used combat practice to bring her back when her mind became overloaded by her new senses. Focus was essential in combat. All that mattered was the here and the now. In combat, staring crowds were just background. If they were not potential threats or potential allies, then they were superfluous, unimportant.

Liliana felt her shoulders, hunched for so long, drop down. She breathed in and let it out slowly, centering herself.

The spider-kin opened her human and second eyes. She did a quick scan of the area to assess her situation, look for allies, weaknesses, the lay of the land.

She stood now on one side of the Dome, in the small extra chamber like a blister on the edge of the circular fighting cage. Tray Bradley stood in a similar chamber on the other side. Another lion-kin in demi-lion form strapped a shield to his arm.

Daniel lingered beside her. The fight would not begin until the two combatants entered the central part of the dome-shaped cage, and the non-combatants left the outer cages.

In her quick scan of the surrounding crowd, a familiar face stood out, his tall, aloof form contrasted with the emotionally charged beast-kin. The Fae prince stood to her right, watching her from just outside the bars, wearing gray slacks and a white synth-silk shirt with folded sleeve ends held by golden cuff links. Two lion-kin in demi-lion form wearing Army uniforms stood to either side of him with their hands on automatic weapons, the only guns she had seen in the hangar. Lieutenant Runningwolf, in short, broad, brown demi-badger form stood behind the prince, completing his protective detail.

Some part of Liliana's mind wondered what affect the nanites had on the stout badger-kin. At least, thanks to Doctor Nudd, he wasn't dying.

She walked up until curved triangles of steel and a few inches were the only thing that separated her from the prince. Daniel stayed at her side.

"What the hell do you think you're doing, Liliana?" Alexander Bennett asked. His voice was pitched low, tight with controlled worry or anger. She couldn't tell which.

"What the hell are you doing here, Alexander Bennet?" she asked him right back. She would not answer the prince's questions.

The memory of how badly he treated the wizard who loved him was still fresh in her mind. The consequences of his casual cruelty might cost lives. Dark paths flowed forward from that moment. If she didn't tame her unruly heart, it might be her in the wizard's place one day.

"I thought I was here to ensure the peaceful succession of the pride-king in my lands. But apparently, I'm here to watch you commit suicide."

"Someone might think you gave a damn," Liliana snapped. "But you have no heart, so that can't be true."

The prince's face darkened with anger or offense. "I have a heart."

"Perhaps the wizard believed that, before you cast him aside like used Kleenex."

"He was no longer useful," the prince stated without inflection.

"I have heard that the fastest way to reach a man's heart is through his stomach, but that is wrong," Liliana commented.

A tiny crease appeared between his brows. "You seem very interested in my heart."

Liliana slanted the sword in her hand through one of the foot-wide triangle spaces of the small cage bars. The sharp tip touched the prince's chest before he could move. "The fastest way to find any man's heart is through the third and fourth rib on the left side."

The two lions beside the prince hesitantly raised their weapons to point in Liliana's direction, but looked around nervously at the beast-kin that surrounded them when they did.

Lieutenant Runningwolf's gun held steady with a bead on Liliana's forehead.

"Stand down," Colonel Bennett ordered, holding up a hand.

His three protectors lowered their weapons but continued to eye Liliana with suspicion, Lt. Runningwolf's finger hovered near the trigger.

Daniel stood tense beside her but said nothing. He didn't know what was going on between her and the powerful Fae, but he clearly had no intention of interfering, even if she killed the prince right there in front of him. Daniel probably assumed she had a good reason.

Liliana wasn't sure he was right. Her reasons for her anger at Alexander Bennett were not entirely rational.

The prince stood very still. His face calm. "Have I given you some reason to be angry with me, Liliana?" His deep voice purred as calm as his blank face.

The spider seer knew that blankness was control of his emotional expression, not a lack of emotion. She had seen beneath the façade.

He felt.

In this moment, she didn't know if he felt angry, hurt, or afraid, but she knew the bored face was a mask he used to hide deep emotions.

One movement of her hand holding a sword tip against his chest would end this magnificent man. Horrified by the thought, she eased the pressure of the sword so it no longer drew blood. "I am angry because you are not the sort of man to be kind to people who love you, even when you don't love them back." She acknowledged the true source of her anger. "I wish you were." Her soft words were nearly lost in the noise of the crowd.

Alexander's voice lowered so only she could hear him. "William was going to kill someone if I didn't put a stop to it." A muscle jumped on the edge of his jaw, spoiling the illusion of perfect calm. "If he killed someone in my service, following my orders ..."

"Then you might as well have committed murder yourself." In his position, she would have separated herself from the wizard with the same haste. Although, she hoped that she'd show a bit more compassion. Liliana pulled her sword tip away from the prince's chest, noting the tiny spot of blood on his white dress shirt. If she had a hand free, she would wipe it away.

The two lions and the badger surrounding the prince sagged in relief. They were soldiers, loyal to the Colonel, and, no doubt, skilled fighters, but no one would like the odds of four against hundreds. If they killed the champion of someone with a legitimate claim to be pride-king, they'd start a war with their own pride.

"There is a high probability that I will not live though the next ten minutes," Liliana blinked human eyes suddenly hot with unshed tears. "If that happens, I will not be there when death comes for you." She risked not only her own life, but his. That hadn't occurred to her until now.

Alexander Bennett reached through the bars. He tilted her chin up to face him, his thumb gentle on her cheek. "Do you regret that?"

"Yes," she whispered. She looked into his deep brown eyes because he forbade her to do what she wanted, look through them to the fascinating, complexly layered soul beneath. The hundreds of beast-kin all around her, the cage that imprisoned her, the lion who would be king standing beside her, the weapon in her hand, all faded to meaninglessness.

Alexander's thumb stroked her cheek.

In all the universe, only that tiny motion mattered.

"I would very much like it if you would kiss me again," Liliana told him.

His lips quirked on both corners. "Survive the fight, and I will," His soft voice travelled only to her ears.

Liliana closed all her eyes for a moment, feeling that callused thumb touching her. It sent electric tingles through her whole body. She and this prince were not done yet. It would be a great tragedy if they both died before exploring the chemistry between them. So, she had to survive today.

She smiled wide, showing him her fangs. "You better make it a good kiss."

He chuckled in a way that made her belly flip. "It will be." He returned her broad fierce smile with one of his own for a moment, but it faded quickly. "You better live to collect it." Now, Liliana could identify the emotion placing the barest wrinkle on his forehead despite his control.

He was worried. For her.

Liliana's heart soared into the rafters of the old hanger. "I will do my best."

"Are you done?" Tray Bradley's gruff voice called from the other side of the dome. He stood inside the dome, and his second had left to join the crowd outside. He held a mace as big as her head, and a massive shield she would have difficulty even lifting.

Liliana studied her enemy with her second eyes that saw in different spectrums. She saw what most others couldn't see beneath the demi-lion's fur. There was extra heat from swelling around Bradley's left knee, a small slash of blood on his left thigh, and another heated swelling under his right eye.

Tray Bradley must have faced at least one other challenger today, perhaps more than one. He showed signs of fatigue, but there had been plenty of time for the big lion to recover from his previous bout. The minor injuries would not slow him down a great deal, but they might give her some weak points she could exploit.

Liliana nodded to Daniel.

He opened the inner door, letting her into the dome proper. The steel cage door clanged behind her.

"I am ready," she said.

The huge lion-kin roared and charged at her.

CHAPTER 9

LION VERSUS SPIDER

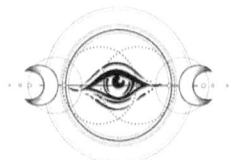

THE WERE-LION THE SIZE OF A MOUNTAIN GORILLA BORE down on the petite spider-kin like a semi-truck barreling toward a doe.

Unlike a doe frozen in headlights, Liliana dodged nimbly to one side, danced past the massive lion and trailed the tip of her sword across his upper left arm, leaving a scarlet path.

If the contest had been to first blood, Liliana would have just won. But she had no illusions this battle would end in anything but her death or the death of Tray Bradley.

Bradley turned on his toes, faster than she expected. He struck at her with the massive mace.

Liliana turned her shield at an angle, so the mace struck it a glancing blow. The force was still enough to throw her back hard against the triangular bars of the dome. She blinked, dazed, her whole body aching.

Her enemy wasted no time following up his advantage. The mace came at her head with crushing force.

Liliana ducked just in time.

The mace CLANGED against the bars, catching some of her hair.

She felt the strands yank free as she danced away from the restricting bars, toward the center of the dome.

Bradley's clawed foot flew out, trying to trip her or strike her legs.

Ha. Don't think so.

She leapt up and over, spinning around in the air. Her dodge turned into a driving thrust toward the lion's body.

Bradley bashed her sword aside with his shield hard enough to rip it from her hands. The sword clattered across the concrete cage floor.

His mace followed up the defense with a powerful attack, spiked head swinging toward her body.

Liliana barely got her shield up in time. She took the full force of the heavy mace driven by the werelion's superhuman power squarely on her shield.

She heard a snap under the crash of metal against metal as the mace connected. Her arm went numb. Her shield, smashed concave by the force of the blow, was ripped off her arm. The blow flung the light spider-kin through the air clear to the other side of the Dome.

Liliana tucked, touched the concrete floor with her right hand, and flipped herself to land on her feet.

Her weapons were gone so she flicked her wrists to pop out her arm blades.

Sickening pain flashed up her left arm as the blade came out on that side. With her second eyes, she could see that both forearm bones were broken. Her arm blades were much tougher and more flexible than bone. The spider-kin staggered a step, steadied her left arm with her right, and flicked the left blade back in, unable to stifle a groan.

More blinding pain hit her, but the unbroken blade stabilized her arm like a living splint. She couldn't use the blade, or the arm. She felt like vomiting.

Tray Bradley bore down on her again from the other side of the circular cage, slowly this time,. His smile grew as he walked. He had all the time in the world.

Seeing his mass, his skill, and assessing her weaponless petite self, down to one functional arm, she felt a wave of hopelessness. She wiped sweat off her upper lip with a hand that shook.

Liliana didn't want to die, but she'd already seen where this path led. An image of her own smashed corpse flashed in her memory.

Behind Bradley, the Fae prince stood, hands white-knuckled on the bars, his fear bare on his face for any to see, his control shattered. If she died today, he would mourn. She saw that on his face. Beyond that, he would die, too, very soon.

She didn't want that beautiful, complex soul to end.

Liliana straightened her back. In order to survive, she couldn't keep going down her current path. She had to change her fate.

I am making a fatal mistake.

She'd fought the lion-kin as if she were a lion-kin. If she had been a lion, she would be a tiny weak lion in a hopeless battle against the fiercest lion in the pride. But while she was her father's daughter, she was also her first mother's daughter.

She was not a tiny weak lion. She was a spider.

As the gigantic werelion accelerated his stride with a wicked fanged smile on his scarred face, mace drawn back for what he expected to be a finishing strike, Liliana leapt up and to the side, left arm hugged into her body to protect it.

She caught one of the bars of the cage with her right hand. She flipped up, body extended and toes pointed, in a one-handed handstand on the side bars. When her feet went through one of the topmost triangles, she hooked her ankles in the bars. She swung forward, popping out her arm blade to slash Bradley across the shoulders as he charged under her.

Bradley roared a lion's rage and pain, shaggy mane shaking.

Liliana flipped to one side. Her slippers touched down on the concrete floor. She attached a silk line to one of the bars of the cage about two feet off the floor. As the lion charged her again, she danced to his left to yank the line taut.

Even as Bradley tripped, he tucked into a roll. He bounced back to his feet on the opposite side of the dome, mace and shield still in place. "Is that all you got?" he taunted. "I'm going to crush you, little bug."

Liliana swallowed, remembering her crushed body in her vision. But she no longer followed that path.

She climbed the inside curve of the cage to the top as fast as she could. Having one functional hand slowed her. She touched her wrist to a cage bar, attaching a line, as Bradley came after her again.

Holding the line in her good hand, she swung from one side of the dome to the other, avoiding the lion by several feet.

He shifted his charge so she couldn't avoid him. To attack her, he was forced to put all his weight on his injured left knee.

The spider-kin bounced off the side of the dome to reverse direction She hit that knee from the unexpected angle with the full weight of her body.

She both heard and felt the sickening crunch, even over the noise of the crowd outside the cage.

Everyone in the hangar heard the lion's roar of pain.

Bradley staggered. For just a moment, his shield lowered.

"This is for Marilyn," the spider-kin whispered. She released her line, landing on the lion's shield. Her body weight forced it down another few inches to expose the lion's neck.

He drew back his mace. If that blow struck her, Liliana would die.

She swept her razor-sharp arm blade across his throat, lightning swift, with every ounce of strength she had behind it.

Blood flew in a circle that caught every spectator in the front row. A bit of warm spray touched Liliana's cheek. The new penny scent of blood overpowered the scent of sweaty lion.

The bushy-maned lion-kin's head slid off backward. His weapon dropped from limp fingers. Liliana rode the twitching body to the ground.

The crowd that had been shouting and growling in a cacophony of noise so ubiquitous, Liliana had long since ceased to hear it, went silent with a collective gasp.

She stood balanced on the lion-kin's shield on top of his massive chest drunk with battle joy. She lifted her face to the ceiling, too high on adrenaline to care that everyone was staring at her. "Daniel Magoro is the king of the lions of North Carolina!" she shouted. "Anyone who says different must face me!"

She opened all her eyes and bared her tiny fangs to her potential opponents. She turned a circle, feet balanced on the shield atop the dead lion beneath her, with the champion lion's blood dripping from her arm blade. "Who challenges Daniel Magoro?" she shouted, daring anyone to answer.

The lions that had spoken for Tray Bradley all dropped their eyes in submission as she looked at them.

One man didn't look away. Colonel Alexander Bennet met her gaze with one as fierce as her own. Some intense emotion that she couldn't name shone from his dark eyes.

Liliana wished she had not given her word not to look into the prince's heart and mind. She would have given anything to know what he thought and felt in that moment.

Arel Magoro's voice broke the tense silence. "Daniel is king!" she shouted.

Every face but Liliana's and Alexander's shifted and roared in a wave of sound so deep it rumbled the spider-kin's belly. It shook the metal supports of the old hangar.

By the cage door, Daniel was mobbed by the jubilant lions who supported him, and a great deal more who had been too afraid to express their support before. Strong, hairy shoulders lifted the big old lion and carried him away. Even most of the lions who had supported Bradley smiled with relieved delight that Daniel would be king instead.

The pride swept Daniel and his family away, out the doors into the parking lot to celebrate under the stars,

Liliana was left standing in a cage with a dead body.

The cage doors were designed to be opened from the outside. With both arms in good shape, the spider-kin could probably have found a way out.

Probably.

Liliana hated cages. Battle joy still sang in her blood from defeating a powerful opponent in single combat, yet she was stymied by a cage.

A pool of blood spread around Bradley's body. There was no way to step off him without getting it on her slippers.

Alexander Bennett opened the outer door of the cage. While Lieutenant Runningwolf held it open, Alexander opened the inner door.

He had to bend down to reach into the dome through the low entrance. He held his hand out to her.

The spider-kin stepped off the dead body, ignoring the puddle of slippery blood she walked through.

She refused to take the prince's hand. She was the pride-king's champion now. She walked out, head high under the cage door that wasn't at all too low for her. Adrenaline in her veins made even the throbbing pain in her arm fade to unimportance.

The prince followed her out of the cage into the echoing emptiness of the hangar.

Liliana swiped at the blood on her cheek, trying to wipe it off, but there was more on her hand. She just smeared it, making even more of a mess.

There was a spot of red on the prince's otherwise pristine white shirt. Liliana had threatened the prince's life. She had also committed bloody murder on a military base right in front of a colonel who commanded a unit who specialized in countering dangerous Others.

She lifted her chin, defying him. She was the pride-king's champion now.

Colonel Alexander Bennett ordered his three guards to drop back some distance from him, and turn around to form a perimeter, watching outward for danger. The two lions obeyed instantly. Liliana was theirs to guard now as much as their commander. But the badger-kin, moved away reluctantly, with many a backward glance.

John Runningwolf seemed to think the most dangerous thing

in the hanger was the petite spider-kin splattered with werelion blood.

Liliana smiled at him, showing fangs. She liked the idea that he might be right. "Are you worried I will kill your commander?"

The badger-kin's voice sounded bland as he wrinkled his nose at her. "There'd be so much paperwork."

With a white handkerchief, the prince wiped Liliana's cheek. When her face was cleaned to his satisfaction, he gently took her right hand. She let him clean the blood off it as best he could with the handkerchief.

Liliana didn't have to wonder for long what lay behind his dark, unreadable eyes. By promising her a kiss, he gave her what she wanted most.

He cupped her face in his hands, leaned in close, hesitating an inch from her lips so the kiss would be her choice.

Liliana closed the tiny distance.

He kissed her gently at first, lips just brushing hers.

A wash of lavender greeted her third eyes as she opened them. Overwhelming relief. Beneath it was the sharp magenta of admiration, and arctic blue of soaring pride as if she were in some way his, and had made him proud. A fleeting thought of her fighting for him was colored with manipulative satisfaction. He'd gained the ally he sought and she was as formidable as he could hope.

But drowning that icy bit of calculation was a volcano of scarlet red desire. Alexander Bennett wanted her. He wanted to own her. He wanted to possess her. He wanted to control her. But most of all, right then, he wanted to sink himself into her body and touch all that she was.

His kiss deepened, growing hungrier, more demanding.

Liliana made a little sound in the back of her throat that she had never heard herself make before. Her knees trembled. The lion had not weakened her with a mace, but this Sidhe prince did it with a kiss.

The spider-kin pushed against his chest with her one good

hand. She needed to take a step back from him to give her head a chance to clear. She licked her lips. Her breath came faster than when she fought. "You are a man of your word."

A broad smile sparkled in his eyes. It looked hungry and dangerous, not at all like the politician's meaningless mask he gave her in his garden.

This Fae prince wanted her. He didn't love her. He probably never would, but he desired the power and fierce, dangerous beauty in her, just as she did in him.

Pete told her before that love might grow over time if given the chance. It was like combat. She risked everything. Love might happen or it might not. She might gain everything she wanted or lose her heart.

"I looked into you," she told Alexander.

"I knew you would." His smile stayed undimmed. He'd allowed her to see his inner self, something he'd threatened to shoot her for before.

"Are you going to start pointing guns at me again?"

His smile turned smaller, still heated, but now crooked with amusement. "Do you still want to find out if I have a heart the bloody way?"

"I know you have a heart. I feel it." It beat fast beneath her fingers.

He covered her small hand with his, holding it tight to his chest.

She let her arm bend so she was not holding him so far away. She didn't want him to be that far away. "Today is my birthday," she told him, not certain why it mattered. She had somehow moved so close to him that she could feel the heat of his body through their clothes.

"Happy birthday." It was the usual social response, but the heat in his voice made the words a mere carrier. "How old are you?"

"One hundred forty-seven."

His smile went crooked again. "You're very spry for your age."

She giggled. "I am young. Spider seers live long lives. My grandmother was born in Egypt before the largest pyramids were built."

She made her decision in that moment. This Fae prince had a heart. Liliana would fight to make it hers. "Take me home," she ordered the prince.

He bowed to her and extended an arm in an old-fashioned gesture, offering escort to a lady.

She took it.

The three bodyguards fell into step around them.

CHAPTER 10

TRUST AND LOYALTY

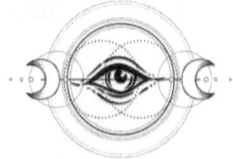

As Alexander Bennett drove her home, bodyguards left behind to celebrate with the pride, Liliana stripped off her bright flower print blouse that was coated in the dead lion's blood.

She wore a black leotard underneath her sapphire blue skirt. The leotard hid the few spots of blood on it. Underneath were warm powder blue tights, now ripped in a couple of places, and matching blue satin ballet slippers she would have to throw away when she got home. The blood stains would never come out of the satin.

The prince, driving manually as seemed to be his habit, had trouble keeping his eyes on the road. It would have been safer if he let the auto-drive take over like Pete usually did. He took her out of the seemingly unguarded gate, although she saw a few of his SET unit's soldiers watching them pass by. Since they were on the opposite side of Fort Liberty from her house, he drove in a wide circle around the large base.

Her skirt had very little blood on it. She used it to make a temporary sling for her broken arm.

While she wrapped and twisted the cloth, she opened her fourth eyes to check on her favorite red wolf. As she expected, Pete, with Doctor Nudd at his side and the legendary sword

Fraegerthach in his hand, killed all four assassins from the order of the Wolfhounds.

It was a good thing he did not need her help. Once the adrenaline rush wore off, Liliana was overwhelmed with exhaustion and pain. As badly as both she and Alexander might desire each other, there was no chance of them consummating anything that night.

"Pete is alive," she informed Alexander.

He raised an eyebrow. "Why wouldn't he be?"

"Four Wolfhounds tried to kill him tonight. Pete was ready for them."

A faint twitch at the corners of his mouth appeared, a sign she now understood that meant he was pleased. "Pete surviving was your doing?" the prince asked her.

"Pete defeated the assassins. He fought valiantly. I warned him and gave him the training he needed so he would be ready. I also made certain that he had his sword tonight."

"William said the sword had been stolen. I assumed Aurore had it by now."

Liliana shook her head. "No, I stole it, not your sister. I gave it back to Pete yesterday. If your wizard had succeeded in taking his sword, Pete would be dead by now. Without it, he could not have defeated the Wolfhounds' protective magic."

The prince's eyes widened for a moment. "I nearly got Pete killed."

"Yes, you did. What I do not understand is why. I know you don't want Pete to die."

Alexander's lips flattened into a thin line. "I was trying to get the sword to my sister so she would stop sending assassins after him."

"You were trying to protect Pete." Liliana smiled. That was a good reason to do the wrong thing. "I said you could not stop the Wolfhounds this time."

"I wasn't going to just let Aurore's lapdogs kill him and do nothing," he almost growled. Most of his expressions were subtle, but he seemed to be very expressive when it came to anger. He glanced at the spider seer. "You told Pete how to thwart William's spell on Giovanni."

"Yes." This could be a dangerous turn of conversation.

"Thank you for that. Did you tell Pete who sent him?" Alexander asked the question in the same bored voice he used when she held a sword tip over his heart. She wasn't fooled. The question was a trap.

"No." Liliana sighed. She could see how her life may have just become far more complicated. "I do not tell Pete your secrets, nor will I tell you his. So, do not ask."

The prince did her the honor of considering things from her side. "You're in a delicate position."

"You should tell Pete who you are."

"I plan to. When the time is right."

"Your sister wants the sword. She will not give up."

"Why? What's so special about that sword?"

"The sword is special in many ways. For one thing, it can pierce all protective magics, even those created by your mother, Queen Titania, or your sister."

"That takes some serious power."

Even with only her human eyes open, Liliana could almost see the calculations happening in his thoughts. "Tell the red wolf who you are," she told him. "Let him know that you have been protecting him. Once he knows you are his ally, the sword will be used in his hands to protect you and yours. Its power will be yours by extension. Neither you, nor any other royal Sidhe must ever possess it. That would be catastrophic."

Every trace of smile disappeared from the prince's face as she spoke. "I don't appreciate being told what to do." His voice had an edge of warning.

She was treading in dangerous territory. Liliana sighed, almost too tired to care. "I make my living giving people advice. Sometimes, I give advice for free. Some people take my advice and prosper from it. Some choose not to, even those who paid me for it." She shrugged with just one shoulder. The other one hurt too much to move. "You can take my advice, or don't."

They drove in silence while the prince thought about that for a while.

Liliana fell asleep.

She woke up when Alexander unbuckled her seatbelt. She opened several eyes to look around. The back of her own house is what she saw. They were in her driveway. When she started to get up, an involuntary moan of pain escaped her. Deep bruises covered more than half her body in addition to the broken arm. Also, she must have twisted her ankle. She didn't even feel it at the time, but now it was swollen and hot.

The prince lifted her out of his car as if she were a small child. "Are you sure you don't need to go to a hospital?"

"Nothing they could do would help. Tell Doctor Nudd about my injuries. He will know what to do."

The door to Liliana's home was only locked at times when she foresaw a reason to lock it.

Alexander opened the door with one arm while holding her full hundred-ten-pound weight in the other. And that was in his human form. In demi-stone form, his strength must rival Pete's in his demi-wolf form.

With some directions, he carried her straight to her bedroom to lay her in bed. He knelt beside the bed to unwrap the satin ribbons around her ankles with nimble hands. His big hands were warm and gentle when they slipped her bloody shoes off. She pulled her legs under the covers as he tucked her in.

"Thank you." For a man she'd never seen bend for anyone, it was far more tender care than she expected. She placed her hand in the center of his chest. Perhaps his heart wasn't as cold as she thought. Or, perhaps his tenderness was a calculated move to win her loyalty. He'd seduced the wizard into his service. She didn't want to fall for that sort of manipulation, but she did want him to kiss her again. The more he did it, the more kisses she craved.

"Does Pete take your advice?" he asked her. He must have been giving her words deep consideration, even while she slept.

"Pete is alive tonight and the assassins your sister sent are dead because he listened to my advice. Sergeant Giovanni is unspelled because Pete trusted me. Eliot planned to kill her, you know, even after he got the sword."

His jaws tightened. A muscle jumped on the side. "I found that out after the fact. I would never intentionally give orders that would get my sergeant killed." His teeth showed in an angry grimace that was neither pain nor a smile. Liliana had a feeling the wizard got off lightly with mere rejection. "I could never trust him." His face turned thoughtful. He brushed her hair back from her face. "Can I trust you?"

"I make mistakes, but I would never give you advice if I didn't think it would benefit you. I will never give you advice that would hurt Pete, though, even if it would benefit you."

"Your loyalty is to Pete first?"

That was a difficult question to answer. Her pull toward this prince of shadows and Green earth seemed to grow stronger every time she spoke with him.

Pete was her best friend. Beyond that, he was a good man. Pete did what he believed was in the best interest of everyone.

Alexander Bennett was not a good man. He was a beautiful man, a compelling and powerful man. In his own way, he was even an honorable man. But in the end, Alexander Bennett would do what was in the best interest of Alexander Bennett.

Liliana knew she should not be angry with the prince for being himself, but she also knew who she would choose to fight beside if the two men became enemies. "My first loyalty is to the Others of Fayetteville. I watch over their lives." She fiddled with the blanket, putting folds of it between her fingers and pulling them out, watching the motion. "Pete is good for Fayetteville. He brings justice to the most dangerous predators, but he does it with compassion and fairness. We need you, too, though." She glanced up at the prince's face for just a moment, then back down at the blanket. "You bring living power to a land that has been fading for a long time. You have the strength of will that the Others of this land need." That was all true, but it avoided the real question, and they both knew it.

"That's the first time you haven't answered a question I asked you."

Liliana sighed. She told him what he wanted to know, even though she knew he wouldn't like it. "I will do what I can to keep Pete safe, even from you."

The prince's face hardened. He drew back from her, hands on the bed as if to stand.

Liliana put a hand on his arm. "You like me because I tell you only the truth. If you want honesty, you have to accept that the unvarnished truth may not always be what you want to hear."

His lips twisted a little, not quite amusement. Irony, perhaps. It made a tiny dimple appear in his cheek. "Fair enough." He settled again, face on level with hers. "I am many things, but I try not to be a hypocrite, at least."

Liliana touched his forehead, tracing the outlines of the crown of silver horns that he wore in his Fae form. She knew the moment when he realized what she was doing, because he snatched her hand, pulling it away from his skin. His huge hand on hers was rough, abrupt, as if he stopped an attack.

"I have looked inside you, Alexander Bennett. I have seen the faces you hide."

He held onto her hand hard, keeping her from getting too close.

She'd seen him, the core and all the complex layers of him. "Knowing you, I desire all that you are. I will risk my own life to keep you safe."

His expression didn't change in any way she could identify, but something softened in his eyes. His grip gentled until he held her hand as if it were a tiny fragile bird he'd caught. His thumb stroked her skin. He swallowed. For a moment, he showed hope and fear and a potent mix of the emotions she'd only seen before boiling under the surface. "That is more than anyone else has ever given me."

In that moment, she didn't doubt that he had a heart. She also understood that while she risked all in this gamble, she wasn't the only one with something at risk.

The Fae prince leaned down to kiss her. Liliana suppressed an inappropriate urge to giggle. It was like a fairy tale, being kissed by a handsome prince while she lay injured in bed. She opened her third eyes and felt a different inappropriate urge.

The flood of scarlet desire she'd seen in him after he watched her fight was back. His heart was filled with a promise of far more than a chaste kiss. "I'll come back when you're feeling better." There was a rough edge to his deep voice.

"Spider-kin heal quickly."

He left with a chuckle. "I hope so."

Chapter 11

Appreciation, Kisses, And Pie

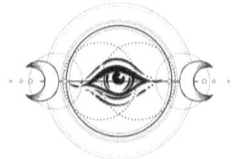

THE NEXT MORNING, LILIANA SLEPT UNTIL 9:37. HER first customer appointment, Janice Willoughby, was at 10 AM. The spider-kin groaned as she rolled out of bed, still in her torn tights and bloodstained leotard. She would have loved to take a very long, hot bath, but she only had a few minutes.

She showered off the lion-kin's blood as quickly as she could, but it still took quite a bit longer than it should have. There was no part of her body that didn't hurt. Her ankle was swollen. Her left arm was useless. She pulled on a clean purple leotard without bothering with tights or shoes, dropped a flowing homemade blouse made of scarves in multiple shades of lavender over it, she pulled on a skirt made of royal purple silk scarves with sequins sewn around their edges.

Another scarf, in red and yellow floral patterns, tied around her shoulder became a sling for her broken arm. Yet another scarf, a cerulean blue stretchy knit, made a serviceable wrap for her swollen ankle.

Her stomach rumbled, but she ignored it. She could already hear insistent knocking at her business door.

The spider-kin limped into the one room of her house that was set aside for her fortune-telling business so she could open the front door.

Janice held a covered serving dish in one hand. The other hand went over her mouth. "Oh, Madame Anna, what happened to you?"

"I was nearly killed by a big lion." Liliana didn't wait for Janice to come in, nor did she bow or do any arm flourishes. She just left the door open and limped over to her normal chair at the little round table with the crystal ball.

"How? I mean, didn't you see him coming? Couldn't you have avoided him?"

"Some lionesses asked me for help. They wanted to hire the Celtic wolf to fight for them, but I told them he was busy last night, so I would fight instead."

"You did that for ..." Janice's hand went over her mouth again. "You could have been ..."

"I had intended to cancel our appointment today, but I overslept. I didn't get a chance to call you."

"Don't worry about that. It's fine. I just wanted to thank you is all. You told me the red wolf would keep my Lou safe. You warned me to take my children and go visit family out of state so we would be safe, too. You were so right, but I guess you know that."

"Yes, I know that."

"Well, so, here. I made you a pumpkin pie." Janice set the pie on the little round table in front of Liliana. "I know it isn't anything special, but ..." She lifted the lid.

The spider seer's stomach rumbled again. "I like pumpkin pie." It was covered in a layer of whipped cream spread smooth, but with little waves in it from the knife.

Janice Willoughby was an excellent cook. Considering Liliana's current mobility issues, she might have to live on that pie for a few days. Standing up in her kitchen to cook was out of the question.

"A pie doesn't seem like enough. I mean, you've done so much for my family."

"You are my best customer. You always pay me well. Pete saved your husband. I only let you know that you could trust him."

"And fought a lion so that Pete would be there when my Lou needed protection."

"I gave you my word that the red wolf would be there."

"Oh, Anna." Janice blinked fast a few times, then threw herself at the spider seer.

Liliana almost punched her best customer out of defensive reflex but managed to stop in time. She grunted in pain as Janice Willoughby hugged her.

The rabbit-kin apologized so profusely that she stumbled over her words.

"It's all right. I am fine." Liliana managed to give her a smile. She patted her shoulder. "I had my own reasons for fighting the lion. My father was lion-kin. I am a child of the pride."

"You're a lion's daughter? If I'd had any idea how dangerous you were, I never would have come to you that first time. But I'm so glad I did."

Liliana smiled at the tablecloth. "I am glad, too."

"Is there anything you need? Anything I can help you with?"

Liliana inhaled the scent of sweet cream and pumpkin. She smelled allspice, too, with just a trace of the sweet bite of fresh ginger. "I'm not going to be able to cook for a few days."

The rabbit-kin patted her unbroken arm carefully. "Don't you worry about a thing. I'll make one of my chicken casseroles and bring it over right away."

"That would be nice." Liliana stood up. "I have to call my other customers to cancel their appointments, then I will go back to bed."

"Oh, of course, you poor dear. I'll get out of your way." Janice left, with several more expressions of sympathy and gratitude.

One thing Liliana liked about the rabbit-kin was that she never had to wonder what Janice meant when she talked. Janice was as skilled at social interaction as Liliana was deficient.

The spider seer ate pie with a spoon right out of the round serving dish while she made her phone calls. She put the remainder of the pie in the kitchen before limping back to her bedroom. She wondered if she could maybe get that long hot soak in a bath now, or if she would rather just go back to sleep.

Someone knocked on her front business door again.

Liliana sighed. She painfully limped back to her workspace.

She opened the door without bothering to look first. If it was an enemy, they could just kill her. She would feel better.

It was Marilyn Bradley, the brown-haired lioness. One hand held a large duffel bag slung over her shoulder. The other held her toddler son's tiny hand.

Liliana tilted her head to the side. "Why are you here, Marilyn Bradley?"

"Oh!" The lioness covered her mouth in shock, just like Janice did when she got her first look at Liliana. For a long moment, the lion-kin stared at her.

The spider-kin hadn't had a chance to look in a mirror, but she suspected she wasn't looking her best. Liliana waited with something she wasn't used to, impatience. Her ankle hurt. She needed to sit down and put it up, preferably with some ice. "Why are you here, Marilyn Bradley?" she asked again.

"I just wanted to ... thank you. And introduce you to my son, Simon."

"Your son's name is Simon?" Liliana looked at the tiny lion-kin. The brown-haired boy glared back at her over his thumb stuck in his mouth.

"I thought you would want to meet him. He's named after my great-grandfather. My grandfather used to tell me stories that I thought he made up. But after what you told me the other day ..." she smiled. "Well, it seems likely that we're related."

"What was your grandfather's name?" Liliana asked.

"Petros Simonson."

"Oh." Liliana blinked as her human eyes watered. "He was my youngest brother." The spider seer extended a hand to the boy. "I am honored to meet you, little nephew. You have my father's name. It is a lot to live up to."

The toddler looked at her hand for a moment, then up at his

mother who nodded encouragingly. He pulled his thumb out of his mouth long enough to squeeze Liliana's hand.

The little boy's hand was slick with saliva and possibly some snot.

Liliana wiped her hand on her skirt. Hopefully, the boy would gain better sanitary habits when he got older. "Was there anything else?" she asked Marilyn. "I am in pain. I would like to lie down."

"Of course. I'm sorry. It's just that we have our lives back because of you and well, we didn't even pay you."

Liliana gave a one-shouldered shrug. "I did not want another unworthy king of lions in Fayetteville. I am pleased that Daniel is king. He will be a good king. I am pleased I was able to help. I would like to lie down now."

"Right. Of course. But here." Marilyn set the duffel bag inside Liliana's door.

Liliana looked inside the bag with her fourth eyes. Money. The bag was full of transferable pay cards, many of them, some marked with large denominations. "Why are you giving me a bag full of money?"

"Andrew Periclum, the previous king, paid Tray a lot for ... for enforcement, I guess. Tray always hid that money away. He called it his retirement plan. Mostly, I think he was hiding it from the IRS. I didn't want any of that money, so I put it all in when we took up a collection to pay the Celtic wolf. The pride donated the rest. Everyone who didn't want Tray to be the next king, even the ones who weren't brave enough to say so in front of the pride, put in as much as they could afford. I thought you should have it."

"Why?"

"Well, you said we should pay you what we thought was fair. For what you did, for me, for Simon, for the whole pride, this isn't nearly enough. We owe you the rest of our lives, but ..." She shrugged. "This is what we have to give. Everyone trusted Arel, Kazi and me to use the money to help the pride. We think you should have it."

"Okay. I am going to lie down now."

Marilyn smiled. "You look like you could use some rest. Thank you, again."

"You're welcome." It was the correct social response, but it didn't feel right. For what she had done, the big bag of money was fair, yes, but at the same time, being paid made it clear to Liliana that the lions thought of her as an outsider. She'd been paid to do them a service. A pride-child serving her pride was not usually paid.

Yet, Marilyn and little Simon were her brother Petros' descendants. The pride was her family. She was now the pride-king's champion as well. She expected Daniel to give her duties once she recovered from the fight.

Getting paid like a hired hand hurt in a different way than her bruises and her broken arm. Clearly, they didn't want a spider in the lion-kin pride.

She watched Marilyn and little Simon get back in the big SUV with Kazi driving.

Liliana blinked tears as they pulled away. Forgetting for the moment about her throbbing ankle, she stared after the car long after it disappeared.

Her fourth eyes and her memory both filled with a vision of the time she'd fallen from the trapeze as a child. She'd bounced too high on the net below. It threw her to the hard-packed dirt where she broke her arm, rather like it was broken now.

Her father dropped down onto the net, bounced perfectly, did a neat flip over the edge, and landed lightly next to her. "Let me see."

"It hurts." She sobbed, cradling her injury.

Her father engulfed her with his powerful arms. That warm, smelly place with her face buried in his sweaty leotard was safer than anywhere else in the world.

"I know it hurts, *kardoula mou*. But you are so very brave to want to fly with your family in the act. Sometimes, it hurts to reach for what you want most."

He stroked her hair for a while as her tears and snot mixed with the sweat on his chest. After the storm died down a bit, he said gently, "Maybe you should wait a few years until you get bigger."

Liliana sniffled. Her tiny face scrunched in frustration. Sometimes words wouldn't come when she was this upset. While pain tried to make her mute, her anger forced words out in a tumble. "Other people get bigger. I'm always small. If I wait to get big, I'll never do anything. I want to fly with you. I don't care. This will heal."

Simon of Nemea smiled down on her with such pride and love that his aura in her third eyes glowed like the blue-white heart of a welding fire.

Grown Liliana smiled to see that expression on her father's face in her fourth vision. She couldn't see the glow of his aura anymore, but she remembered how bright it had been that day.

I am a dome champion, now, Pater. I am the champion of the new pride-king, even though I never stopped being small. You would be so proud.

She'd fought for this pride to be led by a man of honor. She would fight again for her right to be part of it. Maybe she would have to remind Daniel that it was her pride, too.

When she felt better, she would go visit Daniel Magoro to discuss how she would serve the pride now that she was his champion.

Her nephew was his heir. She would have a hand in forging the next pride-king, too.

Liliana closed the door. She looked at the duffel bag full of money. It was a big bag. There was no way she wanted to pick it up right now. But it didn't seem like the best place to leave a bag full of money, right by the door of her shop.

She decided she would move it later. The wounded spider-kin limped back into her living space.

Someone knocked on her back door, just as she closed the door between the business room and the rest of her house.

Liliana sighed. The knock was on her home door this time. If it had been on the business door again, she might have ignored it, but very few people knocked on her back door. They were all too important to ignore.

She limped over and opened the door. "What?"

It was Pete. He looked puzzled. He had a split lip, and a nasty scratch on his neck. "That's the kind of greeting I usually get from Doc Nudd." He looked more closely at her face and whistled. "What happened to you?"

"I need to lie down." The spider seer left the door open. She limped over to her couch. She clearly wasn't going to get that hot bath today.

Pete followed her in. "So, what's the story?"

"I fought a lion-kin last night." She put her sprained ankle up on the arm of the couch. Leaning back, she faced the big, overstuffed armchair that Pete sat in the last time he visited her. "There is beer in the refrigerator," she told him.

"I'm good, but you're not." He hovered over her a little. "Is there something I can do for you?"

"You could get me some ice in a towel for my sprained ankle, and maybe another one for my broken arm?"

"Sure, Lilly." He went into the kitchen. Puttering sounds came from the kitchen, but she didn't bother opening any extra eyes to watch him. "Is that pumpkin pie?"

"Yes. Janice Willoughby made it. It's very good. You can have some if you want."

"No, thanks. I've got enough pie at home to gain twenty pounds." He came back into the living room holding two tied dish towels full of all the ice in her house in corn-based plastic bags. "Lou's wife made pie for you, too?"

"She was thanking me for telling her the red wolf would protect her husband, not kill him."

Pete grinned. "I appreciate that. It would have been a lot harder to protect Lou if he'd been trying to run from me and the Wolfhounds both."

Liliana hissed a breath in through her teeth as Pete placed the ice packs. The ice was very uncomfortable, but it would bring the swelling down on her ankle and numb the pain in her arm. She wished she could use over-the-counter medicines like Normals could. "Can you do something else for me?"

"Sure, Lilly, whatever you need."

"Can you get the duffel bag sitting by my business door and put it in my bedroom closet? I don't want to lift it right now to put it away myself."

Pete got the bag. He hefted it curiously as he brought it in. "What's in here?"

"A whole lot of money."

Pete hesitated for a moment, then walked into her bedroom to set the duffel bag in her closet.

Liliana watched him with her fourth eyes this time, amused.

Pete gingerly picked up the blood-soaked clothes she'd discarded on the floor earlier. She hadn't had the energy to take the blouse and slippers to the trash recycler. They were beyond any hope of laundering. She should turn on the room-bot to take care of it for her.

He came back into the room, looking concerned. "Lilly, why do you have a bag full of money?"

"The wife of the lion-kin that I killed gave it to me."

Pete ran his hand through his thick red hair. He scratched the back of his neck. "Um, Lilly, did you murder a man last night and get paid for it by his wife?"

Liliana grinned, amused by his discomfort. "Are you going to call Detective Jackson to arrest me?"

"I won't, but I'm wondering if I should."

"Some lionesses asked me for help. The new pride-king was chosen last night. A very unworthy man would have become king. He would have killed many people, including those three lionesses, sparking a pride war that would have killed hundreds more."

Pete's pale skin paled a little more. "Yikes. The pride war in South Carolina in the '20's killed over three hundred people, and a couple thousand were injured."

"They wanted to hire my friend, the Celtic wolf, to kill the unworthy lion to prevent that."

"Why didn't you send them to me, then?"

"I promised Janice Willoughby you would protect her husband last night."

Pete got an "aha!" kind of look on his face. He pointed at her. "I can't be in two places at once."

Liliana smiled at his boots. "I watched you and Doctor Nudd fight the Wolfhound pack. You were magnificent."

Pete knelt beside the couch. He squeezed her uninjured hand. "I had an excellent teacher."

She felt warm in spite of the ice on her arm and her ankle.

"Is there anything else I can do for you?"

"I will be fine, Pete. I am tired now. I would like to sleep."

"Okay, I'll let you rest." He leaned in and kissed her forehead.

Liliana closed all her eyes, smiling.

Pete left.

Liliana dozed.

Another knock on her front shop door woke her. She looked, thinking she would just ignore it, but got up instead. It was Janice Willoughby with enough casserole for the spider-kin to eat for days.

Liliana ate some of the delicious warm casserole, then lay back on her couch, not really sleepy anymore, but not interested in doing anything. She didn't even want to open her fourth eyes. She was afraid she might see something important and feel compelled to do something about it.

The spider seer wondered if it might be nice to have a holovision set, or one of the communication centers people had now instead. She had enough money to get one now. She should at least turn on her room-bot so it could pick up her soiled clothes and clean the dirty dishes she'd left in the sink, but even getting up to turn the robot on seemed like too much trouble. If she had a communication center, she could tell her house AI to turn on the room-bot, but that seemed lazy to her any day other than today when half her body was throbbing with agony.

Someone knocked on her home door before she got settled back on the couch with new ice packs. She looked with her fourth eyes.

Doctor Nudd and Siobhan. "Come in!" she shouted. The door was not locked, and she did not want to get up again.

Doctor Nudd and Siobhan brought her medicine. She'd forgotten she had some already. That would have helped. Doctor Nudd brewed chai tea to mix with the powder to hide the bitter flavor.

Liliana drank the medicine-laced tea gratefully.

Doctor Nudd and Siobhan helped themselves to a craft beer each. Once settled on the armchair and the couch arm respectively, they asked her for the story.

By the time she'd explained the essentials, the pain in her wounds had faded to insignificance. She felt rather delighted with everything.

I wonder if this is how my venom makes people feel?

"Thank you, my friends," Liliana said. "You are the best friends in the world, the best friends that anyone ever had."

Siobhan giggled. "Sure, Spider Girl. Glad to see you're feeling better."

Doctor Nudd downed the last of his beer. He patted Liliana's uninjured shoulder. "I'll come back to check on you in a few days to make sure you're back on your feet." He grinned down at her. "The new pride-king's champion will, no doubt, have duties."

Liliana grinned back at his left ear. There was gray and brown hair growing out of it. Doctor Nudd understood. "I'll have duties in the beast-kin court." She giggled. "Just like the Fae prince's Merlin has, and the Fae court Guardian!"

She raised a hand toward Siobhan, two fingers up and crooked.

The sprite hooked two fingers with hers, then pulled.

Liliana pulled back, straightening her fingers as the sprite did. They pointed them at each other and said, "Pow!" at the same time.

The spider seer found this new social ritual as odd as all the other ones she'd learned, but this one was satisfying in the moment. It was nice to have someone else understand how fundamentally her life had changed.

"Later, Champion," Siobhan said on the way out.

"Later, Guardian," Liliana said back.

She asked Doctor Nudd to leave the door open a crack so that whoever came next could just come in. That way she wouldn't have to get up.

Liliana had never in her life had so many people in her house in one day. She felt like she sort of had a party, just not all at once. She giggled to herself.

She closed her eyes for a moment, then looked up, confused by the odd change in light. Her clocks said it was past eight. Her windows were dark. She must have dozed off for a while. Doctor Nudd's medicine was still going strong. She felt no pain and no inclination to move.

A deep voice said her name, "Liliana?"

"Yes?"

Alexander Bennett stood in her entryway holding a gun while looking around her house.

She sighed. "I thought we were past the gun pointing thing."

"Your door was open. I thought something was wrong."

"Nothing is wrong. So many people have been in and out of my house today, I got tired of opening the door."

He closed the door. The lock clicked. "Who was here?" He walked into her living room, still looking around warily as if he expected something dangerous to pop up out of her cupboards.

"Nearly everyone I know."

The spider-kin watched him scope out her living space. He was so tall and his shoulders were so broad that her living room seemed cramped in comparison. Strange that Doctor Nudd was even taller and Pete was just as broad-shouldered, yet neither of them seemed to fill up space like Alexander did.

He relaxed after another moment. Apparently, her bookshelves weren't going to attack. He looked down at the spider-kin stretched out on the couch with her bad arm snugged against her belly and her ankle propped on the couch arm. "You look terrible," he said.

Liliana giggled. "I don't think you're supposed to say that, even if it's true. Isn't there a social rule against it?"

"Undoubtedly." He put the gun in the holster at his hip.

"Why are you here, Alexander? Even spider-kin don't heal that fast."

He chuckled. "I wanted to see if you needed anything. It looks like I was last in line."

"I have pie. And a big bag of money. And good painkillers. I am glad you came, though."

"Is there anything I can do?"

"You could kiss me again. I like it when you kiss me." Liliana pushed the melted bags of ice and the dishtowels on the floor. She held out her good arm to him, making grabby motions with her hand.

The prince smiled at her, one of his tiny, real amused smiles, not his broad fake politician's smile, or the hungry shark smile he gave her after she killed Tray Bradley. "Those must be some really good painkillers."

"I like your smile, too, when it's real."

The prince looked around her living room for a place to sit. He seemed to consider the chair where Pete and Doctor Nudd liked to sit.

He took off his coat and dress uniform jacket. A myriad of colorful ribbons set off the dark blue woolly fabric. He laid them down on the big chair with his hat on top of the neat pile.

His strong arms slipped under the spider-kin's shoulders and knees. Alexander swooped her up off the couch like she was light as a feather. He spun her around and sat on her couch where she had been a moment before, but now her body fitted comfortably against his chest in the crook of his arm.

Liliana giggled. "I like this, too." She snuggled in closer to his broad chest. Her broken left arm was safe in the sling in her lap. Her right hand rested on his chest. She flattened it over his heart where it seemed to belong.

"I'm glad to hear that." His hand stroked her hair back from her face, fingertips gentle on the swollen bruises on that side.

"Are you going to kiss me now?" She looked up at his full mouth with just her human eyes, licking her lips.

"Definitely."

She opened her third eyes as his lips touched hers. He was worried about her. He had been thinking about her all day, both how beautiful and how tiny she was. She'd been so badly injured. He worried that he left her here alone, that if she needed help, no one would know. He should have insisted she go to a hospital. He was both relieved and disconcerted to find she didn't need anything from him.

His concern made her heart soar. Her stoic prince had a heart that she had begun to win.

"You don't need to worry. My friends have been taking good care of me."

"You must have some very good friends."

"I do." The truth of that struck the spider-kin again. She had been alone a long time, long enough that she would never be able to take having friends for granted. "I didn't have any friends at all until I met Pete. I also didn't have to fight widow spiders and really big lions, but I like my life better now."

"Was Pete here?" His body tensed a little. His expression and voice became bland and bored.

"Yes. He moved the bag of money. He put ice packs on me, and he kissed me before he left."

"Pete kissed you? Does Pete kiss you a lot?" His voice still sounded like the answer was unimportant to him, but Liliana wasn't fooled.

She giggled. "You're jealous of Pete."

He raised an eyebrow at her. "You told me you wouldn't look in my head unless we were kissing."

"I didn't need to look." She tapped him on the nose with her fingertip. "I just know."

"You didn't answer my question." His lips pursed in annoyance bordering on anger.

He was so quick to anger. She didn't want him angry with Pete.

Her prince could be a very dangerous man. "He doesn't kiss me like you do."

"What do you mean?"

Liliana gave his unscarred cheek a sisterly peck. "Pete kisses me like that."

"Ah, I see." She felt his body release tension, snuggling her closer. His face lost its hardness.

Liliana smiled at him, wide and wicked, showing him her fangs. "Normally, jealousy is a problem, but I think I like that you were jealous."

"Why would you like that?" He wrinkled his nose in distaste. "Jealousy is an emotion I try hard to avoid."

"You wouldn't be jealous if I wasn't important to you."

He drew up with a blink. "That's ... true."

"You like me because I always tell you the truth." Liliana's hand wandered over the planes of Alexander's chest. She could feel the shape of his large pectoral muscles through his button-down shirt. She loosened his tie until the short end came out of the knot, then tossed the useless piece of fabric on the floor.

He watched, bemused as she struggled to unbutton the old-fashioned buttons on his uniform shirt one-handed and uncoordinated from intoxication. "That's not the only reason I like you," he said, voice so soft it was almost a whisper. He kissed her forehead, but it didn't feel the least bit like Pete's kisses. His lips trailed to her cheek on the side that wasn't bruised, then to her ear.

Liliana wondered if kissing that was not on the lips qualified as kissing that would let her look into him. "I want to know the other reasons. Can I look?"

He chuckled, tickling her ear with his warm breath. "You could just ask."

"I don't always understand what people mean when they use words. When I look inside people, I understand them."

He drew back enough that he could look at her face. "You've already seen inside my head."

"I have seen who you are." Enough of his buttons were undone that she could slip her hand in to feel the heat of his skin through his thin t-shirt over his pounding heart. "I have seen your soul." She ran her hand up his neck to his face, cupping his scarred cheek. "But I only see what you think and feel in the moment when I look. You would have to think about why you like me while I'm looking at you with my third eyes for me to see."

Alexander swallowed as she touched his scars, her fingers careful so as not to hurt when she caressed the bumpy slick skin. His eyelids fluttered closed.

He held her hand against his face. "What is inside my head isn't always pretty. Some of it is dangerous for you to know."

"I already know a great many dangerous secrets, my very dangerous prince, including some of yours. I have never betrayed your secrets. I never will. I try very hard not to betray anyone's secrets."

He opened his eyes. They were filled with some intense emotion, some longing she couldn't identify.

"Let me in," she asked. Her fingertips delicately touched his scars. She wondered what made permanent scars on a Sidhe who could heal nearly any injury. But she didn't look. He would tell her when he was ready.

He nodded. "You can look inside me whenever you wish." Fear flashed in those fathomlessly deep brown eyes.

She looked. He was afraid that each time she looked inside him, she might find something so ugly, so dark that she would no longer want him. But that fear was balanced by a longing, a hope that someone could know him, all the layers, all the secrets and hidden dark corners of his soul, and still want him.

No, not just someone.

Her.

Inside Alexander's mind, Liliana saw herself looking back with exotic eyes like wise and magical jewels. Her head cocked sideways with eyes on the floor, thick wavy dark hair framing an elfin face as she asked him if he would send Wolfhounds to kill Pete. She soared through the air, the essence of grace and power, as if gravity didn't apply to her. She walked out of a cage, splattered with blood, head high like a queen. She trembled and went pliant in Alexander's arms as he kissed her, right after she danced the deadliest lion in the pride to death.

A tender seriousness filled her face as she told him she desired all that he was. She fully intended to risk her life to fight for him. The raw truth of that still shook him to the core.

This man wanted Liliana. He wanted to possess all that power and beauty, unselfconscious grace and honest desire. He wanted her so much he could hardly think of anything else but her.

Liliana had a hard time believing it was true, but she could see it with her own eyes. She couldn't tell a polite lie to save her life, was prone to sudden violence, and had strange eyes that she hid so they wouldn't make people uncomfortable. He liked all those things. Quirks that others saw as odd or disturbing, he saw as desirable.

Liliana slipped her hand up to pull him closer. The fine short hair on the back of his neck tickled her palm. For the first time, rather than just letting him do the kissing, she gave her prince a proper kiss.

As the kiss deepened, she filled her third eyes with the hot red of his desire. She pulled him hard enough against her lips to hurt, and didn't care. She kissed him like she would die if she couldn't, like she needed his lips and tongue to breathe, to live.

He groaned into her mouth, kissing her back with the same desperation. His hand moved up her bare thigh under her skirt until it cupped her bottom.

She ripped the rest of the buttons off his shirt, so her hands could explore his chest. Her fingernails raked against the thin t-shirt material, wishing she could claw it off him so nothing would separate them.

He crushed her tight enough against his hard body to make her cry out involuntarily from the pain. A shock of horror/disgust ran through him like a bucket of ice water over all that fire. He pulled away from the kiss, breathing hard.

"It's all right," Liliana said. He had hurt her, but between the painkillers and the spectacular need inside his head, she was so drunk she didn't care. No one had ever wanted her that much. It made her feel giddier than any drug.

"No, it isn't." A shuddering revulsion doused his passion. He closed his eyes for a moment, took a deep breath and let it out, regaining control. She caught a flash of memories, nothing clear enough to catch more than the impression of pain and sex mixing in a very bad way to make something ugly, before he slammed that mirror of shielding over his mind, shutting her out. "I'd better go."

"I really want to bite you," Liliana said, disappointed. She knew she wasn't thinking clearly with the drugs in her system, but she wasn't sure she'd ever wanted anyone so badly either. This prince of shadows and secrets was the most fascinating man she'd ever met. Waiting until her body healed to claim him seemed like a form of torture.

He raised an eyebrow at that. "You want to bite me?"

"I want to share venom with you very much." She nibbled on the strong column of his throat down to the prominent collarbone that his open shirt revealed. He had so much muscle, she could bite him almost anywhere.

"That's not what I had in mind," he said. His body tensed against her. He would have pulled away from her if he could have without dumping her injured body on the floor. As it was, he took a firm grip of the hair at the base of her neck so he could pull her head away from his skin.

Liliana giggled. "I know exactly what you had in mind. I want that, too. But it would hurt right now, so can I just bite you?" She stroked the short, rough dark hair on his unscarred temple where gray hairs mixed with the black, one of the first signs that he was no longer young. If he let her bite him, he would be hers. The gray would soon fade away. If she had her way, his hair would stay dark forever.

"What would your venom do to me?" His voice returned to unconcerned boredom, hiding how he felt from her.

Since she had permission, she looked. He was afraid. His

knowledge of her species was limited to rumors and legends. He thought she wanted to poison him or bind him against his will like William Eliot's spell.

He didn't know that spider seer venom extended life. Now that she thought about it, Doctor Nudd, his advisor on all things Other, had only known of the healing effects. There were few people left on earth who knew the full truth.

She blinked for a moment, considering. Alexander wanted her, even though he had no idea that she could make him immortal. He didn't want her venom; he just wanted her. That was...wonderful.

"Liliana," he said, pulling her back from where her mind had wandered. "What affect does your bite have?"

"I don't want to poison you, my prince. My venom would make you feel a little bit like I feel from the painkillers. No pain, no worries, only peace and pleasure. And it would help you heal if you were hurt. Spider seer venom is meant to be shared with a lover."

"Would it affect my mind?" This was the question that mattered to him. His greatest fear was being powerless in another's control. He would never risk doing something that would put him in that position.

He trusted her to tell him the truth. She knew he wouldn't like it, but the truth is what she would always give him. "For a few minutes, you would answer me, no matter what I asked, even if the answer were a secret. Also, you would do almost anything I asked. Almost. Your will is strong enough, you could still refuse me if it were important to you."

"What were you planning on telling me to do when I was under the influence of your venom?" His face had blanked into boredom, but his soul roiled with a kaleidoscope of conflicting emotions. Fear fought with disappointment and betrayal for dominance.

"I just wanted to share venom, to taste you and watch the euphoria fill your soul. I hadn't planned on asking you to do anything, but ..." She considered what she would say to him right now if he were under the influence of her venom. She grinned, touching his lips with her fingertips. "I want you to kiss me again."

His lips twitched in amusement under her fingers, so she felt as well as saw the little smile. In his mind, she saw sparkles of relieved and delighted laughter bubble to the surface, wiping away the darker emotions.

"Only you, with a landed Sidhe prince in your power, would ask for nothing more than a kiss. I've never been with someone who had no hidden agenda, who wanted nothing from me beyond myself." He gentled his strong hold on her hair, tucking her head under his chin. For a moment, he just held her, one hand stroking her cheek as his soul's colors softened to a relieved, contented peace. He let out a long breath. "I have a serial killer to catch. I've already stayed longer than I intended. And I think you need rest, Little Spider."

Liliana let her head fall back over his bicep. "I guess so. I don't want to rest, though. I want to bite you and drag you to my bed."

Alexander chuckled as he stood, lifting her effortlessly with him. "I may never let you bite me, but I promise that I will let you drag me to bed another time."

He hated the thought of being controlled by someone else. If she ever wanted his permission to share venom, she should tell him that her venom could extend his lifespan indefinitely.

Liliana said nothing as he carried her to the bedroom, watching the beautiful, shifting red layers of his desire, the sparkle of his amusement, the acid green undercurrent of his fear which was not completely gone.

Alexander wanted her, not her venom.

His mother, Queen Titania, and his sister, Princess Aurore, were both immortal. Many Fae held mortals in contempt. That had stung him his whole life. His own mother ignored his existence because of his human lifespan. Immortality might be an irresistible temptation. If he knew that her venom could extend his life indefinitely, it could change everything between them.

Yet, even under the tongue-loosening influence of Doctor Nudd's wonderful painkillers, she kept that information behind her teeth. She gloried in how badly Alexander wanted her for herself.

His calculating mind might find immortality an irresistible plus, a solid, logical reason to keep her at his side forever. But it wasn't his mind she wanted to win. She wanted his heart.

"You don't want me to tell you what to do?" she teased him.

"I don't want anyone to tell me what to do." His half twist of a smile made the words a tease aimed at himself.

Liliana giggled. "You are a stubborn man."

"And you need to go to bed and heal."

"You are bossy. Very bossy."

He huffed a laugh. "I don't think anyone ever called me that before, but I can't deny its accuracy."

He tucked her in bed, just as he'd done the night before. She could get used to that. "You said I can look inside your head, even when we aren't kissing." She stroked his face with her fingertips, tracing his features, both smooth and scarred. His cheekbones were as sharp as blades.

"That's not the same as allowing you to manipulate my thoughts and actions."

"Not so long ago, you threatened to shoot me if I looked inside you. Today, you gave me permission."

He quirked one side of his mouth, showing that little dimple. "You have me doing a lot of things I never thought I would."

He kissed her once more, a promise as much as a farewell, and left, locking her back door behind himself.

Liliana smiled as she drifted to sleep.

His heart is well-guarded, but I am good at getting past guards.

CHAPTER 12

UNEXPECTED DELIVERY

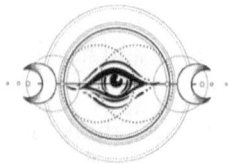

THE NEXT DAY, LILIANA GOT A DELIVERY. SHE SAW IT coming with her fourth eyes.

She took a moment to inhale the sweet scent of the opening rose bud in the vase on her dresser. Alexander had plucked that flower with magic from the bush at the center of his power. Instead of fading, it seemed determined to grow. The red that outlined the ivory petals spread as it opened, becoming even more lovely and releasing more scent.

With reluctance, Liliana limped to her back door to take the package from the drone as it arrived. The little flying machine zipped under her porch roof. It lay a metal box at her feet. She opened the box with her thumbprint, and set it back down, leaving it on her porch. The drone would get it later to take it back to the warehouse. Inside the box, she found a sleek, modern smart phone.

It was not the usual wrist phone that most people used. In fact, while there was an armband in the box, it was just heavy-duty cloth with no electronics in it, simply a way to carry it, not part of its function. There were none of the usual sensors that measured health statistics of the wearer like heart rate, blood glucose level, and oxygen saturation. This phone was flat, like a tablet computer, but smaller. There was no return address on the box, no note, or anything to show who sent it.

The spider seer tried tracing the phone backward in time with her fourth eyes, but that was more difficult to do with objects than with people. She saw the device in hands and machines that built and packaged it. In her living room, she sat in her big recliner chair studying it. She plugged the phone into its charger. That seemed like a logical thing to do. Beyond that, she wasn't sure why she would need such a device. Or how she could possibly make use of it.

Liliana didn't have an official last name, although she used Solifilia, daughter of Solifu in Latin, when required. She had no credit cards or bank account. She bought most of what she wanted at second-hand stores. The house she lived in had been willed to her by her second mother, Ixchel, thirty years ago. She had a sixty-year-old land line phone that she paid for every month via snail mailed pay cards, along with her electricity and water bills.

Getting a cell phone had never been an option she considered before. Cell phone companies wanted all sorts of information that she didn't have. Smart phones had all sorts of functions that had nothing to do with calling people, functions she saw no use for. Besides, until Marilyn Bradley handed her a huge bag of money, she couldn't afford the fees to operate one.

The phone was pretty, though. Olive drab was not a lovely color, but the shiny, lightweight, sturdy metal had some of the utilitarian beauty of a good knife. The smooth front screen was like a black hand mirror.

Could the drone have delivered it to the wrong address by mistake? Not likely, since her thumbprint opened the box. It was probably a gift from someone. It seemed likely the giver was military since it had the color and utilitarian simplicity of a military thing, but many of her clients were soldiers or their family members, so that didn't narrow it down much.

It startled her when the thing rang.

Even with the flashing instructions on the screen saying, Accept

Call with a green circle, or Refuse Call with a red circle, it still took her a few seconds to figure out how to answer it.

"Hello?"

A small hologram of Alexander's head and shoulders, the back of his chair, and the wall behind him appeared inside the phone as if she looked through a window into a tiny, miniature office. "You got the package I sent."

Liliana smiled. "Yes, I did." She opened her fourth eyes so she could see him better while they talked. The actual Alexander in his actual office looked just like the tiny Alexander in the tiny holographic office.

"Don't worry about the data plan. It's paid. The phone is secure military, no tracing, no tapping." He leaned back in his chair, playing idly with a pen. His dress uniform was pressed and tailored. He had a new pure white shirt on with undamaged buttons.

"The phone is a very nice gift. Thank you."

"I have ulterior motives."

"You always do."

He chuckled. "I wanted to be able to check on you without you having to get up to go to your hard-line phone."

"You could check on me again in person like you did last night. I enjoyed that."

"So did I. But I think we should wait until you're fully healed before we see each other again."

Liliana thought that was probably a wise decision, but still wasn't too happy about it. "I will be functional in about a week."

"A week? Your arm is broken."

"In two places, yes. My ankle is also badly sprained, and I have deep bruises over half of my body."

"All that will be fully healed in a week?"

"My left arm will not be as strong for some time, but as I said, spider seers heal quickly."

"That's very impressive."

"I'm glad I could impress you."

"You always do."

Liliana grinned, warm down to her toes.

"I'd like to take you out, then." He looked at the calendar on his computer. "A week from this Friday night. I'll pick you up at seven."

"Take me out? Like a date? Dinner at a fancy restaurant and all that?"

"That is the general idea, yes."

The request seemed odd to Liliana, based on her previous experiences with men who desired her. "Why do you want to take me out on a date? I already want to have sex with you."

He barked a surprised laugh, then leaned forward in his chair, looking into his office communication center. It made his head fill all the space inside the tiny window of the phone screen. "Maybe I want more from you than sex."

Liliana's heart fluttered with nerves. The prince had been impressed by her fighting skill, her dancing, and her honesty, three things she excelled at. "Alexander, I am not so good with crowds and strangers." She didn't want to disappoint him.

He nodded. "I noticed at the hanger. You'll be fine. I'll take care of you." His deep voice filled with a softness that she'd only heard from him a few other times. She didn't want to question that voice. She certainly didn't want to say no to something Alexander seemed to really want.

"Okay. I will expect you at 7:00 next Friday night." Liliana hung up. She fiddled with the scarves that made up her skirt. A date. The spider seer had never been on a single date in her life that didn't end in disaster. She knew where she excelled and where her skills were lacking. Her dating skills were truly abysmal.

She was not alone now, though. She had friends. She would enlist their aid to make sure this date succeeded.

If I can defeat a powerful lion-kin alone, I can manage a simple date with my friends' help. Right?

The spider seer told herself that repeatedly as the week wore on and her injuries faded.

The only distraction she had from worrying about the date was watching the investigation into the brutal killings happening in the forest just outside the boundary of Fort Liberty.

She saw inhumanly long shaggy arms rip people apart, but didn't see anything she thought would really help Pete, Sgt. Giovanni, Lt. Runningwolf, and Alexander. A few of the victims she saw had axes or saws in their hands when they died. They must have been cutting wood for a campfire.

Not all of them, though. Some of the soldiers hadn't been doing anything but drinking too much in a place where intoxication should have been acceptable, the deep woods. But again, she saw great arms rip a beast-kin man's leg clean out of the socket. Something was different this time, though. The big arms she saw doing the killing were stockier. They seemed more ... furry.

Then she saw something else and sighed.

I'm not even healed from the last fight, dammit.

CHAPTER 13

BADGER VERSUS BEAR

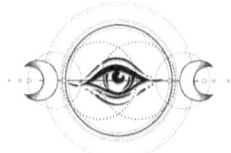

ON THURSDAY, WHEN HER WOUNDS WERE AT LEAST mostly healed, Liliana went to the woods to find Lieutenant Runningwolf. It seemed like this was how her life was going to go from now on. Fighting monsters to protect her friends, healing, then going to fight more monsters.

It was still better than her old life of boring loneliness.

Lieutenant John Runningwolf was not entirely in a category she would call "friend." They barely knew each other. She felt protective of the badger-kin, since unwittingly, he had given Doctor Nudd a few crucial seconds of survival. That had been all it took for help to arrive, so unintentionally, he'd saved the goblin healer's life. Also, John Runningwolf had agreed to keep Liliana out of official reports when she asked. She felt personally indebted to him for that. It was like a Fae favor.

She'd foreseen that she should not fight this enemy at the soldier's side, or the bear-kin would escape.

Liliana chose the appropriate tree in the forest on the edge of Fort Liberty so she could wait for the young Lieutenant to arrive.

An hour or so later, the stocky man crouched under the tree, hiding from a very big bear that obviously was not a normal part of this forest. Small black bears were the only kind native to North Carolina. This bear was huge. Liliana had never seen such a big shaggy brown bear, not even the Russian bear-kin who danced in the circus when she was little.

A mere badger would be no match for such a powerful beast, and this was not a natural bear. It had human intelligence driving those muscles. On top of that, the bear-kin was a killer who tore his victims limb from limb. His big, furry man-bear arms were what Liliana had seen in her most recent vision tearing someone's leg off.

No wonder John Runningwolf trembled, his aura sickly green with terror where he crouched behind the trunk of the tree she sat in.

Liliana dangled a bit of her silk down until it tickled his ear.

The man swatted absent-mindedly at the annoyance, catching his panting breath.

She tickled his ear again. If she dropped down next to him, his startled reaction might give away his position to the giant bear-kin.

Finally, he looked up.

Liliana held her finger to her lips for silence.

His face showed surprise at a comical level, but Liliana didn't dare laugh. He was so flabbergasted to see her sitting in the one tree in a big forest that he chose to hide behind, he momentarily forgot his fear of the bear.

Liliana climbed down a silk line quietly, now that she knew her presence wouldn't startle the young soldier into giving their position away.

She held up a note she'd written on her new phone so he could see. "You can defeat the bear in full badger form, but not in demi-badger form. I will help."

He looked at her for a moment as if judging her sanity, then tapped his wrist phone. He showed her what he'd typed. "Not a chance."

Liliana tapped the screen, running her fingers under two words. "Badger form."

Lieutenant Runningwolf indicated a space between his two

outstretched hands, about three feet long, and pointed at himself. Then pointed in the general direction of the bear and put his hands up as high as he could reach.

Liliana already knew that badgers were far smaller than bears, especially gigantic bears like that one. She rolled her eyes, just her first eyes. The others couldn't make that expression.

She tapped the screen again, then tapped her forehead between her open fourth eyes.

The soldier looked at her fourth eyes, large and pupilless with pale, opalescent colors swirling slowly. He looked at the sky for a moment in an expression that clearly said, "Why me?" without words. Then, he started unbuttoning his shirt.

The bear seemed to sense them somehow, despite the silence of their exchange. He started snuffling his way in their direction.

John Runningwolf undressed faster. He shot Liliana a look, with tight, angry lips and glary eyes that eloquently said Liliana better be right about this, or assuming he survived, he was going to make her pay.

Liliana gave him a gesture she'd seen Pete use, thumb up, to indicate everything would all be fine.

The badger-kin's eyes narrowed in suspicion.

The grin she gave him felt frozen and forced, but she maintained the "Everything will all be fine," hand gesture. She had seen this battle earlier with her fourth eyes. Everything would definitely not all be fine.

Lieutenant John Runningwolf didn't look like he believed her gesture of reassurance. This was sensible, but there wasn't a lot of choice as the bear-kin got closer. He pulled off his boots and pants, dropped to all fours and changed. His body sprouted long, bristly brown fur on the sides. His nose stretched into an upturned point as a long white stripe painted itself up his forehead. Arms became stubby legs that ended in long claws. The already short soldier shrank to a creature less than a foot tall and just as wide with round furry ears.

His badger form was actually kind of cute. Liliana might be socially inept, but she would never speak that thought aloud.

As the brown badger rushed out of concealment toward the giant bear, Liliana hoped John Runningwolf would eventually forgive her.

The badger circled the tree to get behind the big bear.

The bear's first indication that he wasn't alone were badger fangs sinking into his hind leg.

The bear roared. It tried to fling off the clinging irritant, but the badger's jaws locked hard on bear meat. The massive bear stood on its hind legs and shifted.

Huge bear paws grew fingers as big around as Liliana's wrists. The bear's muzzle shortened and legs lengthened. Shoulders, still covered in a shaggy brown pelt, broadened as the monster's three meters of height gained another full meter. The werebear became nearly as big as the stone giant Lilly and John Runningwolf fought together. It roared with rage and pain.

Now that the monster had hands, he reached down to grab the badger attached to his heel.

Runningwolf let go before the bear could grab him. He dodged back away from the clawed paw hands as big as his body. Long badger fangs snapped at the pursuing fingers, keeping the bearman's hands warily at bay.

But badgers weren't built for running speed. He didn't even try to escape the werebear's long strides. The demi-bear swatted at him, but the nimble badger dodged.

Lieutenant Runningwolf did the only thing he could. He dug at the ground with his claws making a slight depression and flattened his already flat body into it making himself flush with the ground.

When the bearman kicked at him, long badger claws clung to the ground, refusing to be budged. The more the bear tried to hit him, the deeper the badger's claws dug into the ground, and the harder he hung on to roots, rocks, or just plain dirt.

The big werebear tried stomping on the badger, but by then the smaller creature's entire body was below the grade of the rest of the ground. The bear's foot was far larger than the badger was wide. The giant couldn't get its big foot to do much damage.

While the bear became increasingly frustrated and enraged, pounding, clawing, and stomping on the half-buried badger, Liliana crept through the tree branches to the net of webbing she'd prepared.

The edges of the web were weighted with stones. She pulled the single line that dislodged all the stones just as the demi-bear reared up to try a double-fisted smash on the battered badger.

The net entangled the werebear's entire upper body, including both his arms.

As the bear-kin stumbled back, Runningwolf took his chance to race out of his half burrow and bite the bear's ankle again.

The bear-kin struggled frantically, flailing in the net, entangling his arms more thoroughly. He fell onto his butt, lifted his leg into the air, badger still attached, and slammed John Runningwolf into a tree.

Liliana winced in sympathy.

The blow knocked the badger loose, but when he got up from where he landed, his bared teeth were bloody. The badger-kin had taken a chunk of the bear with him.

The werebear's broad muzzle stuck out through a hole in the net. He tried to bite Runningwolf where he crouched snarling and hissing.

The badger looked like it would be just a mouthful for the monster, but Runningwolf twisted his body to avoid being bear lunch. Instead, he chomped down hard with vicious badger teeth on the bear's lip.

The giant bearman made an amazingly high-pitched sound for such a big, growly beast-kin. Yelling, he rolled onto his back. He tried to grab the badger, but the net entangled his arms.

Runningwolf stood on his chest. He shifted the grip of his teeth to bite the bear's whole muzzle, puncturing deep into his nose.

"AHHH," the werebear howled. His frantic struggles entangled him even more in the net until he could barely move. Blood seeped down like thick red tears as the bear made whining pain noises. "Sthtop! Pleathe! I give up!" he pleaded.

Liliana climbed down out of the tree.

Runningwolf growled, refusing to release the demi-bear's muzzle.

The bear-kin whined like a cub. "I thwear. I won't fight anymore. Just let go of my nothe!"

The badger released his grip on the bear's face. Runningwolf didn't budge, however, from his position, squat body standing with all four feet on the demi-bear's chest. The bear lay with arms entangled, helpless while the badger snarled in his face. Eye to eye with the predator that weighed more than ten times what he did, John Runningwolf snapped his teeth.

The gigantic bear whimpered in terror beneath him as he wet himself.

Liliana wrinkled her nose. She wrapped web line around the bear's ankles, tying some lines to her net, and anchoring it all to a couple of sturdy tree trunks.

When she was sure the bear-kin was no longer a danger, she slowly stepped backward until her back encountered a nearby tree. She watched warily the smaller, but infinitely more dangerous predator now aflame with a bonfire of fire orange anger in her third vision.

John Runningwolf turned the attention of his beady black eyes to her.

The badger-kin climbed off the body of the demi-bear, who shrank down to human form, holding his mangled face and weeping in agony.

Liliana knew her bonds would hold even on the bear-kin's smaller, human form, so she ignored him. At the moment, he was far from the most dangerous creature in the clearing.

The squat, flat, scratched, bloody, and enraged badger stalked stiffly toward her, his snarl showing four long fangs dripping bear blood.

Liliana held out John Runningwolf's pants. "You did win and you are not dead."

The badger stared at her, snarling and hissing for a few more seconds. Finally, he huffed, snagged the pants with one long claw, and dragged them behind a tree still grumbling.

Lieutenant John Runningwolf in human form, barefoot and shirtless, came out from behind the tree a few moments later, snarling nearly as much as his badger form had been.

Liliana looked at the claw slashes, deep bruises, and blood smears covering his entire body. She gave a wan smile. "You did defeat the bear-kin."

"I hate you."

Liliana shrugged. That was understandable. "I said you could win in badger form, not that it would be easy."

"You said you would help." John Runningwolf put one hand against a tree trunk, then sank to the ground as if his legs would no longer hold him up.

Liliana pointed at the webbing net that held the bear-kin helpless.

John Runningwolf snarled at her again. "Is this revenge for holding you at gunpoint at the pride-king challenge?"

Liliana sat down next to him, back to the same tree, fairly certain now that the badger-kin wouldn't attack her. If nothing else, he was too tired to be bothered. "All my friends tried to kill me at least once before we became friends." She put a sympathetic hand on an uninjured part of his arm. "I am sorry. I knew the bear-kin would rip you apart if you fought him in demi-badger form as you intended. I couldn't help you fight directly because my left arm is still weak from being broken when I fought Tray Bradley. The bear would have gotten away if I tried."

The badger-kin grunted a grudging acknowledgement. "Backup is on the way. I called it in before I trailed him. I found a hunk of fur at the last crime scene so I knew the killer's scent. Pete identified the fur as Kodiak bear. I came back alone to have a look at the scene again and caught a whiff of bear."

Deep bear claw swipes gouged into John Runningwolf's ribs. Despite being deep enough to show the glint of white bones, the wounds didn't bleed. A smear of blood showed where it had bled for only a moment before stopping.

New flesh covered the bones as she watched. The ragged edges of torn skin slowly sealed together. Liliana blinked her first eyes. She tried opening the rest of her eyes to see what was happening, but none of her various forms of vision could show her microscopic machines knitting his flesh together.

Lieutenant Runningwolf looked down at the slashes. "Yeah." After a moment, he added, "I'm stronger, too."

"This is what Andrew Periclum intended with his nanite experiments. You are the only one who gained the advantages he was trying to invent for all Others."

The soldier huffed a tired version of his previous growl. "He didn't care if he killed a bunch of us, including me, in the process."

They sat together for a long time. Only the soft weeping of the injured bear-kin broke the silence until they both heard military police making their crashing, clumsy way toward them through the underbrush.

Liliana stood to leave. "Goodbye, John Runningwolf. I'm glad you didn't die."

John Runningwolf looked up at her from his seat in the leaf mould. "Just John is fine."

Liliana smiled. "My friends call me Lilly. I think I would like it if you called me Lilly."

"Lilly." He nodded. "Thank you, I guess. For saving my life."

"You are welcome."

She looked forward in time to see if his life was safe now and saw another death. "You are Alexander's protector. When Officer West offers to guard him, say yes. If you guard him at that time, you will die, even if I save Alexander. If Officer West guards him, Officer West might die, but I might still be able to save him. Alexander will live, at least long enough for me to fight for him."

A bright grin split his bruised and bloody face. Liliana had all her eyes open and saw the sparkle of amusement that complemented it. "I know how much you don't care in the least about the Colonel or how he feels about you."

Liliana felt her cheeks flush and her ears get hot. She didn't know what to say to that, so she climbed the tree and left the area via interconnected branches.

John's coughing laughter followed her.

CHAPTER 14

ROYAL DATE

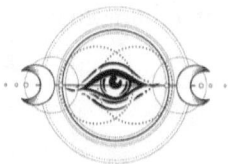

THE NEXT MORNING WAS FRIDAY. SHE'D MADE NO appointments. She had the whole day free. Liliana knew what she had to do. She grabbed a handful of the pay cards out of the bag of money that Marilyn gave her, put the new cell phone Alexander gave her in the teal velvet drawstring bag that matched her cloak, and caught a cab to the Willoughby's house.

The people in Janice Willoughby's neighborhood put extra effort into keeping their lawns green. Nature cooperated with them vividly this spring. The tall shady trees sheltered colorful hostas. Early blooming flowers like irises and daffodils lined the sidewalks. Each house had a nice big front porch, most with chairs or porch swings on them to enjoy the lovely weather of Fayetteville.

In the Willoughby's driveway sat a toddler's bright red toy car and a couple of bicycles of various sizes. Liliana cast a wary glance at the big tree with the tire swing. The grass grew particularly green and lush around it.

Janice answered the door when Liliana knocked. "Madame Anna? What are you doing here?"

"You should call me Lilly."

"I thought your name was Anna." Little Kayden, who was about the same age as Marilyn's son, Simon, peeked out at the spider-kin around his mother's leg.

"My name is Liliana. My clients call me Madame Anna. My friends call me Lilly. You should call me Lilly."

Janice smiled brightly. "Oh, that's so sweet. Thank you, Ma ... um ... Lilly." Her hand dropped to Kayden's head in a caress that seemed automatic.

"I need help." Liliana stroked the velvet of her wrap. The little boy's hand stroked the denim seam of his mom's pants leg.

"You've been such a great help to me," Janice Willoughby said. "Anything you need. Just name it."

"I need to be pretty."

"But you're already pretty." The rabbit-kin bristled. "Who said you weren't pretty?" She seemed ready to fight whoever dared to say such a heinous lie.

Liliana smiled at Janice's knees, warmed by the rabbit's protective instinct, even if it was misplaced. "I have a date tonight."

Kayden grinned back at her, peeking around his mother's knee.

"Oh, Anna, I mean, Lilly!" Janice clapped her hands together and bounced on her toes in their sneakers. "You have a boyfriend? Girlfriend?"

"Boyfriend," Liliana clarified. She winked at Kayden.

He scrunched up half his face trying to wink back.

The rabbit-kin bounced even more, making her ponytail swing. "That's wonderful." She pulled Liliana into her house by the hand. "Tell me everything. Where did you meet? What's he like?"

Kayden ran away as Liliana followed Janice into a living room littered with puzzles and toys. Wendy the dog barked at the spider-kin until Janice shushed her by tossing a stuffed animal. The very big, shaggy blonde dog made the toy squeak repeatedly as she bounded into another room.

"I met him in a parking lot." Liliana found that first question easy to answer.

"In a parking lot?"

Since she didn't want to elaborate, she tried to answer the other more difficult question – what was Alexander like. "He is complex and intriguing, tall and handsome, scarred in body and soul but stronger for it. He is smart and honorable, but very dangerous. He makes my knees wobbly when he kisses me."

"Well, that all sounds wonderful, except for the dangerous part." Janice steered the spider-kin around a Lego construction that looked and moved kind of like her room-bot. She pulled the spider-kin toward the communication center in one corner of the room.

"I like dangerous men." Liliana found Janice's living room as alien as a moonscape. "It's a species trait. My sister Isabella married a Komodo dragon-kin assassin. My father Simon was a lion-kin prince. One of my mother's sisters married Ghengis Khan."

"Well, I can help you get ready for your date, but I don't think I particularly want to meet your new boyfriend."

"He would not harm you. He strictly follows rules and laws, whenever they don't interfere with his best interests."

"That's um, good to know, I guess." She started punching buttons that brought up holo-projected menus above the comm center. "So, do you have a budget for this that we need to stick to?"

Liliana showed her the handful of pay cards she'd pulled out at random. Many of them were pre-loaded cards with specific denominations stamped on the front.

The rabbit-kin laughed. "With that, I could get you ready for a date with a king."

"He is only a prince," Liliana told her.

The rabbit-kin looked at Liliana for a long moment. "You have a date with a tall, handsome, dangerous prince, who you met in a parking lot?"

"Is his rank important to date preparations? My father and first mother taught me proper royal court etiquette, but I did not think any of that applied at this point."

Janice snorted. "Having never dated a handsome prince, I don't really know. Knowing men, though, if he's kissed you enough to make your knees wobbly, then I suspect you're past worrying about how to do a proper curtsey."

"That's good, but I already know how to do that anyway."

In a matter of a few minutes, the rabbit-kin used the comm center to call one of her neighbors to watch her children for the day and instructed the house AI to make several appointments.

Liliana found the disembodied voice disturbing. She decided that no matter how much money she had, she wouldn't purchase a house AI. The soulless, chillingly polite voice reminded her of HAL 9000 from Arthur C. Clarke's 2001.

Janice and Liliana spent the entire day getting ready for the spider-kin's date. Janice took Liliana to Raleigh for shopping first, to pick out a new dress, a matching bra and panties set, new shoes, and jewelry, and a tiny, beaded pocketbook that she particularly liked. A salon was next. Her hair and fingernails were carefully trimmed, shaped, and adorned.

The spider seer also got her makeup done for her. She bought all the makeup. She asked the woman to show her how to do it herself, including a less dramatic style for days when she wasn't going to a fancy restaurant. Until then, Liliana hadn't known there were different ways to do makeup based on the occasion or time of day. She had only ever used stage makeup in her circus days, but now she felt a powerful need to be extra pretty as often as possible.

The spider-kin could not imagine trying to learn all this date related stuff without a friend like Janice to help her. While various strangers poked and prodded, Janice bombarded her with dating advice.

Janice and Lou Willoughby had a happy marriage. The rabbit-kin knew far more about relationships than Liliana could possibly learn in one day, but she listened, and tried to remember all of the many rules and cautions. It was a lot to absorb and much of it made no sense. Some of it even seemed contradictory.

When Janice dropped her at home at six, one hour before the date was due to start, Liliana sat on the edge of her armchair carefully. She was afraid to move for fear she would mess up something that she had paid a ridiculous amount of money for someone to prettify. She opened her fourth eyes. Afraid to look into the future at her date for fear she would see disaster, Liliana decided to watch her prince instead, to see how his day had gone.

She missed some important things while being primped. Detective Jackson questioned the Kodiak-kin that John subdued while Alexander observed behind a one-way mirror. The big man from Alaska got some of the details wrong about the various victims who had been ripped apart while they were camping on the southeast edge of Fort Liberty along the banks of Bones Creek.

The evidence said that they'd caught the culprit. Detective Jackson accessed his arrest records from Alaska. They showed he had a history of angry brawls. He knew two of the victims.

Only two?

Liliana used her fourth eyes to look back at all six victims. The first four had saws or axes in their hands when they were attacked.

Why did most of the victims have cutting tools?

She saw each of the first four victims cutting living tree branches for firewood. Then a roar of rage, screams and blood and ... Liliana closed her fourth eyes shuddering.

Focus on the hands and arms of the killer. She took a deep breath, steeled herself, and looked again. The long arms that tore at the victims were bark-covered, the bark peeling in strips to give it a shaggy appearance.

Ah, a Fae. Or something? It looked like an actual tree. Definitely not a bear-kin.

With that in mind, she asked another question: *Why? Why did this Fae attack four campers?*

A forest spirit, a Green man, woke in a vision with the barely faded colors of the recent past. He'd been sleeping for decades in an ancient hickory that housed his spirit. Many of the trees in that forest had faces within. They were dormant dryads and other Fae. When he saw the campers callously hacking at trees that might be sleeping people, the old man lost in a world he didn't understand, went mad with rage.

She saw Alexander standing next to Detective Jackson as she

spoke to reporters, "There is no further danger. The murderer is in the custody of Fayetteville police."

"We were happy to help with the investigation," Alexander added. "We're confident the forests are safe again."

That was not accurate, but it wasn't Alexander or Detective Jackson's fault. They had no way to know. Liliana would have to tell them.

The angry forest spirit had roots sunk in the land that chose Alexander. The Fae prince should be able to calm him, convince him to end his killing spree.

The insistent knock on her door finally brought her back to herself. She looked at her clocks. It was 7:13. Either Alexander was late, or he had been knocking on her door for a while.

She looked out with her fourth eyes. The prince was about to knock her door down.

Liliana quickly opened the door. "I am sorry. I was lost in time."

Alexander stopped, shoulder still turned to shove the door. "I thought something happened to you." His eyes raked over her from the toes of her ballet slippers, up her slender legs, bare, rather than wearing her usual tights. The hem of her new dress was so short it barely covered the lacy underwear. The dipping sweetheart neckline barely covered the lacy push-up bra that matched the underwear and enhanced her modest décolletage. Her hair, as black as the satin dress, was pinned up in softly draped ringlets with sparkling emerald and diamond hair pins that matched the dangly earrings and delicate choker necklace she wore.

Liliana thought having her hair up made her neck look like a giraffe's. Her face was all exposed with her gigantic cheekbones. And the makeup the woman at the salon used made her eyes look huge. She looked like a cartoon dressed for a funeral.

Janice had insisted that a "little black dress" was just the thing for a fancy date, but Liliana always preferred bright colors. The emerald necklace and hair pins were the only part of the outfit the spider seer actually liked. The shoes were nice, too. Janice insisted that Liliana should get high heels, but she'd drawn the line there.

She couldn't fight, climb, or run in high heels. So, instead, Liliana got a new pair of black satin ballet slippers with extra-long ribbons that crisscrossed her calves all the way up to her knees.

Alexander stared at her for several seconds, his face full of some dark emotion. She thought maybe he was angry.

"I'm sorry," Liliana said.

"For what?"

"For...not really knowing how to dress for a date."

His hands fisted at his sides. That definitely looked like anger. She must have really messed up, and they hadn't even made it out the door yet. "Liliana, look in my head right now."

"I thought you didn't like it when I did that."

"Just do it."

She opened her third eyes to see the image of herself burning in Alexander's mind like a torch flame with the blaze of his passion. His one strongest thought was that she wanted to have sex with him, and her bed was only a few feet away. Only three things kept him from sweeping her up and carrying her straight back to her bed. One was his iron self-control, which allowed him to let the other two rule his actions. He had promised both her and himself that they would have at least one proper date. He wanted to know more about her than that she made him feel like a horny teenager and she could kill the strongest lion-kin in the pride.

Neither of those would have been enough to restrain him without the third reason. He didn't want to risk the short-term psychological effects of her venom. The idea of losing control of his mind and his actions, even for a few minutes, disturbed him deeply. Even so, his deep desire made him wonder if it might not be so bad to lose control for a while with her.

Liliana smiled, delighted. "I did okay, then."

"You look breathtaking." He extended his arm like a perfect gentleman, but she'd seen the barely restrained fire behind his brown eyes.

He had given her a compliment. She was supposed to complement him in return. He wore his dress blues, the jacket so dark it was almost black, the pants brighter blue with a gold stripe down the outside of his legs. "You always look elegant. You look even more elegant than usual."

That seemed acceptable to him. So far, so good.

The car waiting for them wasn't camouflage painted and didn't have gigantic tires. It was sleek and small with a long, curved hood that flowed into a smaller curved cab and trunk. It reminded her of cars she hadn't seen in many years, but this one was practically an artistic sculpture with wheels. It was a lovely shade of green like pine needles.

Alexander held the door for her as she sat down low in a cream-colored leather interior. The dash had analog gauges. There was no sign of a screen or an auto-drive.

"I like this car," Liliana said. "I don't think I've ever seen a car like this."

He started it up with a soft *vroom* that most cars these days didn't make. "My dad was big on Jaguars. It's a classic E-Type in British racing green. We used to work on it together when I was a kid." He pulled away from Liliana's house, his car smoothly taking the corners. "When they changed the emission laws, I modified the engine to run on hydrogen and hybridized it. The trunk is full of batteries."

Liliana petted the leather interior. "It's lovely. My second mother was jaguar-kin."

He chuckled. "My father would probably have been delighted to meet her."

Liliana smiled to herself, imagining what Ixchel would have thought of a man whose favorite kind of car was this graceful, agile vehicle named after her kind. She would have been intrigued, at least.

They didn't speak as Alexander drove to Raleigh, driving with a hint of a smile, both hands on the wheel. He seemed relaxed, content to guide the pretty machine along their route.

Liliana checked on the Green man. He'd settled to sleep near the roots of a dryad's tree. He would do no more harm tonight.

Alexander looked over at her at some point. His lips curved in a small, pleased smile.

Liliana tilted her head. "What did I do that pleased you?"

"I just realized another thing I like about you."

"What is that?"

"When you have nothing to say, you don't say anything. You don't feel the need to fill silence with meaningless words."

"People who do that can be very tiring." While grateful to her friend for all her help, the day had been exhausting with Janice talking to her every moment. Liliana much preferred the nice rabbit-kin woman in smaller doses. "When do they ever have time to think?"

Alexander chuckled. "Exactly."

The restaurant he took Liliana to was crowded in the front with people waiting. The spider-kin made a small sound of distress. She tried to hide behind the prince's taller body.

He put an arm around her shoulders to pull her in close to his side instead.

Liliana closed all her eyes. She let him guide her. She focused on keeping her hands still. Janice had admonished her repeatedly not to play with her clothes. Apparently, it was unladylike. Liliana had to avoid doing it during her date or she would embarrass Alexander.

She opened one human eye as he stopped walking.

He spoke to a tall, elegant woman who wore a black dress a lot like Liliana's, except the woman was tall enough in her spike heels to almost look the prince in the eyes. The top of Liliana's head didn't even reach his shoulder. The woman looked comfortable in her black dress.

The spider seer had to remind herself that the prince had his arm around her, not the other lady.

"Reservation for two. Bennett."

"Yes, of course, Colonel. We have your table ready."

His strong arm on her shoulder guided her out of the crowd of waiting people. They passed through a softly lit restaurant filled with diners and bustling servers. They stopped at a table in the very back next to a window. It looked out onto porch seating that was empty in the chilly evening. The table was cradled in a shallow alcove that isolated it from the rest of the restaurant. No one would be able to see or hear them once they sat down, as if they had dinner entirely alone.

Liliana smiled up at her prince. He'd said he would take care of her.

Alexander managed to look smug, despite his expression remaining virtually unchanged.

"You knew I had trouble with crowds."

"You did mention it, and I saw your difficulty in the hangar."

"Thank you." It was incredibly considerate of him. It probably cost a small fortune to reserve this specific table in such a popular restaurant.

The menu was all in French, which was familiar, but the food was still mostly unfamiliar. She had eaten very simply when she lived in Europe. Circus people didn't have a lot of money to spend on fancy food.

Alexander ordered for them both in French.

The waiter answered in French, asking if they would like any appetizers, and what sort of wine they wanted.

In the same language, Liliana requested the toast with tapenade appetizer. If the other food was too strange or too rich, at least she could eat the bread and olive paste.

"*Parlez-vous français?* Alexander asked her, surprised.

"*Oui. Ma mère m'a appris à parler Français.*"

"How many languages do you speak?"

"Only eight, fluently." Liliana shrugged. "I know some Russian and Norwegian and a smattering of some other languages, but mostly just the curse words and simple things like 'Hello' and 'Where is the train station?' I'm not fluent, but I know a little Romani. When I was young, I had many Romani friends." Friends long gone.

"Which eight do you speak fluently?"

"As I said, my mother taught me French. She also taught me

German and English. I only learned a little of her native Egyptian, sadly, not enough to be fluent. I learned Greek, Latin, and Arabic from my father. My second mother taught me Spanish and Portuguese as well as a Peruvian Indian dialect that I do not remember well, but I could probably pick up again if I were around people who spoke it."

"You continue to surprise me. Have you travelled a lot?"

"I have not left the United States for the last eighty years. I have been in Fayetteville for nearly four decades."

He shook his head with a wry expression. "You barely look twenty, but you're over twice my age. That's difficult to reconcile. Where were you before you came to the states? And what made you decide to come?"

"I grew up in a travelling circus. We toured all over Europe and into Russia for many years. When World War II made most of Europe unsafe for us, the whole circus came over on a big boat. Himmler's red wolves killed my parents and many of my family and friends. There was a bounty on the heads of all spider seers. The Roma were being rounded up into camps. My first mother's visions saw they would all die there." Liliana carefully did not open any eyes. She didn't want to see into that awful time again.

"No secrets were safe from spider seers," Liliana said softly. "So both the allies and the axis powers wanted us dead. Nearly every spider seer I knew of was slain. My second mother smuggled me out of Europe hidden in a cage with two of my lion-kin brothers and some true lions." Liliana fiddled with the tablecloth under the table where it wouldn't be obvious. She would never forget that time of her life, but she hadn't actively thought about it in many years. The constant presence of fear and grief had faded with time.

Alexander held his hand out to her across the table. She let the tablecloth go and took his hand instead. His long fingers held hers, rubbing gently. She watched the movement. It was soothing, like her scarves, but warmer, better.

"Considering how you danced and how you fought Bradley, I'm

not surprised you had a circus background. Even when fighting for your life, you looked like you were performing."

Liliana was grateful for the shift to less painful ground. She took a breath, let the old sadness go, and smiled up at the ribbons on his chest. She knew he enjoyed watching her fight, even though he had been afraid she would die. "I wish you had seen me fight Pete. When I fought the lion, I was confined by the dome cage. My battle with the Celtic wolf was like being on the trapeze again."

"You fought Pete?"

"That is how we met. He thought I was a murderer. He tried to kill me."

Alexander's jaw clenched. "I'm sorry about that. I should have trusted you when you said you weren't the killer."

She shrugged. "You didn't know me."

"Why didn't Pete kill you?"

"I defeated him."

"Why didn't you kill him, then?" Alexander leaned forward. He seemed fascinated by the story.

"I looked into him and didn't want to kill him. He has a compassionate soul filled with love for Ben Harper."

"How did you convince him you weren't a murderer?"

"I bit him."

Alexander's face went through a series of subtle expressions. Liliana recognized, surprise, then anger, curiosity, then back to anger. Anger seemed to be the one emotion the prince expressed freely. "You bit him." His voice showed no emotion at all.

Liliana had begun to learn more about him. When his voice went all bland and flat, he was carefully hiding his often very intense feelings. "The killer Pete sought was a spider-kin who killed her victims by biting them. I bit him to prove that my bite was not deadly, so I could not be the killer."

"And he let you?"

Her cheeks heated with shame. "He did not. I ..." Liliana swallowed a sip of water, took a deep breath, and admitted what she had done. "I forced him." She ran the tablecloth between her fingers under the table where she hoped Alexander wouldn't notice. The linen fabric was rough, but the movement was soothing in its familiarity. She looked down at her lap, watching the movement.

"That bothers you," he observed neutrally.

"Pete has forgiven me, but it is not an act I am proud of."

He nodded slightly. "I'm glad."

"You're glad that I bit Pete against his will?"

"I'm glad that you're ashamed of it, even though you were under extreme circumstances."

Oh. Alexander had been keeping his distance from her ever since she told him she wanted to bite him. "I give you my word that I will not bite you unless you give me permission."

His lips twisted in that way that made a dimple appear on one side. Not amusement, irony. "I already know that you keep your word scrupulously. If you'd said that earlier, we might not have left your house."

Liliana smiled as she remembered what he was thinking when he picked her up. "I really do want to bite you, though. If we talk, learn more about each other, then you might let me."

He sipped his wine, then set down the glass. "Liliana, I don't think there are enough words in the world to convince me." Colonel Alexander Bennett was not a man who liked giving up control.

"I have three years. I am patient."

"What happens in three years?"

"In three years, I will be one hundred fifty, an adult, and my body will change. If I have not chosen a mate, my body will impel me to mate with the nearest strong, fierce male to produce a spider seer child. I would much prefer to choose my mate."

Alexander chuckled and leaned back in his chair. "You know, it's generally considered bad form to discuss children on the first date."

Liliana cocked her head sideways. She had broken an important social dating rule. Somewhere in the endless stream of words Janice Willoughby flooded her with, the rabbit-kin had mentioned that rule. She said something about it scaring men away. Liliana considered the unseelie prince smiling at her over his wine glass with banked heat in his eyes. "You are not easily frightened."

"No, I'm not." He took a sip of wine. "Three years."

"If you and I are still together in three years, then I will choose you to be the father of my daughter." The spider seer desperately wished either that she could open her third eyes in the public restaurant to look into his mind and heart, or that he would be more overtly expressive. Her prince was all subtlety and hidden layered motives. He was far more accustomed to hiding his emotions than expressing them. She had to work hard even at the best of times to parse the complex language of expression.

"Can't you just look into the future and see if I will be?"

"It's difficult to look into my own future. My actions alter it constantly. Plus, your future is very hazy. Several paths of probability lead to your death within the next week. Some of those paths lead to my death as well. Death tends to overwhelm my sight. I have a hard time seeing more than flickers of possibility past that point."

"I'd nearly forgotten what you said in the parking garage when I confronted Periclum. I didn't take your warning seriously at first. Now, I know to always take what you tell me seriously." He sipped wine thoughtfully. "So, either I'll die in the next week, or you'll save me, and spend the next three years trying to convince me to let you bite me." A ghost of a smile teased the edges of his mouth.

"I hope it will not take that long. I really want to bite you."

His lips quirked up further. "I gather biting is sexual for you?"

Liliana thought about that for a moment. "It is more intimate than a kiss, but not like sex."

"How is it different?"

"It is an expression of emotional attachment, just as sex can be. Sharing venom is how a spider seer binds her mate to her. Seer magic affects the paths of fate. Once we share venom, our fates will be linked. When we have shared venom for a long time," Liliana hesitated. She didn't want to mention the extension of his life but needed him to know as much else about it as possible. "Our lives will be bound to one another forever."

"I'll never let anyone put a binding spell on me, Liliana."

"It's not like a wizard's binding spell. The effects are far more subtle. There is no element of coercion. Fate will simply make our life paths intersect frequently. We will often meet unexpectedly. We will find ourselves in endeavors where we will be more successful together than apart. Things will happen that make it easier or more advantageous for us to spend time together." The non-physical effects of venom were subtle enough that most people thought they were coincidental. That made it difficult to explain. "Have you known people who desired each other, but never seemed to get together at the right time, or who got jobs on opposite sides of the country and never saw each other again, as if fate were against them being together?"

Alexander nodded. "I've seen that happen."

"Venom causes the opposite effect. It will never force us to be together, but it will make being together easier. It will make it so that if we choose to stay together, that choice will not be sabotaged by chance events. Chance will instead flow in our favor."

"You bit Pete. How has it affected him?"

Liliana looked down. "My life and his have been closely intertwined since I bit him. It might not have been so strong an effect if I bit him only once, but I bit him again, with his permission, to save his life when the widow spider venom nearly killed him. If we do not share venom again, the effect will eventually wear off. For now, though, even though his heart belongs to Ben Harper, Pete is also mine."

Alexander leaned forward. He smiled his small, pleased smile. "You want to bite me so you can claim me as yours."

"I have seen inside you. You want to claim me as yours as well. You want to use sex to do it. I want to use venom."

"So, you don't want to have sex with me after all?" His eyes sparkled with amusement. He was teasing her.

"I want sex with you so much I can barely think of anything

else." She grinned back at him. "But I also very much want to bite you."

"I'll consider it."

"I'll be patient."

The tapenade arrived. Liliana cheerfully bit into the crunchy toast, wondering how hard it would be to make this at home. The difficult part would be getting the olives that grew so well in Greece and Italy imported here. The flavors reminded her of green islands and sea so blue it almost hurt to look at.

She would enjoy having it more often.

She saw the same enjoyment on Alexander's face.

Liliana remembered a piece of advice that Janice gave her about dating. She had been answering questions all evening, like she was accustomed to, but that meant her own life had been the main subject of discussion. Janice advised her to ask her date questions, to get him talking about his own life. She said that men preferred to talk about themselves. If she thought about it, there were a lot of things she wanted to know about Alexander.

"You have European Fae court manners, you speak French as if it were native to you, but you said your family is from North Carolina for generations." It wasn't quite a question, but it put into words some of what she wondered about him.

"My father was career military. He went into the diplomatic corps after he put in his thirty years." Alexander crunched and swallowed a small round of crusty bread coated in colorful olive paste. "I grew up speaking French as much as English. My father was stationed in Algeria for a while, then Switzerland. He had a diplomatic post for many years in Belgium after he retired from the service. I went to school there. I've spent some time on the ground in Chad, as well. We have French, German and Arabic in common. I'm also fluent in Russian, Pashto, and Swahili, and I speak enough Spanish to get by."

"When did your father meet your mother?"

Liliana saw a muscle jump as Alexander's jaw clenched. "They got together when he was still active military, posted in Poland.

When the Queen of Air and Darkness dallied with a mortal, as she had done hundreds of times before, she never expected to get pregnant. Fae have children so rarely." He drank half a glass of wine at once. "She wanted nothing to do with a mortal child who would die in less than a century."

The spider seer reached across the table. She held Alexander's hand, rubbing his fingers the way he had done hers.

He looked up suddenly as if she startled him but didn't pull his hand away.

Liliana thought Janice might have been wrong about that piece of dating advice. Her prince seemed far more comfortable when her life was the subject of conversation, not his. She should steer the conversation onto less painful ground, as he had done for her, but there was one more thing she really wanted to know. "Did your father know who she was?"

He shook his head. "He knew she was Fae. His best friend in the service was beast-kin, so he knew about Others. He knew what a Fae was, but he didn't know ..." His grip on Liliana's hand tightened a little. "They killed him for having a queen's son, and he never even knew. She was just a beautiful Fae he had a fling with once. A few months later, she handed him a baby and told him it was his."

"I'm sorry," Liliana said. "How old were you when he was killed?"

"Sixteen." He smiled at her, a broad, entirely false smile, shrugged as if it didn't matter, and pulled his hand away from hers to pour himself some more wine. "It was a long time ago."

Even Liliana could understand such a blatant attempt to change the subject. She tried to think of something to ask that would follow logically in the flow of conversation but would not pry at the painful subject of his father's death when he was an adolescent. "How old are you now?" was the best she could come up with.

His smile faded to something a little more genuine. "Isn't there a social rule against asking that?" He was teasing her by using her own phrasing back at her.

"I think that rule only applies to women," she teased back. "And

I already told you how old I was, so, you owe me an answer for balance."

He chuckled, then bowed his head to her to concede the point. "I'm fifty-eight."

"You look like you are not yet forty."

Alexander shrugged and sipped more wine. "Fae blood is good for something."

"The land chose you. Sleeping Fae are awakening in a hundred-mile radius and wandering into Fayetteville looking for a leader. I would say your Fae blood is stronger than your mother credits."

"Titania doesn't doubt the strength of my blood since it's hers. She simply sees it as fleeting, and therefore unimportant." He shrugged. "With my short life expectancy, no European Fae court will ever recognize mine. They will simply assume they can outlive me and take what they want from my wrinkled corpse."

Liliana fell silent, considering that. The server brought their food.

Should she tell the prince that her venom would extend his life indefinitely? She probably should, but she didn't want to. She considered him a strong possibility for a potential life mate. She could not imagine spending her life with someone who stayed with her only because of the calculated advantages of her venom. Yet, it would fundamentally change his life. He should have the right to choose immortality in full knowledge. Perhaps, he already had chosen. "There are various magics that extend life. Do you want a Fae lifespan? Have you considered seeking one of those magics out?"

He nodded. His face blanked. His feelings on this subject must be very deep. "I have. Magic always has a price. I haven't found any form of immortality that has a price I'm willing to pay."

Liliana fell silent while she ate her meal.

He wanted immortality. Most methods that extended the lives of mortals involved dark, blood magic. He wasn't willing to sacrifice the lives of others to extend his own. She was glad to know that there was a limit to what he would do to get what he wanted. She was also very glad that he had already chosen to seek immortality.

If he became her mate, then he would be as long-lived as a spider-kin. There was no blood magic involved. Liliana was the price for the magic. But she was unwilling to be a means to an end. He would either choose her or not, for herself. She would not use immortality as a bargaining chip. But if he chose her, then she could give him something special, something he wanted very badly. She smiled to herself.

The food was delicious, although very rich. She ate less than half of it.

"Alexander?" she asked, finally, as she realized she was just pushing food from one side of her plate to the other. She knew that dates were intended to help people know each other better in order to enhance their relationship. She did know more about Alexander now than she had before. He knew more about her as well. On dates in the past, nearly everything she said had damaged her relationships, rather than enhancing them. This time, even her comment about the blood fire time and children had not seemed to dissuade Alexander from wanting her. She wondered if asking him personal questions had made him uncomfortable enough that he no longer desired her. "Do you still want to have sex with me?"

He set his fork down. His stare had that hard, dark look that was almost like anger, but not. "Absolutely."

"This has been the least disastrous date I have ever been on. I would like to go home with you now and have sex."

He raised a hand to get the attention of one of the servers. "Check, please."

The server brought a tablet computer. Alexander authorized payment with his thumbprint.

"I had intended to take you dancing," Alexander said as he escorted her to his car.

"I like dancing. Right now, I would rather go to your home and have sex. You can dance with me another time."

He chuckled as he got in the car. "You have no idea how much I appreciate your honesty right now." The trip back to Fort Liberty went much faster than Liliana thought was possible. He risked getting a speeding ticket.

"Oh," Liliana said as they sped through traffic. "I almost forgot to tell you something important. You and Detective Jackson were wrong."

"Wrong about what?"

She quoted, "The murderer is in custody. There is no further danger. The forests around Fayetteville are safe again."

"The bear-kin wasn't the killer?"

"The Kodiak-kin that John Runningwolf captured killed two of the men, but he was imitating the method of the other murders for a personal vendetta."

"A copycat." He nodded minimally. "Who is the real killer, then?"

"Many trees in the forest around Bones Creek are waking up as your influence spreads. A Green man woke before most. He did most of the killing. But the entire forest will slowly wake now. You must speak with the dryads and sylphs, the Green man and the goblins. They will all awaken at once if you ask them to. You should also have the foresters warn people not to cut green wood when they camp."

His hands tightened on the steering wheel. "The trees are waking up because of me. Those deaths are on my head."

"The land chose you." Liliana said. "You did not choose." She put a hand on his arm. "It is true that your aura has been magnified by your bond with the land, but the land doesn't just make you stronger, you make the land stronger. As your bond deepens with Fort Liberty and Fayetteville, the land will flourish. As the land flourishes, beast-kin will be drawn to it. Fae sleeping in plant or mineral form will awaken. This is not your fault. It simply is. The Green man chose to kill because the campers hurt the sleeping dryads. That is not your fault either."

He sighed. "Thank you for that, but if the land had chosen someone who knew the effects of land bonding a little better, this wouldn't have happened."

Liliana squeezed his bicep. "The Green soul of the earth chooses. Your sister Aurore, no doubt, knows all about the effects of land bonding. The land didn't choose her."

"Much to her annoyance, no land in her five hundred years of life has ever chosen her."

Liliana considered that. "You worked the land with your hands, bled to nurture neglected plants. I suspect these are things that Aurore has never done."

Alexander barked a laugh. "I can't imagine her getting dirt under her fingernails on purpose."

"The killings are not your fault. But it is your responsibility, as the land ruler, to go to the forest, to help those awakening to adapt to the new century. You must order them to be at peace with the Normals."

"Tonight?" he asked.

"No one will die tonight. Tomorrow, though, speak to the forest, so no more people will die.

"I'll take care of it first thing tomorrow."

An issue occurred to Liliana. "Some of the ones sleeping in that forest are European seelie or unseelie Fae. Many more are native and have no concept of that separation. You will need to decide if you will banish the seelie Fae, but they have lived here longer than you or I. The native Fae have been here far longer than that."

Alexander was silent for a while as they travelled. "If the seelie Fae will accept an unseelie ruler, they can stay. I'll take Lieutenant Runningwolf with me. That should be a sign to the native Fae that the old wars are over. They're welcome as long as they follow modern laws."

Liliana nodded approval and patted his arm.

"That's what you meant, isn't it?"

Liliana cocked her head sideways. She looked at him from the corners of her human eyes, not sure what he was talking about.

"When you said you would give me useful advice and I could choose to follow it or not."

"Yes. That is exactly what I meant."

"You give Pete advice like this all the time?"

She nodded. "I always give Pete advice if he or those he cares about are in immediate danger. Also, when he asks me. And sometimes just because I know it will help."

"Do you see any danger like that now?"

"There is a strong possibility that you and Pete will come to blows if you don't soon share with him who you are. Even if you survive the murderer, someone he trusts will tell him dark things about you. He will believe them and seek your life."

Alexander nodded, face grim. "I always knew that was a possibility. Celtic wolves and unseelie are natural enemies. William warned me repeatedly not to get too close to him."

Liliana made a rude snorting noise that her first mother would have admonished her for making. "William Eliot was a terrible source of information. Our red wolf has no enmity toward you or any unseelie. But if you will not share your truth with him, he has no way to refute the lies others might tell him."

Alexander raised an eyebrow. "Our red wolf?"

"I know you think of Pete as yours, just as I do. Telling him who you are would make both your lives less complicated."

"I'll tell him when the time is right."

Liliana sighed. *Why am I attracted to stubborn men?*

CHAPTER 15

FINALLY

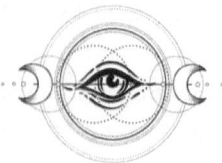

LILIANA WAITED IMPATIENTLY UNTIL ALEXANDER PARKED his car in the garage of his house. As soon as the car stopped moving, she opened her door and went over the hood, careful not to scratch or dent the pretty car.

As Alexander stood up and shut the car door, he turned to face her. With her standing on the hood of the car, his face was at roughly the level of her neckline.

She bent down to kiss him, delighting in being taller than him. One hand found the back of his neck, but the crisp, short hair was far too short to fill her hand with it like he liked to do with hers. It tickled her palm as her lips met his. He had to look up, the angle a new experience for them both. They explored the touch of lips, the joining of breath, a glory that she'd craved for so long. Now, there was no hurry. The night was theirs.

She pulled back after a moment, all eyes open so she could look down at him. Her hands traced the shape of his face, following her multi-layered vision. Scarlet passion burned through the complex interlocking ice crystals of his usually logical, controlled surface. Her hands felt the warmth of soft skin overlain in her vision with the shimmer of hard obsidian. Silver horns like the ghost of a crown surrounded his brow. "You are so beautiful."

A firework sparkle of amusement accompanied the deepening red of desire. He delighted in her ability to make him laugh, even if it only showed outwardly in an upward quirk of lips and a huff of warm breath. "I think that's my line."

She saw a mirror of herself in his mind, his view of her. She drew in her breath sharply. The woman in his mind was stunning, his desire for her overwhelming. He didn't want Liliana's venom. He didn't want Liliana's vision. He didn't want a spider seer ally.

He wanted Liliana.

She blinked her first eyes as they filled almost to overflowing. So much desire, just for her. She ran her thumb across his full lips.

Long lashes brushed his cheeks as his eyes fluttered shut, breath hitching.

She kissed him again. In that moment, there was no other option.

His hands that had been resting on her hips went around them, cupping her bottom, pulling her closer.

She hooked one arm around his neck. The other explored his chest while her weight dropped into his hands, all without breaking the kiss.

He lifted her down as he stepped back, her entire front warmed by his body, his big hands holding her full weight without strain.

She wrapped her legs around his waist to hold herself up, so he could use his hands elsewhere. Her mouth opened to the heat of his tongue.

One hand stroked up her back. Calloused skin skimmed over the thin satin of her dress and up the nape of her neck left bare by her high hairstyle.

She shivered. His thick tongue stroked inside her mouth. "Mmmph." A moan escaped her.

He turned and took a step to get to his garage door, bracing her back on the wall beside it. His hard body pressed heavily against every inch of her.

She pushed his jacket off over his shoulders.

He let go of her long enough to let it slide off to the ground behind him. The elegant dress uniform jacket made a messy pile on the concrete garage floor behind him.

His broad palms stroked up the outside of her thighs where they wrapped around his waist, sliding under her skirt to the lace and silk of her panties.

One hand slid under her, supporting her as he pulled back from the wall, the other hand opened the door to his house. The big hand under her with fingers long enough to encircle her waist, touched her through thin material.

She squirmed in his grip, unable to be still, wanting so much more.

Not for a single moment did either of them stop kissing, mouths sliding, exploring textures of heat and wet. They each demanded more of the other.

His eyes stayed closed, sunk in the sensations of kiss and touch bombarding him. Hers were open. She saw his kitchen lit by moonlight shining in through the broad glass of his sliding back patio door with the open curtain.

He didn't need eyes in his own house, immaculately free of clutter. His steps were sure as he set her bottom on his kitchen counter.

His lips left hers finally. His mouth scorched a shivery path down her throat, hot tongue and the brush of teeth that gave her goose bumps.

Her hands, which had been frantically unbuttoning his shirt, stilled as the hot path of his lips and tongue dipped into her cleavage. His big hands cupped her small breasts so he could kiss them more easily. His thumbs stroked her nipples.

She threw her head back, closing all her eyes for a moment to just feel his lips on the top of her breasts. When his hands squeezed gently, she made a sound like she did in the dome when a giant lion slammed a mace into her shield, a groaning whuff of expelled air.

That. "I want more of that."

He chuckled against her breast, "Happy to oblige, my lady. But I think this is in the way." He unzipped her dress, his fingertips tracing a shivery path down her back. When his hands came up, he brought the dress up too, pulling it over her head.

As he tossed her new dress aside, she didn't feel cold, just relieved to have less clothes between them. The cool air on her skin caressed her, as soothing as if she were burning with fever.

He pulled her bra down some on both sides, until her breasts rested above the lacy material. He did that delightful gentle squeeze with his hands again.

Liliana moaned, "Yes."

While his hands continued massaging in a way that made her arch her back to press herself into him, his hot mouth closed over her nipple, tongue stroking, and swirling.

She cradled his head to her chest for a moment, glorying in the wet heat, but wanting more.

When she couldn't stand it anymore, she took one of his big hands in hers. She pulled it down from her breast, guiding his long fingers to the very wet panties between her legs.

"There. Touch me there."

He chuckled again. "I can see I will never have to guess what you want." He pushed his other hand down her back, sliding it under her panties and her bottom. He lifted her full weight in one hand so he could use the other to pull the bit of black lace down. When he set her back down, her bare cheeks touched cold granite countertop.

He slipped her panties over her ribbon-wrapped calves, stepping back to get the cloth off both feet, but keeping one hand on her hip to stabilize her on the counter's edge.

After he tossed the panties aside, not even looking where they went, his gaze fell hot and hard on her. His hands scorched her skin, one on the outside of her thigh, the other on her knee, thumb stroking her inner thigh in a tiny caress that felt like an electric connection to her center.

He stopped moving.

She opened all her eyes to see him staring at her.

In his mind was only her. She sat on his kitchen counter, naked but for her ballet slippers and a lacey scrap of bra that held her breasts high. Her disheveled hair curled thick to frame her elfin face. Jewels sparkled in that silken dark cloud nearly as bright as her many-colored eyes. His soul glowed with something so intense, it made the red desire shade white hot at the center. "You are so beautiful."

She smiled, giving him back his own words. "I think that was my line."

He laughed, a full brilliant smile of unsuppressed joy brightening his face and his soul. Then his grin turned mischievous, his dark eyes sparkled in the moonlight, and he came close again.

She expected another kiss, but he dropped to his knees. She got her kiss, just not where she expected it. "Oh!" She clung to his head as his tongue speared into her, licking and stroking, just as it had her mouth.

"Unh." She made that sound like someone knocked the breath out of her. "Yes," she whispered. "Yes." She shuddered to her toes.

He licked into her, his hands pushing her legs more open, thumbs stroking her inner thighs, closer and closer. One thumb finally stroked through her thick curly hair to find the most sensitive part of her.

Her body jerked as his strong thumb stroked across that nub, his tongue buried in her.

"Yes," she almost sobbed.

He licked up from inside her and stroked over that nub with his tongue. Then back to stroking her wet clitoris with his thumb while his thick tongue pushed inside her.

She leaned back on her hands, braced her heels against the cabinet doors below her. Her hips rocked without conscious thought. "More." She whimpered softly, not even sure what she wanted more of. This just wasn't quite enough.

His thumb and tongue never stopped alternating their assault on her clitoris, but his other hand stroked in. A single long finger slowly sank into her very wet sex.

She dropped back to leaning on her elbows on his kitchen island, knocking off a small appliance of some sort. It fell with a loud crash they both ignored. She pushed her sex forward, rubbing against his face. "More!" She lost herself in sensation that was magnificent and intense.

Almost, almost.

He sank another long, thick finger into her, and she screamed.

Warmth converged from her thighs into her center before exploding. Her hips arched up off the counter, bucking against his hands and face. Her body squeezed his fingers. Her belly muscles tightened in spasmodic rhythm. Electric, pulsing fire licked up every inch of her skin. Her nipples ached. Her fingers grabbed white-knuckled onto the edge of the counter as her body shook.

Alexander's tongue stroked her clit, chasing her as she jerked. His fingers plunged slowly in and out. His other hand held tight to her hip to keep up with her bucking body.

The sensation went on for long seconds as she whimpered with the intensity. She never, ever wanted it to stop. Her shuddering finally slowed, the intensity of his tongue becoming almost too much.

Still, she wanted so much more.

She sat up with a soft growl and pulled his head up from her body by the ears.

He was laughing at her. That shark smile lit his face and his sparkling soul lit her third vision.

It made her grin back at him, flashing fangs in a smile that was far more hungry than amused. She wished so hard she hadn't agreed not to bite him. His long, muscular neck showed down to the collarbone where his shirt was unbuttoned to the waist, thin t-shirt underneath. She wanted to bite him, so much. She wanted him, so much.

Grabbing the lapels of his opened shirt, she pulled him in for a wet kiss that tasted of her own body. He smelled like gun oil, expensive cologne, and delicious musk of aroused man.

She popped the remaining two buttons of his shirt so she could pull it over his ridiculously broad shoulders. While he put his arms behind him to pull the sleeves off over his hands, she popped an arm blade out long enough to cut the neck of his t-shirt. His eyes widened for a moment in surprise, just as she took hold of his t-shirt neck with both hands and did what she'd been dying to do. She ripped it in half, finally baring his magnificent chest.

He licked his lips, breath catching as she tore his clothes in her impatience. He'd already dropped his shirt on the kitchen floor. He yanked off the remaining scrap of t-shirt cloth before pulling her into his arms, mouth meeting hers in a devouring kiss.

She wrapped her legs around him, but let her body down lower, so her wet sensitive sex rubbed against the hard bulge, straining the taught fabric of his pants.

He groaned into her mouth. As he carried her toward the bedroom, he tried to toe off his dress shoes.

Liliana undulated against him, feeling her center rub almost painfully against the hardness under the rough cloth. Her peaked nipples were tickled by hair as they touched the muscular glory of his chest.

A startled grunt escaped him as he stumbled, throwing a hand out to catch himself against a wall. He staggered into his bedroom. His knees hit his big bed blindly, making him fall forward with her bouncing and laughing underneath him.

She'd made her suave prince more than a little clumsy.

Alexander growled at her as he fumbled with his belt. He shoved his pants down and off.

The sparkle of amusement in his aura told her he thought it was funny, too, but was too intensely aroused to laugh. He leaned over her on his elbows. His body nudged against her center.

Liliana's smile fell away. She reached down between them, grasping him, so she could move his tip against her clit a few times to glory in the sensation.

He groaned. All his weight rested on one elbow as he grasped her arm. "I can't take much of that." His deep voice had gone husky and rough.

"I can take all of that," Liliana countered. Her hand encircled him. She stroked along the velvet skin over rock hard length. Positioning him at her entrance, she said, "Give me all."

Alexander swallowed, face inches from hers. He stared down at her eyes as his hips shifted slowly forward, careful, despite the shudder running through his entire body. "I'm not a small man. I could hurt you."

Liliana grinned, for once, delighted to lose herself in his dark eyes. "I'm tougher than I look."

He huffed a chuckle. "You certainly are." His face went serious for a moment. He gently pushed a lock of hair off her cheek. Shining white shone in the center of him again. His soul reminded her of the rose in the vase on her desk at home, pure white in the center with scarlet surrounding in overlapping waves of vibrant color.

He kissed her, soft and tender. Then he pulled back to watch her face as he pushed into her, little by little.

As his broad shaft entered her, she closed all but her human eyes. The delicious sensation was almost overwhelming. Through slitted eyes and lashes, she watched her prince's handsome face, jaw clenched hard, fighting for control that had always seemed to come so easily to him.

She opened her hips as wide as she could to take him in. He was a big man, as he said. He stretched her deliciously. She had a weird, momentary image flash, just in her memory since her fourth eyes were closed. Her older sister, Isabella, intoxicated the night before her wedding, giggled with young Liliana. She whispered that spider seers were built to handle powerful men, the bigger the man, the better. The drunken Isabella told her baby sister more than the adolescent spider-kin ever wanted to know about how large her soon-to-be brother-in-law, Rizki, was in areas she never wanted to think about in relationship to the Komodo dragon-kin.

Liliana grinned at her prince, being so careful not to hurt her even as he shuddered with need. She palmed one truly exceptional butt cheek with each hand, hooked her ankles around the backs of his legs and pulled him in.

He slid smoothly into her slick channel, as deep as she wanted.

Alexander squeaked, higher pitched than any sound she'd ever heard him make. He looked at her, eyes wide.

"I can take all of you," she said. She undulated her hips, moving him inside her. Her voice went breathier when she added, "I want all of you." She moved her hips again. "Don't hold back."

He groaned. "You amaze me. Just when I think you can't be any more ..."

"Talk less. Move more." Liliana ground against him again.

He chuckled, which felt really interesting. "Happy to oblige, my lady." Then, finally, he started to move, long slow withdrawal, then a slow plunge into her again.

"Oh." So intense, so much. All of it at once. Perfect. "More."

He did it again, then again, each time pulling out a little faster and plunging in hard enough she would probably have bruises from his hip bones hitting her inner thighs.

It was so much better than just biting him.

Liliana hooked her arms under his, around his chest and back. She held on as her magnificent man pushed into her, hitting her sensitive clit with every thrust. Sweat slicked the skin of his back under her hands. His muscles bunched and rolled beneath her fingers. His body brutally pushed hers to limits she'd never felt before.

She rocked her hips to meet him. Her body matched his rhythm so each hard thrust penetrated as deep as she could get it.

This man should be mine. Will be mine. I want him forever.

"Mine," she murmured. *Mine, mine, mine.* Her body gloried in the feel of him filling her. He pushed her toward more and more pleasure that skated on the edge of pain. She tossed her head and writhed as he thrust, as if they fought. She chased the climbing pleasure.

So good. So good. Almost.

She found it. Liliana threw her head back and yelled as her body bucked. Heat exploded and pulsed through her again, too intense to quietly contain.

Alexander grunted like she'd hit him. His rhythm stuttered as he struggled to push into her body as it squeezed him in a hard drumbeat.

He plunged into her as deep as he could go and shuddered.

She felt him spasming inside her. It set off a second explosion in her when the first hadn't even finished. "Alexander!"

They groaned and shook together for a long, incredible moment.

Eventually, the spasms slowed to little aftershocks every time they shifted. Finally, the pulses of fire burned down to warm coals that spread liquid relaxation throughout Liliana's body.

Alexander slid his long arms under her.

She straightened one leg, seeing his intention in his mind.

He rolled onto his back, taking her with him, so she lay on his broad chest.

Her hands stroked those magnificent pectorals without thought. Despite shredding his shirt to get to them, she still hadn't gotten to really touch them until now.

He held her close, wordless for a long moment, bodies still joined as he slowly softened inside her.

She propped herself up on one arm so she could look down into his face. Her other hand stroked his chest. Satisfaction colored his soul. The moonlight through the bedroom window silvered the edges of his high cheekbones and forehead on the unscarred side like his face was an artistic portrait in charcoal and chalk. Liliana had never seen anything more beautiful. "Are you sure I can't bite you?"

He grinned at her, broad, relaxed, and genuine. "You want me to be yours. I heard you."

"I have never wanted anything or anyone more in my life." Liliana could not be anything but honest. The truth of the words resonated with every inch of her complete self, cuddled against him. Her heart wanted him. Her body wanted him. Alexander should be hers.

His grin vanished, replaced by something like awe. "I'm not sure I've ever met anyone I wanted more either."

"So, I can bite you?" Liliana felt hope spark. If she bit him, she would never lose him to chance. Fate would be on their side.

He stroked her hair, pulling one of the emerald and diamond hairpins loose that had partially fallen out. He set it on the nightstand without looking. His bright soul darkened with uncertainty and a shading of fear. "No, Little Spider. I know how much you want it. But I don't think I can allow it."

Liliana stroked his face reassuringly. "I will only bite you when you are ready, when you are sure that you wish to be mine." It was odd, but he was the only one who wasn't sure. Her heart had apparently decided for her without consulting her multi-faceted mind.

The fear and uncertainty cleared from his aura. "What if I want you to be mine, instead?" A hint of smile touched his lips.

"If you are mine, then I am yours, obviously." Liliana's hand drifted. She wished she could touch his abs with her fingers, but she was laying on them. As she stroked down his side, he jerked and quivered.

She looked at him with all her eyes. That shouldn't have hurt.

His lips were tight. His face looked angry. "Don't." But his aura sparkled with suppressed laughter.

"You're ticklish."

"I am not." But it was a lie.

She grinned and stroked him in that spot again, squeezing a bit with the tips of her fingers.

He snorted a laugh, muscles bunching, then grabbed at her hand.

She evaded. She managed to squeeze once more, eliciting another laugh that she joined in with, even as he caught her wrists.

He put both wrists in one hand and pushed them over her head so he could find all her ticklish spots with the other.

She squirmed and squealed.

They both laughed until they were breathless and fell asleep in each other's arms.

CHAPTER 16

TO SAVE A PRINCE

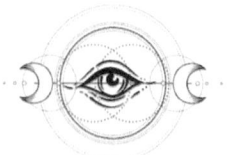

LILIANA LAY AWAKE SOME HOURS LATER, SNUGGLED IN the strong arms of her prince. His warm breath against the top of her head puffed steady and deep with sleep. His long body spooned around her made her feel very small and oddly, very safe.

But it wasn't her life that was endangered. It was his. In a matter of days, an assassin would come to end his life.

Talking about her parents at dinner brought up old feelings that she had all but forgotten. Himmler, the son of a seelie princess and a human, with the aid of the red wolves of Germany, had all but destroyed the spider seer race. Her first mother, her father, two of her brothers, their children, and so many of the friends of her youth. What few had known was that Himmler sought a sword. In the hands of a Sidhe, that sword could amplify Fae power to godlike levels.

Now, a killer came for Alexander, her beautiful prince whose heart beat faster when she touched him. The enemy believed Alexander had the sword. Fraegarthach would make him a god, and it would destroy him. Liliana would never let that sword anywhere near her prince.

Up until he defeated the Wolfhounds, Pete needed the sword to survive, but now, it was a liability. Fraegarthach needed to leave. As long as it was in Fayetteville, it threatened her prince's life and his deepest self.

But that was a fear for another day.

Something had fundamentally changed in Alexander's future. She no longer saw him dying from a single gunshot to the head in his own kitchen as his most probable future. That possibility was gone. A far more certain vision now took it's place. Alexander sat bound to a chair. He was being beaten in a place she didn't recognize. It was somewhere with a high window with no glass. His path had changed, but it still led to his death. Now, instead of fighting someone she had a high probability of defeating, she would face a different opponent. She still could not see her opponent's face, but she did see him killing her in some of her visions. She might not be able to beat this new murderer.

As she saw big fists and hairy human forearms crash into her prince's face, she at least knew the gender of her new opponent. A man. A big man.

This killer didn't just seek Alexander's death, though. He thought her prince had the sword. The killer would hurt him to try to force him to tell where it was. The probability that she would win that fight was even less than when she fought Tray Bradley. This was a far more formidable enemy than the slender person who killed Alexander in his kitchen in her previous vision. Plus, her left arm would still be weak from the bad break. Her best chance lay in finding a way to stop him without fighting him directly.

The possibility of dying while fighting for Alexander's life was not what kept her awake long into the night, though.

In all her visions now, whether she lived or died, whether she fought or stopped the killer another way, she always saw Alexander's body bloody on the floor. Sergeant Giovanni put two fingers to his throat to check for his pulse, shook her head, and said, "He's dead."

She could no longer see a future where her prince survived.

Just a day ago, there had been a good probability that he would live. She must have done something that changed the possible futures. It must have happened today. She didn't know what she had done wrong. Something she'd done that day was a mistake.

Alexander would pay the price.

She blinked tears. There had to be something she missed. There must be a path where he could be saved.

"Hey," Alexander mumbled softly. "What's wrong? Did you see something?"

"It is something I do not see that worries me." Liliana held his big hand close against her chest, rubbing his fingers for comfort. His other arm was under her head. His bicep was her pillow.

"What don't you see?"

"You. I see myself fighting for you. Sometimes I win and survive, but I do not see you alive after that, even if I defeat your attacker."

"I don't like the idea of you fighting for me if you're not sure you can win."

He always seemed to ignore the danger to himself. It was as if he didn't care, but he said he believed her. Maybe he was just so used to his life being in danger that it didn't perturb him.

"I decided to fight for you when you had only kissed me once."

"And now?" His thumb stroked between her breasts, over her heart.

"A dozen angry trolls could not stop me from fighting for you."

He chuckled and hugged her tighter against his body. "Be careful then." He placed a kiss on the top of her shoulder.

They were both silent for a time, but his breathing didn't steady and slow. Alexander lay awake now as well. "What can you tell me about it?" he asked after a while. Maybe he was not as unconcerned about his fate as he seemed.

"Something significant has changed. I no longer see a small, black-gloved hand, probably a woman, and a single fatal shot that catches you by surprise. Now, I see a man, a killer who believes you have Pete's sword. He will suppress your magic so you can't fight back, torture you for information, then kill you. I changed something. I made it worse, somehow."

"What's so special about Pete's sword that everyone is after it?"

"It is Fraegarthach, the Answerer."

His body stiffened. He lifted up onto one elbow to look down at her, stealing away her nice bicep pillow. "Fraegarthach has been lost for two millennia."

She opened her second eyes so she could see him as well. "Not lost. Hidden for generations by a pack of Celtic wolves. Pete is the last of the pack. The others are all dead."

"No wonder Aurore wanted it so badly. Pete has the sword now, doesn't he?" His voice had that bored, flat tone that he used when he sought to hide his emotions.

"Do not seek the sword, my prince. I knew that you would desire its power, much as you desire immortality, but as you said, there is always a price. The price for Fraegarthach is far too high." Her view of his face through her second eyes was awash in colors that she had no name for, eerie and yet, still beautiful. She could see the crown of silver horns as a flickering aura. His face reflected oddly, as if it were much harder than human flesh.

His lips quirked and that dimple in his cheek appeared. "Apparently, the price for not having it is death."

"Some things are worse than death."

"I can't let Aurore get her hands on it, Little Spider. She's already tried to kill Pete for it more than once. I have to do something or eventually, she'll succeed."

He was trying to convince her to help him get the sword. He was a master manipulator, yet she was not fooled. His argument had a flaw. It depended on Pete's life being more important to Liliana than Alexander's own life. To her astonishment, that was no longer true. "The sword, itself, will protect Pete, as will I. That sword must never again be held by a royal Sidhe."

She shifted onto her back to face him with human eyes. "One rampaging Green man is a consequence of a Sidhe prince bonding to the land here. If you or your sister held Fraegarthach, every Fae in a hundred miles would awaken at once, mountain giants, elementals, dragons, the horrors of native stories we never heard, creatures that have been gone so long we no longer even have legends of them. The longer you held it, the wider that circle of Green power would become. Six people lost their lives from just one angry, confused Green man."

"It would give the wielder the power of a god," he said softly. His bland tone could not hide his desire for that power from her third eyes.

She touched his face, tracing the scars that marred his perfect skin. "The laws of physics would break down. Chaos would reign." There were few things her prince desired as much as power. One was order, and oddly for a soldier, another was peace. "The moment one Fae laid claim to that power, every other Fae of royal blood, seelie or unseelie, would seek to take it. You would be the spark that ignited another great war."

He grimaced in distaste, but his mind still searched for ways to make the sword his.

"My parents and older brothers are dead because a Fae sought that power. I suspect Pete's parents and maybe his entire pack was killed because of it." She didn't dare open her fourth eyes, not wanting to see the consequences of such a rash action. "How many would die, do you think? Would you, a young prince still cementing his power base, be one of them? Are you ready to do battle against every other Sidhe in the world?"

His jaw firmed with a kind of stubbornness that refused to back down even if all the world stood against him.

She stroked the hard muscle of his jaw with her thumb. "My help is yours for most things, but I will not help you destroy yourself and rip the world apart."

"Fraegarthach is a Fae sword of power. It wouldn't kill me." There was a hint of question in his voice.

"No, but it would deeply, fundamentally change you. All that you are now would be gone. A monster would live in your skin. I like you as you are, my prince of shadows and secrets."

He settled back with a sigh pulling her close against him. "Then I suppose it's a good thing you and Pete didn't let me get it."

Liliana kept silent. She knew the desire for the power of

Fraegarthach had not left her prince. Alexander would seek the sword again. It was his nature to seek power.

I accept that.

She understood who and what he was. So far, his lust for power had been less strong than his desire to protect his people. He sent the wizard to get the sword from Pete thinking that would save the red wolf from being hunted constantly by his sister's assassins. He'd sought a path to the sword without bloodshed. He couldn't have known how William Eliot would twist his orders.

After a while, Alexander slept.

Liliana did not sleep until dawn lightened the windows. She searched every possible path of the future, fought to get past the images of torture and death to see another way. She couldn't understand why her prince would die now when before, there had been a chance for her to save him.

What changed? What did she do wrong? More importantly, what could she do to fix it before it was too late?

Finally, exhaustion dragged her under its spell.

CHAPTER 17

MORNING REVELATIONS

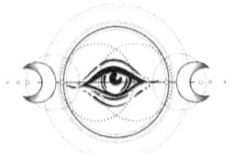

LILIANA WOKE TO A KNOCK ON THE DOOR, CONFUSED AT first because she wasn't certain if it came from her front business door or her back home door. The muscular form of Alexander Bennett moved quietly around the room.

Liliana looked backward in time a bit with her fourth eyes so she could see more of him walking around naked, then shirtless. It was a sad thing to cover up that many beautiful muscles.

He leaned down and kissed her cheek where it barely stuck out above the covers. "I'll get it. It's Runningwolf. We've got a standing eight o'clock meeting here to go over the plan for the day."

"On Saturday?"

"I called him back to duty when I first got up. He must have already been up to get here so fast." Alexander knelt down beside the bed so they were face to face.

Reflexively, Liliana, shifted her first eyes' gaze to his right shoulder as she always did when people tried to make eye contact, but found it wasn't that strong a compulsion. She could look at his cheek or his lips. He had very nice lips that made her think of how they felt on her skin.

His big hand pushed her messy jumble of hair aside, baring one of her second eyes. He leaned down and whispered in her ear, his warm breath making her shiver. "Someone gave me some good advice about how to deal with the awakening forest and the angry Green man."

Liliana smiled, warmth filling her from toes to hair.

Alexander kissed her on the neck before he left the room to answer the door.

With her fourth eyes, Liliana watched him go. His backside was as magnificent as his chest. She stretched lazily, warm and happy and drowsy, starting to doze back off as she watched him.

Alexander bent to pick up his shoes from the hallway as he walked. He dropped them neatly under the little bench by the front door in their usual place.

Lieutenant John Runningwolf saluted smartly when he opened the door. "Good morning, sir."

Alexander returned the salute before inviting the young soldier in. "Coffee?"

John grinned. "Yes, sir, absolutely and always." He doffed his cap and tucked it under a strap on his shoulder as he came in. "Sergeant Giovanni and that civilian Detective Jackson are fairly certain now that the Kodiak-kin was a copycat. He's had no contact that we know of with any of the victims, other than those last two."

Alexander walked into the kitchen while they talked. "The culprit's a Green man who recently woke up. He's probably not even from this century, so Jackson's not going to find anything on him."

In the kitchen, her prince went to pull open the refrigerator. There was a scrap of black satiny cloth and lace hanging on the handle.

Liliana giggled, awake now, so she got up out of bed. The interaction in the next room was far too interesting for her to sleep through it.

The colonel paused for only a moment. He removed the panties, tucked them in his pocket, and opened the refrigerator door as if nothing happened. "We'll need to go to the Bones Creek forest, in the area where the killings took place." His voice hadn't changed.

John's cheek made an odd sort of tick. He started to snicker, but Alexander stared at him in a way that made the smile vanish. He cleared his throat, "Um, sure, um, yes, sir."

"I intend to use my bond with the land to wake up all the sleeping Fae in the area and lay down the law. Those people don't know the rules, or the changes that time has made." Alexander poured a glass of orange juice for himself. He punched buttons on the front of an express coffeemaker on his counter.

John held out a hand. "They don't know the land has a ruler, now."

"Exactly." Alexander placed a mug of hot coffee in his outstretched hand.

The young soldier walked around the kitchen island to a barstool. He paused for a moment, staring at the living room.

Liliana wondered what he was looking at and looked herself. A blender was shattered all over the floor by the island. Liliana's new black dress was half on the arm of the couch, half on the floor. Her bra hung from the corner of an end table.

"I'll need you and Nudd there," Alexander said, ignoring the direction of his Lieutenant's gaze. "Brief Detective Jackson. I want her to know what's going on. It's an asset having someone in local law enforcement who knows what's really happening. She can provide cover when necessary. The press already thinks we caught the killer. Best if we can keep it that way. I'll take care of the Green man, myself, if she approves."

Alexander bent down, picked his dress shirt up off the kitchen floor. He folded it in half neatly on the kitchen counter. "Inform Siobhan as well. This is an official court action, so we'll need our Guardian." Alexander paused for a moment. "And Pete. He's off today, but he'll come in if you tell him its related to the recent killings."

John nodded, still staring at the mess of Alexander's usually photo-ready living room. "Pete, okay. Sure. Um."

Liliana giggled again as she searched through Alexander's closet. She'd fallen asleep in her ballet slippers, but that was the only thing she was currently wearing.

John pushed some of the chunks of broken blender aside with his boot. He lifted a scrap of torn cloth off the barstool he was about to sit on. His face made some weird contortions as he struggled not to smile. Holding up the torn scrap that used to be Alexander's t-shirt, he looked at his commanding officer with a poorly suppressed smirk and raised eyebrows. "Something you want to tell me, sir?"

Alexander looked at him, face blank and serious. "No, there isn't."

John shrugged and tossed the scrap of material behind him to land on the couch. He glanced at the dress and bra. "Was she anyone I know?"

"Would you like to spend the rest of your tour as a gate guard?"

John winced. "Fine, so we bring in Pete. I don't see how you're going to avoid letting him know what you are."

Alexander nodded. "I've been advised that I should come clean with Pete about my nature."

"Didn't that Eliot guy tell you it was a super bad idea because of the whole Celtic wolf unseelie thing? Possibly, a battle to the death level of bad?"

"I've gotten new advice that I trust more than I trusted Eliot's advice."

Liliana bounced on her toes a little, her grin broad enough to crack her face in half as she chose something to wear. She didn't think anything of Alexander's in camo would be appropriate since she wasn't a soldier, and they all looked like mud and algae anyway.

"You finally got together with Liliana," John said with a knowing smirk.

Alexander narrowed his eyes. "Why do you say that?"

Liliana figured now was as good a time as any to come out since apparently John already knew she was there.

As he glanced toward her, his smile broadened. "Lucky guess."

She walked in front of the kitchen island, behind John's barstool. Along with her new black ballet slippers with the long ribbons that wrapped up to her knees, she wore one of Alexander's white dress shirts that fell down to her knees to meet the ribbons.

Normally she would be uncomfortable wearing so little in front of two men, but in her current state of mind, she couldn't be bothered to care.

"Good morning, John." She carefully avoided the chunky bits of machinery and broken glass on the floor from the blender so she could sit down on the barstool next to him.

"So you really don't care what the Colonel thinks of you, I see. Not at all."

Liliana lifted one finger without looking at him in a gesture that had served her well for decades on this continent.

John lost his battle to hold in his laughter.

Ignoring him, Alexander asked her, "Would you like some tea?"

"But you don't drink tea," Liliana said, confused. "You had none the last time I visited you."

Alexander opened the cupboard above and to the right of his sink. The entire bottom shelf was filled with little square tins of many kinds of loose-leaf teas, each with what looked like an ink stamp on the beige labels of a woman in a Victorian dress merged with a gear where her legs should be. Tea Punk Teas.

Liliana couldn't decide which amazing flavor to choose. Some were familiar flavors like jasmine green and masala chai and something called Earl Grey De La Crème. Oh, that sounds delicious. Others were completely new.

She chose the one that seemed most appropriately named for her current situation. "Elixir D'Amour."

Alexander's mouth made that pleased little twitch at the corners that she loved. This morning, his understated smile was less subtle than usual.

John buried his own smile behind his cup of coffee.

Later that morning, after Alexander had given her a quick lift to her house to put on proper clothes, they drove out to the forest near Bones Creek where the murders had taken place.

By the time Liliana and Alexander arrived, John had already gathered several people. The lovely campsite with the trickling stream on one side, a huge, centuries-old cypress with what looked like a lightning scar providing shade, and a stunning view of the surrounding hillsides had been stained a few days ago with the blood of a pair of soldiers, two friends who camped there on their day off.

Siobhan, Doctor Nudd, Detective Jackson, several members of Alexander's Special Enemies and Tactics (SET) unit – everyone they needed was there, except Pete.

Liliana and Alexander had just hiked the short distance down the forest trail from where they parked the cars when Pete's van arrived behind them. Liliana had been watching for it with her fourth eyes.

She felt a little odd about using her spider eyes with so many people around, but they were all either Others, or Normals like Detective Jackson, who were comfortable around Others. A few were even her clients. Not having to hide what she was among so many felt a little daring and scary, but...liberating.

She saw Sergeant Giovanni get out of the van with Pete. Liliana vaguely remembered that the two had planned to play a virtual reality laser tag game together on their day off.

As Giovanni and Pete came up the trail from Pete's van, they were arguing. Liliana stopped on the edge of the trees a fair distance from the SET squad to watch them with her fourth vision.

She touched Alexander's arm, stopping him from joining his soldiers. Softly, she said, "Sergeant Giovanni is very loudly griping about how horrible Eliot was. She thought he might be her next husband. She never would have dated him if she'd known he had Other ancestry. She is arguing that Others of any kind can't be trusted."

Alexander asked, "Are you going to advise me on what to do about that?"

"I am not. I am terrible at relationships. I don't know how to fix this. I just thought you should know there is a problem. Sergeant Giovanni is dear to you. Pete is her closest friend and she loves him. She admires and is loyal to you." Liliana pointed at the group of people waiting a short distance away. "But everyone here is some kind of Other except Detective Jackson. And Sergeant Giovanni is saying this loudly enough for some of them to hear."

She pointed at John Runningwolf, standing in front of the small squad of SET soldiers in demi-badger form, his round ears folded back and prominent fangs bared slightly. Several of the others in demi-plant, demi-stone, or demi-animal form, also showed signs of anger. Keen hearing was a common trait in many Others.

"Sergeant Giovanni is now talking about Andrew Periclum. He seemed like just another soldier, a doctor even. He had so little concern for anyone that he did deadly experiments on his own people. Others have no real compassion, even for their own kind. They're all basically sociopaths."

A muscle jumped in the side of Alexander's jaw. They were close enough to the trail in the quiet of the forest that they could hear the two arguing now. Liliana no longer needed to repeat the ugly words to Alexander.

"Doc Periclum was a sociopath. Sure. I'm not saying he wasn't." Pete's voice was getting louder as they neared. "But that doesn't mean all Others are evil, just because that one person was. That's like saying all Italians like chocolate just because you do."

"Others are beasts and plants, though. They don't have real souls. Them passing as people most of the time makes them all big liars to boot." At that moment, Sergeant Giovanni who was in the lead, stepped into the clearing and looked around. She saw a large group of Others from her Colonel's special unit, plus Siobhan and Doctor Nudd in human form, all looking at her.

Her olive complexion darkened with a flush of blood, but instead of ducking her head in shame, she lifted her chin defiantly.

She ignored the group, and smartly saluted Colonel Bennett, despite wearing civilian clothes.

Alexander stood there for a moment, not answering her salute, so she was stuck standing at attention and saluting. "I wasn't aware of how strongly you felt about Others, Sergeant."

"I apologize, sir. I shouldn't have aired my personal feelings like that. I never would have if I'd been on duty. I had no idea anyone but Pete could hear me."

Alexander sighed. He returned Sergeant Giovanni's salute half-heartedly so she could put her arm down. "I'll put you in for a transfer on Monday."

Sergeant Giovanni's face looked like Alexander slapped her. "Sir, I ... I'm really sorry. I've never let my personal opinions keep me from working well with them before, though. I swear I can still do my job."

"You misunderstand me," Alexander said. "I assume you won't wish to work for someone who isn't human, who lacks compassion or a soul." He paused for a moment while Sergeant Giovanni sputtered a little, then added, "Someone like me."

She stopped, still. "But ... you're not..."

"I am." He looked up where Pete hung back a little. "I had intended to discuss this with you privately, but it seems keeping my identity secret has caused more than one issue on my team."

Pete stepped up beside Sergeant Giovanni. He glanced to the side and a few feet away where Liliana watched them with her second and fourth eyes. Her human eyes were aimed at her feet. Pete's face was thoughtful, as if doing math in his head. He looked at Alexander. "You're the Fae prince Lilly mentioned."

Alexander nodded to him. "I gather she told you there was one in the area, but not who it was."

"I don't tell people's secrets." Liliana stepped up beside Alexander, human eyes on the grass and leaves on the ground between Sergeant Giovanni and Pete. She believed they would not come to blows, but to her surprise, she found herself preparing to defend Alexander from Pete if the worst happened. Not the other way around.

Alexander seemed far less concerned with Pete's reaction than with Zoe Giovanni's. He faced his sergeant, who had followed him loyally from assignment to assignment for years, believing he was human. "I am Other."

Sergeant Giovanni shook her head in denial.

"My father was human, but my mother was a queen of the Sidhe."

"Sir, you don't have to say that to show what I did wrong. I know I messed up, but I also know you're human. You've always been human."

"Why? Because I care about the people I lead? Because I have protected you—and you, me?"

She tightened her lips in a thin, angry line. "Because Others aren't like you, sir. I know I was out of line. I understand if you need to send me away from your SET unit, but you don't have to lie to me."

Alexander unbuckled his belt and handed it to Liliana who wasn't sure what she was supposed to do with it. He handed her his hat as well. She put it on, since that seemed like the only logical thing to do with a hat. He removed his camouflaged shirt and dull green t-shirt. He handed her those as well. She hung them on the nearest branch.

His gaze never left Giovanni as he shifted, growing more than a foot in height, plus a few inches more if you counted the crown of silver horns. His flesh became glassy black sharp-edged stone. Here, in the sunshine, up close, Liliana noticed a shimmer of green within him, like in rainbow obsidian, but slowly swirling like the colors in her fourth eyes.

Sergeant Giovanni's face paled. She covered her mouth with her hand. Her head shook in denial.

"My nature is dangerous for anyone to know," Alexander told Giovanni. "I never wanted you to be in danger because of me, so, I kept it to myself. It was never my intention to deceive you."

Pete smiled a little sadly. "There are a lot of good reasons to hide what you are. One of my closest friends thinks Others aren't even really people." Pete took a deep breath before he stepped around so that he stood beside Alexander, facing Giovanni. "It's why I didn't tell you, either, Zoe."

"Didn't tell me ...Oh." She shook her head again. "You're not one of them." The statement was certain.

Pete gave her a rueful shrug.

"You're not! You can't be." She didn't sound completely certain. "I've met your parents."

Pete grimaced. "I was adopted. I'm wolf-kin. You and I were pretty close before I found out how you feel, and then ..." He shrugged. "I'm sorry, I just ... I love how easy we are with each other. I didn't want to lose that."

Giovanni's jaw set. Her dark eyes flashed. Her aura blazed equal parts orange with anger and the pale unclean yellow of pain. "Fine. Fine. You both put one over on the gullible Normie. Bet you thought it was hilarious listening to me rant about Others." She drew herself to attention. "I'll accept that transfer on Monday, ... sir." The last word sounded sarcastic. She marched back up the trail the way she came.

Alexander watched her go, his living stone face oddly more expressive of the sorrow and pain coloring his aura than his controlled human face was.

Pete took a couple of steps after her. "It wasn't like that, Zoe." But she ignored him and kept walking. After a moment, he stopped, letting her go. His shoulders slumped in defeat.

Liliana watched Sergeant Giovanni on the trail back to the cars. She let tears fall silently once she was far enough away she didn't think anyone would see them. Liliana's heart ached for the woman who just lost the two people she cared about most because she couldn't let go of her prejudices.

Alexander walked up behind Pete. He put a giant stone hand on the wolf-kin's shoulder, his face and aura filled with sadness. "It's bad for morale to have someone with those attitudes working with my soldiers. I didn't know or I would have found a gentler way to have her reassigned."

Pete looked up at the graceful living statue of volcanic glass. He nodded agreement. "She was always the consummate professional on the job. I'm not surprised you didn't know." He turned to face Alexander. "Liliana told me the local Fae prince was unseelie."

"Is that going to be a problem?" Alexander pulled his hand away from Pete's shoulder and showed him his empty, weaponless palms, tension in the sculpted statue shoulders.

Pete shrugged. "Doc Nudd's been like a second father to me. He's unseelie. I really don't care."

Alexander made a graceful gesture with his hand. "Nudd told me that. I should have listened. He has always given me wise counsel. But I've had enough unpleasant experiences with seelie and their allies that I was hesitant."

Siobhan piped up behind them. "The Colonel got bad advice from that Eliot git for a while is all."

Pete glared at her. "You knew?"

Siobhan grinned. "Lilly's not the only one who can keep a secret."

Liliana wrapped Alexander's belt around her hand, fiddling with the canvas end and the metal tip. She looked at her hands as she ran it between her fingers. "There have been a lot of revelations today. There is something else. The Kodiak-kin killed only two people."

Detective Jackson hadn't said much up to then. She'd been looking a bit unsure of why she was there, but that got her attention. "Yeah, I knew that, actually. Do you have some sort of a lead? Did you see something, Lilly?"

"I did."

The giant living statue of Alexander glanced down at Detective Jackson, who stood no taller than Liliana, about waist high in his current form. He gave the petite Normal a respectful half nod. "I would appreciate it if you let the press continue to think the killer is in custody."

Detective Jackson's eyes narrowed at the giant, regal figure. "Justice for murderers is my area, Colonel. I'm not letting a killer go free to end someone else's life on your say so." She put her hands on her hips, not backing down in the least from the giant of oily black stone. "Why would you even think I'd mislead the press?"

"I suspect the answer to that question is going to be obvious in a few minutes." He glanced at Liliana. "You're certain I can wake the forest?"

Liliana nodded. "I have seen you do it in the near future. I have no idea how you will do it."

Alexander's expression twisted to irony. Even in demi-stone form, the expression made a dimple in his cheek. It was adorable. At least, Liliana thought so.

"Wake up the forest?" Pete said as they walked to rejoin the larger group.

Doctor Nudd joined them in a few long strides. "I've seen it done only twice in the millennia of my lifetime. A land ruler can awaken all sleeping Fae in an area at once and speak to them. They'll all hear what he says."

Pete blinked. "A land ruler. Like a king or a queen?"

"Any Fae that is land bonded." Nudd nodded to the tall obsidian figure. "Our prince should theoretically be able to do it."

"Theoretically," Alexander stated drily.

"What do you want us to do, sir?" Lieutenant Runningwolf gestured at the double line of mismatched Others all in demi-form, standing at parade rest with automatic rifles, customized to the unusual size and shape of each, held with butt resting on the ground at their sides. Each wore a military uniform that was apparently made like Pete's clothes, with stretching or loose sections to allow shifting from human form to demi. Some had slits in the back to allow wings or extra limbs to protrude like Siobhan's jackets.

"You're my backup." Alexander gestured to the double line of soldiers. "I'm hoping this will go peacefully, but at least one of the creatures in this forest is a serial killer. If some of the beings awakened are not happy about me giving them orders, it may come down to a show of force."

"Yes, sir." Lieutenant Runningwolf's long striped badger muzzle dipped in a nod. He turned to face the squad of twenty Others in two neat rows of ten each, all in demi form. "You heard the Colonel." His deep, growly voice snapped. "Shoulder arms."

The men and women, beast-kin and Fae, seelie and unseelie, moved as one to lift their weapons so they leaned against their shoulders, in a stance that looked precise despite their varied heights and shapes. It was a position that would make it easy for them to stand for long periods, while keeping the weapons at the ready.

"You may need to fight instantly, when given the order," the badger-kin continued, speaking with authority to creatures twice his size or more in some cases. "However, you will do nothing unless attacked or given the order. Until then, hold steady and strong. No sign of fear or any other emotion. You are statues until you hear an order otherwise. Understood?"

"Yes, sir." The SET squad chorused.

Lieutenant Runningwolf nodded in acknowledgement. He did a neat about face, his own weapon held across his body, at the ready. "We're ready when you are, Colonel."

A nod of the great crowned head looked majestic, but the dimple and familiar tiny quirk at the corner of the Fae prince's lips made Lilly smile.

Chapter 18

Awakening The Forest

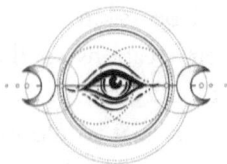

Alexander stepped in front of the two rows of men, with John Runningwolf just to the right and slightly behind him, guarding one flank. Liliana stepped up to the same position on his left. Being in front of so many strangers was uncomfortable, but no amount of discomfort could induce her to leave Alexander's flank unguarded.

Detective Jackson chose to stand beside Liliana, unintentionally perhaps, also taking a protective position.

The small figure of Siobhan in human form, all three foot ten of her, stood in her leather jacket with her machine pistol in hand, directly in front of Alexander.

It was an odd position for a court guardian. Normally, they stood behind the one they guarded, far too large to stand in front of their charges. Siobhan was small enough that she could stand directly between her prince and danger, without obscuring more than his knees.

Doctor Nudd was still walking all around them, halting occasionally and touching a leaf or the bark of a tree. His craggy face was even more wrinkled than usual as he studied the birds and squirrels as if they held some secret he needed to know.

Alexander called to him, "Merlin."

The Merlin of the court was the wisest advisor to the ruler. His position was usually right at the ruler's side, close enough to whisper important information in his ear. At some point in history, the Merlin also became expected to be the most powerful wizard of the court.

Dr. Nudd dropped to one knee in front of the silver-crowned obsidian statue in camo pants. Siobhan stepped to one side to make room, watching the forest warily with her machine pistol in hand, unconcerned about Nudd being near the prince she guarded.

Alexander put a living black stone hand on his shoulder. "I am uncertain how this is done. Is there some information you could give me?"

Nudd ran a hand through his curly hair, making it even more messy than usual. "I don't think you'll have any trouble waking this forest up. It already feels like it's watching us."

Liliana nodded. "The Green here is rich and strong." Her third eyes saw the pulsing flow just beneath the grass being pulled into every tree, especially the big cyprus that shaded them. Green men only made their homes in the most magical of forests. The longer they stayed in a forest, the more magical it became. The fact that one slept here with his family made her wonder if once it had been a place of power. And if the trees here would like it to be so again.

Nudd scratched his bristly cheek in need of a shave. "My concern is that this forest, when awake, may be more than we bargained for."

Outwardly, the living statue of oily black stone seemed regal and still, but Liliana could see ripples of unease, shivers of beige uncertainty on the edges of Alexander's aura. "You and the land are one, my prince." Liliana touched his smooth stone arm and squeezed. "Call the Green. For you, it will come joyously, like a hound eager for the hunt."

He took hold of the hand on his arm to draw her to his side, from the position of a flanking guard to the position of a queen or ...a consort. *Oh. Right.* She hadn't considered the implications of becoming a landed prince's lover.

His stone hand was oddly warm in hers. "This is the first time I've done anything like this. My court has been largely theoretical until now. Nudd has been giving me guidance about how it is normally done, but this. This will begin it. After this..."

Liliana looked up high to his eyes, a deep shimmering green. "Nudd has taught you how to be a king. Now you must choose what kind of king you will become," Liliana said.

His eyes closed as his aura stretched down into the earth from the soles of his boots, and came back up a hundred-fold stronger. Deep green whorls of power circled his legs like a slow-motion tornado. It didn't cling to him only. It spread to Siobhan and Nudd who still knelt in front of him, to Liliana beside him, and John a step back on his other side. The earth power even reached a smoky tendril to the one human among them, Detective Shonda Jackson, who sucked in a breath when the magic caressed and sunk into her skin. The flow of power continued to the two lines of Other men and women standing at the ready behind their commanding officer.

As the Green coursed through Liliana, the energy charged her body like electricity through a wire. She found her weight on her toes, feeling light and strong, as if she could leap twenty feet straight up to land on the high branches above her if she chose.

When all of Alexander's allies were intertwined with the ghostly wisps of Green power, he spoke one word. His voice rumbled the soles of Liliana's feet, the same voice she'd heard him use before to command obedience.

"AWAKEN."

And the forest obeyed.

Chapter 19

Living Green

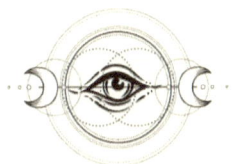

Liliana watched, all eight eyes open. She saw the Green that swirled around her knees spread out from her prince's boots, just beneath the surface of the ground like streams flowing from a spring.

The forest stirred. All around them, trees swayed on a day with no wind. Outcroppings of rock shifted and gained human shapes. In one spot the earth itself heaved into a mound that grew arms and a head and opened its eyes. The water of the creek flowed backward. It lifted into the graceful shape of a woman. A small fish swam down her leg from her midsection and vanished in the rest of the creek.

With her fourth eyes, Liliana saw the green man who had been sleeping in a small hickory grove a quarter mile away. His bushy-bearded face lit up with joy as the sapling whose roots he slept on stretched and yawned. The sapling became a little girl, perhaps eight or nine. Nearby another hickory creaked as it arched and shook its limbs into arms. Its many twigs took shape as a wild cloud of hair down to a lady's barky knees. The green man shifted from human form to a thick old hickory demi-form to embrace the lady. The little girl climbed them both so she could sit on what must be her mother's shoulder.

As the Green flow of power gushed further, a hillside moved, lifting a hoary head. It turned a face like a crude sculpture of stone and dirt with bushes in place of eyebrows. It didn't stand, thank goodness. The boulders rolling off its shoulders might have crushed someone.

Some distance away a far larger hillside opened a single eye to regard them.

Liliana swallowed. That single eye was easily larger than her house. She glanced at Alexander, Detective Jackson, and John Runningwolf. They hadn't noticed the giant eye. They were too busy nervously eying the closer creatures surrounding them; huge tree spirits, rock trolls, and some creatures she had no name for like the earth man.

Not all of them were as joyous as the Green man and his family. Many looked angry at being disturbed. They faced the little group with clenched fists of wood or stone.

The majestic ancient cypress growing beside the stream bared white spikes of teeth even as a face formed in the craggy bark above the fissure in the trunk. The treeman creaked as he painfully wrenched his knees up out of the mud. He shifted form, shrinking into a tall, muscular man with dusky-skin and untamed long black hair wearing only an old-fashioned pair of pants made of homespun cloth. A horrible inflamed, half-healed wound, still dripping blood down his flanks formed where the crack in the old cypress' trunk had been. Mud covered his pants legs. His now human teeth were bared in a snarl as he faced the double line of Other soldiers with their modern rifles and their camouflage uniforms.

The man who had been the cypress lifted a hand. The trees surrounding the little group, the ones that had not awakened to more humanoid forms, bent their branches in hooks that reached toward them with sharp, grabbing branches. The man's hand bent in tense claws as if he would rip them apart from several feet away.

Alexander's polished black statue face showed no fear on the surface, but his aura changed to sickly green as the world came to life, and the life showed overwhelmingly hostile intentions.

Liliana knew that if Alexander couldn't control this angry Fae mob, no one could. She had no doubt her own aura would be flashing with acid green if any of the many species of Fae had the right kind of vision to see it.

John's voice rang out. "Rear rank, about FACE. SET squad, Ready ARMS."

The back line of soldiers neatly turned in place so half the soldiers watched their backs. All the soldiers shifted their weapons from leaning casually on their shoulders to up in their hands, ready to be aimed.

The soldiers in the front line shifted to aim at the half-dressed wounded man who seemed to be turning the trees of the forest into weapons against them.

"Flash protection position." Siobhan's high voice pierced the angry rumbling and the waving rustle of leaves that wasn't caused by wind.

Behind Liliana and beside her everyone clenched their eyes shut, faced the ground, and with weapons in the crooks of their elbows, plugged their ears with their fingers.

Siobhan primed her small machine gun like a pump shotgun, yelled, "Flash out," and fired.

Liliana hastily copied everyone else, including Alexander. She closed all her eyes, plugged her ears and bent her head down just before Siobhan pulled the trigger. Around her, even Detective Jackson, who probably didn't know why she was doing it, copied the action.

It surprised Liliana that this time the precautions were more effective. Apparently, the stun grenade had less of an impact in an open forest than a tile-floored restaurant.

She looked up right afterward to see what effect Siobhan's weapon had on the dangerous cypress Fae.

The man with the nasty wounds screamed. The stun grenade probably went off right in front of him. He put his arms over his face, staggered, and fell to his knees.

Around them, the trees stopped trying to attack them. Some of the humanoid creatures shook their heads or put their hands over their ears, some fell off their feet, or roots, or whatever. The more sensitive the Fae's ears and eyes, and the closer they were to the explosion, the more intense the effects. But many of the Fae, especially those in stone forms, just looked angrier. Rock trolls took grinding steps toward them with clenched fists.

The hill giant shook its great head, showering the surrounding area with dirt and stones.

The giant eye on the hill that nearly qualified as a mountain blinked.

"Hold fire!" Lt. Runningwolf shouted, the sound booming to be heard over ringing ears.

There weren't many weapons useful against such large stone creatures as the rock trolls. Nothing short of mining explosives would bother the hill giant. Never mind whatever that was in the massive hillside behind it. The trolls didn't have any clear weak points either, like Spearfinger had. If it came to a fight, as well-trained and well-armed as they were, the SET squad might take some of the Fae with them, but they would most likely all die.

The best option is for this not to become a battle.

That wasn't what they came for, in any case.

Liliana reached out for Alexander's long stone fingers. "You are part of the land that nurtured their rest, my prince. Speak and the people of the land will listen."

His hand briefly squeezed hers, but he didn't look at her. Instead, a single command rang out, echoing through the ground at her feet like a minor earthquake as he said, "STOP."

All around them, the stone, earth, water, and plant beings that had started to look like an angry mob, froze.

"BE AT PEACE."

The creatures blinked stone or bark or dirt or liquid eyes. Their fists unclenched. They looked around them as if waking from a dream.

A demi-crabapple tree, clenched her twiggy fists again. She

stepped toward them. She said something in a language Liliana didn't know.

Behind her, she could see with her second eyes, as the front row of soldiers shifted their aim to point at the brightly blooming sentient tree that stood quivering with acid green fear and determination in her aura.

Doctor Nudd stood on Alexander's other side, still in human form. "Gaelic, my liege," he said softly. "She says she is seelie. She asks if her and her kin can leave, or if you intend to kill them. She'll fight if she has to."

Alexander nodded, but instead of having Nudd translate for him, he spoke to his Guardian. "Siobhan, tell her that her people are welcome to stay, just as all the unseelie are. They can go back to sleep, leave, or join the modern world. They will have to accept an unseelie land-ruler, but this is not an unseelie court. This land draws no lines of blood between night and day. This isn't Europe."

Seelie flower-sprite Siobhan spoke in her high-pitched voice in a lilting, musically accented version of the same language the blooming tree had used. When the tree-woman said something short and probably rude in a grumbling, skeptical voice, Siobhan put a hand to her own chest, then gestured to Pete.

The red-headed man shifted larger and broader his muzzle and tall ears pushing out, showing his red-furred demi-wolf form.

The flowering tree woman put her hand over her mouth as she recognized the red wolf's race.

"I told her, highness." Siobhan spoke to Alexander in English loud enough for everyone to hear. "When she called me a liar, I told her I was a seelie sprite and Pete was a Celtic wolf, and we were both a respected part of your court."

"The lesser one is joking, surely." A tall, slender pine goblin spoke up in clear French. "Your choice, of course, if you choose not to obliterate them, but surely you don't allow Seelie scum in your court."

Alexander answered in the same language. "Siobhan is a court Guardian." His stone nostrils flared. A small red coal of anger lit the center of his deep green eyes. "You will speak to her with respect if you intend to remain in my lands."

The pine goblin laughed. "That little weed? A Guardian?" He laughed harder, slapping his woody thigh.

Alexander's face didn't change, except possibly to become more grim.

Siobhan's expression twisted like she'd eaten something sour. "Can I kill him, highness?" she asked Alexander in French. She pumped the lower part of her weapon, just as she had before firing the stun grenade. "Make an example of one, and the others will fall in line."

Liliana cocked her head to one side, confused. The stun grenades were not lethal, and Alexander had not given Siobhan permission to use more deadly grenades as far as Liliana knew.

She looked at Siobhan with all eyes open.

Oh. The threat is a lie.

Alexander's black stone lips twitched at the corner in amusement. "It would be effective, no doubt, Guardian, but would not convey our desire for peaceful coexistence." He held up a hand. "Do not blow the pine goblin into splinters for his insolence."

"Mmmph. Yes, sir." Siobhan lowered the muzzle of her gun reluctantly.

The pine goblin looked nervously at the weapon. He glanced at the ancient native man of power who was still on his knees shaking his head and blinking watering eyes repeatedly, likely unable to hear any of their conversation.

"You should probably apologize to my Guardian," Alexander said, mildly. "She has been known to take retribution for slights out in blood. Unofficially, of course."

The tall pine looked like he'd swallowed a bug. "My apologies, of course, Guardian." The words sounded like they were drug out of him painfully.

Siobhan glared at him. "Accepted." She spoke with the same reluctance.

"Green man, I would speak with you." Alexander pointed at the elder hickory, even though he had just arrived with his family and was at the far back edge of the crowd.

His wife made a sound of distress. She reached for him with clinging twigs as he pulled away. He straightened, shifted to his smaller human form, and walked to stand in front of Siobhan who did not allow the man any closer to Alexander.

He dropped to one knee, trembling. "My liege." He spoke in an accented English that sounded like it came straight from England. The words and the gesture both acknowledged Alexander as ruler.

"You are the Green man of this forest. All can feel the richness of Green in it. But the land that feeds it is mine. I will not tolerate murder of seelie, unseelie, or beast-kin on this land without cause, nor especially of Normals. They do not understand their transgressions. You have slain them when their only crime was ignorance."

The old man with his bushy beard in faded clothes from a previous century swallowed and nodded. "I was confused and afraid, but those are not good reasons to kill the innocent. I submit to your punishment." He bowed his head, putting one hand on the ground as if he expected to be beheaded.

Much to Liliana's surprise, Detective Jackson stepped forward. "I represent the human law here, which you broke."

There was a murmur among those watching as they realized a Normal human stood among the Fae prince's court.

The old man sat back on his heels. He looked up at the petite policewoman.

"You murdered four people. Why?"

"I was just..." He swallowed. "They cut limbs from green trees. I'd forgotten which ones were my wife and daughter. I thought they hurt my little girl." The shaggy-bearded man blinked and tears fell. "She and her mother nearly died of the influenza. I brought them here to heal. The Green was fading everywhere, but this place still had some power. I used my magic to pull as much of the Green as I could, but no matter what I did, it wasn't strong enough to do anything but keep them alive in tree form. Only in the last decade has it started to help them heal again. They were nearly well. To survive so much, then be cut down by some insensitive idiot. I just ..." He shook his head and tears fell again. "I wasn't really in my right mind at that point. When I saw that soldier cut a sapling that might have been my little girl, I just... I'm sorry. I'm so sorry."

Detective Jackson sighed and rubbed her temples. "Do you intend to continue killing campers or anyone else?"

"No, ma'am. I know they didn't deserve what I did." He looked to Alexander. "Please, just take care of my family, sire. They were not in any way responsible."

Detective Jackson looked up at Alexander, who gestured to her that the decision was hers. "Well, it's not like I could drag you into a court of law." She nodded. "All right. Protecting your child is a hard thing to argue with. As far as the press and my bosses are concerned, the bear did it." She glared down at the weeping old hickory. "I'll let it go. But if anyone in this forest gets so much as a scratch from now on, I'll know who to blame and where to find you."

The old man looked up at her with dawning wonder, then looked up at Alexander.

He gave a confirming nod. "Detective Jackson represents the human law in this place. If she forgives your actions, then I do as well."

The man's beard was split by a brilliant smile. "Thank you, ma'am. Thank you, sire. I swear, this will be the safest forest for miles around."

As the Green man joined his relieved family, Alexander addressed the now quiescent crowd.

"If you wish to leave this realm, I will not stop you. If you wish to remain, you will swear allegiance to me. After that, you may sleep again or wake as you choose. If you wish to rejoin mortal society, we will arrange for you to be taught and given what is necessary to pass as a Normal from this time."

He repeated the English statement in all his languages. Liliana repeated it in the two she knew that he didn't. Nudd repeated it in

Gaelic and another tongue she didn't recognize. John repeated it in two more languages she didn't know.

Alexander's voice deepened again until it vibrated through the earth. "I RULE HERE NOW. IS THAT CLEAR?"

Everyone nodded and the old-world Fae lined up to swear fealty. The hill giant nodded, huge stone eyes focused on Alexander. "I SWEAR." The giant's voice rumbled like an avalanche, then it laid back down. As its eyes closed, it lost its human face, becoming nothing more than a hill again.

On the cliff face behind the giant, Liliana was relieved to see that great eye close and vanish as if it had never been. She wasn't sure Alexander or anyone else saw it.

The ancient cypress man on his knees with the horrific wounds shuddered. He looked up at Alexander, face filled with rage and sorrow, eyes full of impotent tears. His hearing was probably still damaged, and his sight limited to only the edges around big blotches of white, but the language of the earth was one all Fae heard and understood.

There were a lot of Fae who had moved to surround the cypress Fae. The ones in human form all had the facial features of native Americans.

The ancient cypress growled a few soft syllables that Liliana didn't know. His shoulders sagged in a defeated shrug. He seemed unable to hear anything but the words Alexander spoke through the Green.

"*Nvwadohiyada*," John Runningwolf said to him and to the dark-haired people around him who still had angry or wary faces. "Peace to you."

Those among the crowd reacted to John when he said that one word. The woman in the creek was among them. She stepped onto shore, taking a human shape in a blue and green dress with a bell-shaped skirt and corset forming a V at her waist. Shiny black hair was parted in a perfect line with little twisted buns over each ear framing a broad face with native American features. The other native Fae moved to stand with the woman who stood straight-backed and chin high. In oddly accented, but clear, crisp English, she said, "We will not leave this land, no matter who rules. Many of us hid in our other forms when they told us we must go. We will fight to stay."

Alexander shook his head. "I'm not asking anyone to leave. That was a long time ago. If you wish to join society again, my people will help you make new homes here. I only ask that you obey modern law." He gestured at Detective Jackson. "Find your place in Normal society or continue your sleep here. As you choose."

The woman nodded to Alexander, then to John with a look of relief. "*Dudanilvtsv*. Agreed."

She turned to speak to the other native Fae rapidly in a language Liliana didn't know.

Alexander looked at John for a translation.

He shrugged. "I only know a few words of old Cherokee Tsalagi."

Alexander raised a stone eyebrow. "I suspect it would be a good idea to learn more."

"Yes, sir. There's some basics on line, I think." John pointed at the cypress Fae still on his knees, tears streaming from his eyes . "I know some of the old plains Indian trade hand language, too?" He made it a question to Alexander.

"Do what you can." Alexander nodded permission for him to leave his post.

John turned behind him. "SET squad is yours, Corporal. Absolutely no firing unless one of us is directly attacked or the Colonel orders it."

A young fox-kin with three tails stepped forward. "Yes, sir."

Lieutenant Runningwolf slung his weapon over his shoulder by its carry strap, shifted to his less intimidating human form, and walked toward the man who had been a great spreading cypress by the creek with scars that looked like lightning strikes.

The rest of the non-native Fae stood peacefully in a line in front of the prince under Siobhan's, Pete's, and Detective Jackson's watchful eyes.

Liliana wanted to go to the cypress man. His anguish tore at her heart. Defeat and hopelessness saturated every line of his body and his aura. "He needs healing," she said softly, touching Doctor Nudd's hand. "And not just of the body."

After getting a nod of permission from Alexander, Doctor Nudd joined John. "Perhaps I can be of assistance?"

John nodded. "He sure looks like he could use a doctor."

Carefully, and slowly, hands out, they approached the wounded native cypress Fae.

Liliana couldn't help. She had to watch with her first and third eyes the line of Fae approaching her prince. Each dropped to a knee or some semblance of a knee, and stated what they wanted to do, whether sleep again or join society, stay or leave. If they intended to stay, Alexander asked for an oath of fealty to himself, and an oath to follow the modern laws of the land, both Normal and Other. The second oath he required the Fae to swear to Detective Jackson, as a representative of the human law, much to her surprise. And theirs.

Liliana's third eyes let her spot honesty or deception, which she murmured to Alexander so he would know the true depth of emotion of those who swore loyalty to him.

With her fourth eyes, she watched John and Doctor Nudd slowly approach the cypress Fae, yearning to help him herself. The power and pain that radiated from him was compelling and heart breaking.

The man watched them warily, still blinking with tears still flowing, but his eyes now tracked the big custom automatic weapon John carried.

"Hang up a sec, Doc." John lifted the carry strap slowly over his head and deliberately laid the weapon on the ground in front of the ancient Fae.

"*Nvwadohiyada.*" John repeated the word he'd said before. "Peace. We don't have to fight." He held up his empty hands.

The native cypress Fae shook his head slightly. He pointed to his ear. Blood trickled down the side of his neck.

John winced in sympathy. "He took that flashbang right in the face."

"I can help." Nudd held out a hand toward the man's face. "If you will permit me?" He eased carefully closer, making sure the man saw every movement. He gave him every opportunity to avoid his touch.

The cypress Fae clenched his jaw. His body tensed as if expecting some sort of attack, but he let Nudd touch the side of his face.

The old oak goblin closed his eyes. His healing magic flowed like water freed from a dam. Green light gushed from his fingertips and washed over the cypress Fae. The glow didn't just soak into his ears, but flowed over his whole body, suffusing him in healing light so bright it lit the entire clearing, outshining the sun in broad daylight.

The rest of the awakened creatures gasped in awe, both native and immigrant.

The ancient Fae stiffened for a moment, then sagged, eyes drooping with deep relief. He murmured something in a language Liliana didn't understand, then blinked. "Doctor." He spoke in accented English. He raised a filthy hand that shook to touch the gnarled hand on the side of his head. He squeezed Nudd's hand, a look of gratitude on his face. "The pain is ... gone now. I hear and see clearly again." He touched his chest and belly where not even scars remained of the horrible gaping wounds he'd had before.

Nudd looked at his own hand with astonishment. His gift had never manifested so powerfully.

"Sorry about the stun grenade," John said.

The cypress man's eyebrows scrunched for a moment, then cleared. "The weapon of light and sound."

John nodded.

"I would have killed you all if the tiny warrior hadn't used it."

John grinned. "Well, then maybe not that sorry."

The old Fae huffed, not quite a laugh. He wiped tears from his cheeks. His face showed no lines. He had to be centuries old, but he looked no older than a man in his early thirties. He looked at John Runningwolf for a moment. "You are Sioux?"

John nodded. "Lakota."

"Why do you serve a white man?"

John's grin widened. "The Colonel's a long way from white, even in human form."

"His power feels like the people from across the sea."

Nudd explained. "His mother is a powerful Fae queen in Europe, but his father's ancestors were Normals brought here against their will. No part of him is an invader or conqueror to this place. His father, grandfather, and great grandfather were all born within a hundred miles of where we stand. His ancestors lived by coaxing food from the earth with their hands. This land chose him."

The cypress Fae closed his eyes as if what Nudd said caused him physical pain. "Four generations. So long." He opened his eyes and his face was angry again. "And where are the principle people? Where are the people who were here for dozens of generations before that?"

John shrugged. "My girlfriend in college was Eastern Cherokee. She grew up near Maggie Valley."

The old Fae gave a puzzled look.

"In the mountains, to the northwest about, um, about two- or three-days' ride on horseback. I think. Pretty area."

"Did they fight the ones who wanted to take our homes?"

"Eh, not really, no. The ones who didn't go on the forced march mostly hid. Some of us Sioux fought, but all the wars all the tribes fought against the Europeans are over now, and um…" John rubbed the velvet short hair on the back of his neck. "We lost."

The snarl appeared on the cypress Fae's face for a moment, but then he sagged. "Lost. Long ago. While I slept and heard only the wind and the song of the brook. While I waited to die or for healing that didn't come."

"Yeah. Pretty much." John gave him a sad look. "Things were bad for the Cherokee for a while. They got scattered all over. A lot of people died about two hundred years ago. About the time you went to sleep, I'd guess."

"There was a village near here. Farms, homes. A young woman showed me newspapers. After just a little bit of practice, I could read them."

John grinned. "Yeah, that was pretty cool. The Cherokee Phoenix. They still publish, although it's in English these days."

The man's shoulders sagged again.

John shrugged. "The world changed. Not much point in being angry about what happened two hundred years ago. It eats you up inside, without bothering the people who did it in the slightest since they're mostly long dead."

"Two hundred years ago." The cypress Fae closed his eyes again.

"Why did you sleep so long?"

"I was dying in body, tired in spirit. Bleeding inside and out. I thought to sleep forever here."

John looked around the glade with the brook, the view of the hills, the fresh, alive feeling that indicated strong Green in the area. He nodded. "Not a bad place for that. If you want, you can go right back to sleep. No one's stopping you."

The man looked up at the sky. He let the dappled sun shine on his face and took a deep breath. "I am alive." He nodded to Doctor Nudd. "Thanks to a healer of the people who invaded, I am hale. I have slept enough."

Liliana's attention was drawn back to her third vision, which she had focused on the line of people waiting to speak to Alexander. She saw a flare of orange rage as the pine-goblin who sneered at Siobhan earlier came close. Outwardly, he seemed as respectful as the others.

The spider seer stepped past the petite native wild hydrangea sprite swearing a heartfelt oath to the new land ruler, as if merely walking along the line. Her footsteps were as silent as she could make them. She stopped directly behind the goblin.

When the goblin stepped forward for his turn, he dropped to his knees with a flare of triumph and rage. He bared yellow spikey teeth at Siobhan where she stood in front of Alexander's knees. As he touched the ground with his hand, Liliana felt the roots of the many trees move under the earth. Ignoring the sudden tight grip on her ankle, she popped out her arm blade and cut off the arm/branch that touched the earth just above what passed for an elbow.

The pine goblin had only a moment to look startled at his forearm and hand laying on the grass. Around them, the roots that had shot out of the ground now waved aimlessly. The barrel of Siobhan's automatic weapon came up to his forehead and fired.

The muffled *brrrdddttt* of automatic weapon fire exploded his head in sap and bark and splinters. It left no doubt that Siobhan's ammunition was effective against Fae.

Alexander smiled dangerously showing silver needle teeth, lifted his own hand, and the roots that had been trying to grab him and everyone near him, switched their target. The roots pulled the pine goblin's still twitching corpse rapidly under the earth which moved out of the way to make space.

Liliana saw no sign even of fatigue in her prince as he gestured to smooth the ground again. Within moments, the area was covered with bright grass and wildflowers, as if the pine goblin had never been. The Green in this area channeled through her prince made them all strong.

He looked up at the rest of the waiting Fae, those who had sworn to him and those who hadn't yet. They all showed signs of shock, some with the beginnings of fear, some with anger. "In case anyone else intends to use this chance to get close to me and cause harm, you should know that my consort sees into your souls and knows your true intent."

Liliana tensed for a moment as she knew everyone would be staring at her now. But it was a tactic. Like when she stared down every lion who might have called challenge. She could not show fear or nerves. This was a form of combat.

She turned to face the crowd, threw back her hair with all eyes wide, and bared her fangs at them all.

Everyone, even the rock trolls cringed when her eightfold gaze fell on them.

It was weird to discover that as much as she hated being stared at, nearly everyone else there showed deep unease when she stared back at them with all her eyes unashamedly open. A heady feeling filled her. For once other people could be made uncomfortable by HER stare.

While Liliana swept her stare across the crowd, fangs bared and arm blades out, Siobhan popped out the magazine from her Kel-Tec and pulled a new one out of a pocket of her baggy pants.

The Fae, led by the pretty little hydrangea sprite, all started kneeling where they stood, showing respect, or possibly just fear, not just to Alexander, but to Liliana.

None showed anything in their auras that Liliana could identify as hostility or challenge. Not after the pine goblin's very sudden death.

"Like I said, make an example of one." Siobhan popped the new magazine into place, ready to fire again.

"Mmm." Alexander sighed. "I'd hoped to avoid that, but I can't argue that you were not correct."

When Liliana's many-eyed stare fell on the native cypress Fae, he looked back with admiration in his aura and a nod of respect. "The consort of the man you serve." He spoke to John and pointed at Liliana with his chin. "That one who sees souls and severs limbs. Also, your tiny Guardian, the one who chose to use a weapon that did no lasting harm to stop me, rather than the one that explodes heads. They are like *yunwi tsunsdi*."

Nudd looked confused.

"Little people," John explained. "Invisible nature spirits. Kind of badass. A few let me see them up in the mountains. Just show them proper respect and you'll be okay. Usually."

"I suspect people frequently underestimate such small warriors." The cypress Fae had an odd smile on his face as he looked at Liliana.

She nodded back to him, a half bow.

Nudd grinned. "People always underestimate Siobhan and Liliana."

John grinned. "Siobhan is the sprite. She made all our weapons and she kept me from getting knifed in the back at a bar." John pointed. "That's Liliana. She killed the biggest werelion I've ever seen. Sliced his head right off with one of those blades on her arms."

Nudd added, "Siobhan saved my life once when the local king of the lion-kin pride tried to kill me. She fought him to a standstill one on one, sword to sword. Liliana saved all of us from getting blown up and burned alive shortly after that."

"Those are tales I would like to hear," the cypress Fae said with the beginning of a tired smile. He got to his feet. He stood straight with a look of wonder as he moved without pain, tall, slender body whole and unmarked. The smile faded. "I see that Elohi loves the beautiful man of shimmering black stone. Her spirit flows strong through him and answers his call. But I cannot swear to obey a foreign chief. Especially when I know so little about him."

"Let's talk to Colonel Bennet about that." John shrugged. "I suspect the two of you can work something out. What's your name?"

"I am Agasga."

"Lieutenant John Runningwolf. This is Doctor Nudd."

Agasga nodded to the craggy man who appeared to be centuries older than him. "I am in your debt." He touched his unmarked chest and abdomen gingerly. "I did not think to live to see another day. You have given me a new century."

Doctor Nudd didn't know if the native Fae used the same system of barter, favor for favor that the European Fae did, but Agasga had acknowledged a debt. "I would ask a favor of you in return. Let the old enmity go. Live in the modern peace."

"That is not so easy a favor to grant." His eyes were dark pits for a moment, looking back into another time. "You don't know what I have seen." Then he sighed. "But I will try."

"You can stay with me while you get adapted to the modern era.

I have plenty of room." Nudd held his hands up. "If you wish, of course."

"You offer me your home when your people's ancestors took mine." The cypress Fae huffed a small chuckle that didn't seem like he thought anything was funny. "The world has greatly changed while I slept."

Liliana smiled, admiring Agasga's resilience to so quickly accept the changes in the world. Not to mention his rather magnificent, lithe build and the firm squares in his healed belly. Sharp cheekbones and a prominent nose might have made him look severe, but his eyes were large with thick lashes that almost looked feminine.

Even this ancient wounded warrior would live in the modern peace Alexander offered. Pride swelled in her chest as she looked up at her obsidian prince.

Alexander accepted pledges of fealty and obedience to a rule of law and all around her, the many kinds of people calmed. Some even smiled. There was a feeling of hope for a better future. Alexander was going to be a great king.

If she could keep him from being murdered.

CHAPTER 20

LOSING TIME

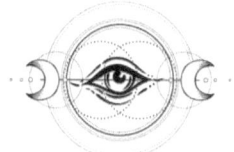

LILIANA SPENT THE REST OF THE WEEK IN A FRAZZLE, searching and searching, but nothing changed. When she got up on the morning he would die, she sniffed the rose Alexander gave her and her eyes burned. It had bloomed wide, almost completely open. The petals were more than half red. The rich scent reminded her of how much she would lose if she couldn't find a path where Alexander lived.

She fought to claim Alexander's heart as hers, but it was a two-edged sword. Her heart already ached to be close to him always. The thought of failing him ripped at her soul.

And that was to say nothing of the land. She still didn't know what would happen to the land that had bonded so strongly with the prince if he died. The Green kept getting stronger in Fayetteville. Alexander clearly caused that. If he died, would the land grieve? Would the Green fade and die with him?

Would I?

She met Pete and Siobhan at the Starbucks down the street from her house each morning to see if they had learned anything new that might help. Detective Shonda Jackson had been recruited to try to find information about the assassin that would come for Alexander.

Siobhan and Pete were also worried about Ben. The teacher was becoming suspicious of Pete's nature. The more hints that Ben Harper got that Pete was somehow different, combined with his glimpses of the peculiar nature of some of the children he taught, the more disturbed he became. Pete's beloved wasn't sleeping due to nightmares.

Liliana could relate.

She asked Janice Willoughby the day before to talk to Ben now that his eyes had begun to open. Give him a friendly face to answer his questions. Help him past the point where he questioned his own sanity.

In all her searching, she had seen another, unexpected danger. A woman would threaten not Pete's life, but his heart. She wouldn't kill Pete, but he might kill her, and he would regret it. She would make him cry either way.

In any other situation, the spider seer would have spent time exploring the woman's past and future to learn who she was, and why she would so deeply affect her favorite red wolf. But, for now, she had other things on her mind. Pete's heart was endangered, but her prince's life was endangered.

She went to the coffee house. She sipped a chai tea latte and wished her head would stop pounding while she waited for Pete and Siobhan.

Siobhan came in the door with Pete on her heels. Her bright red hair was spiked more than usual on top, giving her a startled look. Pete wore his carrot-red hair spiked a little on top as well. The sprite's eyes in human form were bright blue, as were Pete's. It occurred to Liliana that the diminutive woman and the average-sized man gave the impression they might be related. Red hair and blue eyes was an unusual color combination.

Liliana remembered an image of a lock of red hair slipping out from under a black baseball cap. In all the frantic searching her fourth eyes had done over the last few days, she didn't remember where she'd seen that flash of vision.

"Hey, Lilly. How ya doing?" Siobhan said.

"I have not slept in two days," she answered the sprite. "My left arm aches and someone I care about, maybe more than one, will get murdered today. I can't figure out how to save them."

The sprite snorted. "Remind me never to ask you anything until after I've had coffee."

Pete paused to hold the door for a woman and her two children. When he finally came in, he looked at Liliana and whistled softly. "You don't look so good, Lilly. Is everything okay?"

Liliana burst into tears. "Everything is not okay."

Pete sat in the chair next to her, putting an arm around her shoulders.

The spider-kin buried her face in his chest and got his shirt wet while he patted her back.

After a few moments, she sniffled. Siobhan handed her a bunch of napkins. Liliana blew her nose and fought to get control of herself. "Do not kill the next person who points a gun at you," she told Pete, in between sniffles. "You will deeply regret it if you kill her." She did not know who the woman was, but she had seen Pete weeping heartbroken sobs over the woman's body. With that warning, she could at least spare one person dear to her some pain.

"Okay, Lilly. I promise."

The day had come when her prince would be tortured and murdered.. She had searched all night and all the previous day the various paths of probability, seeking some option, any option that would save Alexander. She found nothing new, but she couldn't stop searching.

Pete and Siobhan had no help to offer her, so she went home again and resumed her search. She stared at the blank wall next to her armchair with her exhausted fourth eyes showing her over and over, images of Alexander bloody on the floor. It was like watching her parents and her older brothers die again and again when she was too young to do anything about it.

She woke to bright sunshine slanting through her big living room picture window that faced west. Afternoon sunshine. She looked at her clocks. It was 4:23. She had slept away most of the crucial day.

The spider seer scrambled to her feet. She called a cab with the smart phone that Alexander gave her. She had to get to his home first and wait for his killer.

She peeked with her fourth eyes to see when the killer would arrive at Alexander's house, and saw that he wouldn't. She saw again a room with a tall window with no glass and Alexander tied to a chair.

Liliana sighed and called Alexander.

When his head and shoulders in his camouflage uniform appeared in the window of the phone, she said, "Changing your path will not stop the assassin."

"So you said, Little Spider, but I wasn't about to simply go home and wait to be killed."

"You could have tried locking your door," Liliana pointed out. "I told you that if you tried to avoid this, it could become far worse."

Alexander pinched the bridge of his nose. "Detective Jackson wanted to put me in protective police custody."

Liliana felt strangely warmed by that information. "Detective Jackson listens when I tell her someone's life is in danger. She has been digging up information, trying to catch your killer before he can hurt you."

"I appreciate the sentiment, but I feel safer on my own base, surrounded by tens of thousands of soldiers, state of the art security, and with earth and fire at my command. To get to me, this killer will have to get through ten stories of electronic security, booby traps, and other-kin soldiers from my SET unit ready and waiting, including Lieutenant Runningwolf. The detective and three of Fayetteville's finest are here with me as well."

"The more people who stand between you and your murderer, the more people will die. I warned you that you could make it worse. A few of your best soldiers will die now, and Officer West. I like Officer West."

"I've broken my patterns. The detective and I have gone to considerable effort to keep my location secret."

Liliana nodded. "That would seem like a good plan. I have no idea why it won't work. I only know that it won't."

He gave her that twisted shadow of a grin that made a dimple in his cheek. "Sometimes honesty is not very comforting, Little Spider."

Liliana swallowed. She tried to think of something to tell him that was both true and reassuring. "Your influence has expanded since you calmed the Bones Creek forest people. As long as you're within twenty miles of the base, earth and fire will answer you now."

He chuckled. "I considered going somewhere off base, to throw off the attacker. If I'd known that, I might have."

"It would not have helped. It just would have made it harder for me to get to you. It will already be difficult."

"I considered that. Every gate guard on duty today has your description and orders to let you through immediately without question. They won't require you to pass through any of the scanners. I had them program all the electronic security systems to let you through as well, and to erase any recordings made of you as you pass."

"Thank you. That will help. Stay alive, my prince. I will find a way." Liliana hoped that was not a lie.

Chapter 21

Not Alexander

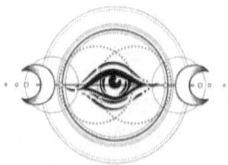

Liliana trusted Alexander's word that no recording of her would be kept when she entered Fort Liberty, and she was in a hurry. So, she did something slightly terrifying and jogged directly to the front gate of the base only a few blocks from her house.

Camera drones hovered overhead, but when they saw her, they moved on without pausing. The petite spider-kin took a place in the line of slowly moving military vehicles with their imposing silhouettes and gigantic tires. It chafed at her, the time she spent waiting for each vehicle to be inspected, scanned, and the ID of the driver checked.

But she'd entered Fort Liberty improperly before resulting in a blazing headache from a nasty sound weapon, shrapnel in her thigh, and a bullet wound through her side. Bypassing the guards without injury or discovery had taken careful timing and patience. She had none of that now. She stomped on her impatience and her nerves, staring at the many scanners and cameras, telling herself again that Alexander Bennett was a man who kept his word.

She pulled the ID card that had only her name on it. Alexander told her to show it to the gate guards and she would be permitted entrance.

The massive vehicle in front of her pulled forward. It was finally her turn. She held the ID card up in front of her face and stared at her feet while two armed gate guards approached her.

"Lady, you can't come in through this entrance," the first man said officiously.

Liliana huddled in on herself and thrust the ID card out more firmly in the faces of the two guards.

He continued without a glance at the card. "This entrance is only for military–"

The other guard interrupted him. "You're clear, ma'am." He waved his arms. "Let her through. She's got full access at any time."

"But ..." the first guard said.

"She's with Colonel Bennett's people. Orders came through this morning. Special clearance. Way above our pay grade."

Looking at Liliana, arm wrapped around herself, human eyes staring at the pavement between her feet. "This can't possibly be the woman we were told to ..."

The other guard pointed at the ID card Liliana still held up.

Finally, the first guard looked at it. His face paled. "Apologies, ma'am."

The second guard asked with a trace of deference. "Ma'am, is there anything you need from us?"

"There is a building on base, tall like a tower, but it has no glass in the higher windows. It is important that I get there quickly."

"The fire tower," one guard said. "That's clear on the other side of the base."

"Um, we'll call someone and see if we can get you a car," the other guard said.

Cars were coming out the other side of the gate. One stopped, the window rolled down and a familiar voice said, "I'll take her there."

Liliana was surprised to see Sgt. Giovanni in an ordinary car.

"Well, get in already." The sergeant's voice was flat and tired.

Liliana got in.

Without a word, Sergeant Giovanni did a quick U-turn and

went back in through the gate. The guards waved her through. They drove in silence.

The auto-drive moved them smoothly through the streets of the base the size of a small town. Sergeant Giovanni clenched her jaws tight. She refused to look at Liliana after she entered in the destination. "You're here because Colonel Bennett is in danger. He told us something about a killer coming before..." She trailed off.

"Yes. A man is coming to kill him. He will die today if I can't get there in time to fight the murderer."

The car rounded a corner. They passed the statue of a soldier that Liliana had seen on her nightmare run through the base. It looked considerably less forbidding as she drove past it with no one shooting at her.

They said little as more of the base slid past the window, but Sergeant Giovanni seemed to be getting more and more agitated. Liliana could hear her teeth grinding together. "Are you sleeping with the colonel?" she asked finally.

"Yes." Liliana wondered if that was really a question the sergeant wanted answered. "He is mine." That was perhaps optimistic, but if she had anything to say about the matter, it would be true.

Another few moments of silence slid past along with the hospital that Liliana had prevented from blowing up.

Finally, Sergeant Giovanni growled through her clenched teeth. "If you break his heart, I'll break your legs."

Smiling, Liliana glanced up at the military police sergeant.

Sergeant Giovanni glanced back at Liliana. "What are you smiling about. You don't think I'm serious?"

"No, I think you are very serious, Sergeant Giovanni. That was a shovel speech." Liliana's smile broadened.

"Damn right it was."

"The thing is, Pete and Colonel Bennett are both under the impression that now that you know they are both Others, you do not care about them anymore."

Sergeant Giovanni ducked her head. Liliana heard her teeth

grind again. "That's bullshit. The colonel is the one who told me to transfer because he didn't want me around anymore."

"Alexander is under the impression that you do not want to be near him or his unit because he and many of the soldiers under his command are Others."

"Yeah, well, maybe he's right." Sergeant Giovanni's words were surly.

Liliana didn't need her third eyes to show her the shading of pain that lay beneath. "He is not right."

"How do you know?"

"Because people only give shovel speeches for people they care about."

The car pulled up and parked in front of a tall concrete building with windows empty of glass and filled with armed soldiers looking out.

Sergeant Giovanni looked at Liliana oddly. "Do you love him?"

Liliana studied the sergeant's rank insignia on her collar. "Sergeant Giovanni, my intention is to go into that building and fight a killer who has somehow circumvented an entire Army base and a landed Fae prince with power over earth and fire. I know the killer is a better fighter than me. I am not at full strength, but I would give my life many times over if I knew it would just be enough to save him."

She looked at Liliana for a moment. "My name is Zoe." A look of determination tightened her jaw. "No one is killing the Colonel if I can help stop it in any way."

They went into the building side by side.

Four armed guards stood in front of the entrance to the building. They pointed weapons at Liliana and Zoe as they approached. "Password," one said.

The two women looked at each other. Zoe shrugged.

"I am Liliana. Alexander said I would be permitted to come. He did not mention a password."

The guards lowered their weapons. "The colonel told us to let you in."

Liliana stepped forward, but the guard who had spoken stepped in front of Zoe. "Sergeant, you're not cleared to be here. You'll have to wait outside."

Zoe squeezed her lips together tightly, then nodded. Liliana knew that if she was turned away, the soldier who had served Alexander faithfully for many years would drive off the base. After a few days of leave, she would be transferred somewhere else.

Liliana objected. "She needs to come with me. She has something important to tell your colonel."

Zoe looked at Liliana, face expressionless.

Liliana looked back, meeting her eyes for a moment.

Zoe nodded. The guards let them both enter the odd tower with no glass in the windows. Another half dozen guards, including Lieutenant John Runningwolf, were in the large room inside. Bare concrete floors and gray cinderblock walls made it feel like a prison.

"Where is Alexander?" Liliana asked the stocky badger-kin.

"He's fine. In the next room with Detective Jackson." He pointed with his thumb to a door behind him, thick new-pale wood, with heavy bars drilled into the cinder block on either side to hold it.

Opening her fourth eyes, Liliana looked for Alexander. She saw him in a room with gray cinderblock walls and an empty window behind him. He was tied to a chair, with a bloody scrape on his cheek. While she watched, a fist impacted his face, rocking his head to the side. The spider seer flinched. The vision had the sharp clarity of present time. What she saw was happening, now. "Open the door. Alexander is in trouble."

"That's not possible," John said. "I've been standing right here for an hour. There's no other way in."

In Liliana's fourth vision, someone broke one of Alexander's fingers. He grunted in pain, teeth gritted to hold back a scream.

Liliana pushed past the young soldier. She tried to figure out how to make the giant locking mechanism move. "Open this door!"

"Let her in, Runningwolf," Zoe said. "The colonel gave her full access. At least let her see that he's okay."

"All right." The big badger-kin slung his rifle over his shoulder. He punched in a combination on a device he pulled out of his pocket. A loud metallic click sounded. He used his considerable strength to push the mechanism of the huge lock, causing the metal bars to move out of the wall. Finally, the door swung open.

Liliana rushed in, Zoe and John right behind her.

Inside was a small gray room with a simple couch and chair. Alexander sat in the chair, looking up from the report in his hand. Detective Shonda Jackson had a thermos of some hot beverage in one hand and a pistol aimed at them in the other.

"Just me," John said. "Liliana is here. She wanted to see that the colonel was okay."

"I'm fine," Alexander said. "No need to worry."

Liliana blinked her human eyes for a moment, relief and confusion flooding her in equal measure. She was certain the vision she saw had been of the present, yet here was Alexander. He was not tied to a chair with a bleeding, broken nose. She looked around the room. There was no window in this room. She had seen an empty, glassless window frame behind him in her vision. He had been tied to a metal chair. There was no metal chair in this room.

"But ..." Liliana's eyes had never failed her so completely.

"It's all right, Lilly. Your vision must have been wrong." Alexander's deep voice held a gentle tone.

A cold chill made the hair on Liliana's arms stand up. Alexander did not call her Lilly.

"And a good thing, I'd say," Detective Jackson added as she put her pistol back in the holster on her belt and sipped her drink. "Don't stress about it. Even a really accurate fortune-teller gets things wrong now and then."

Liliana opened all her eyes. She looked at the tall man who sounded, smelled, moved like Alexander, but wasn't. Her third eyes showed her a flat, barely visible shimmer of silvery light in a silhouette around his body. What she did not see was a complex layering of the colors of ice and passion, ruthless confidence and old pain, cool control and anger. She did not see Alexander's soul. "That is not Alexander."

The thing in front of her with Alexander's face frowned, then looked at the badger-kin soldier who stood next to her. "She's delusional."

Lieutenant John Runningwolf looked at Liliana, his dark brows furrowed. "Why would you even say that?"

Detective Jackson shook her head. "I've been at his side all afternoon."

"I've had eyes on the Colonel since this morning, aside from that one hour I let Officer West watch over him." Liliana had advised him herself to allow that since she'd seen him die in visions where he didn't take that short break.

Liliana searched with her fourth eyes. *Where is the real Alexander?* While all three pairs of her other eyes showed her the room she stood in with John, Zoe, and Detective Jackson, her fourth vision showed her the room with the empty window.

The heavy bulk of Officer West's hard fist hit a bound Alexander in the belly making his breath cough out harshly. The vision was as sharp as Liliana's vision of the false Alexander and the people who stood next to her. This was happening, right now. But not here.

The false Alexander gave an order to John. "Escort her out, Lieutenant. The enemy must have gotten to her somehow."

"Yes, sir." He took Liliana's arm in a firm grip. "Come with me."

Liliana tried to yank herself loose, but the werebadger was too strong. She could attack him but there were a half dozen other shifters in the room right outside the door who would attack her if she moved against their Lieutenant. She had no desire to harm John, in any case.

Zoe Giovanni got a sour look on her face. "Sir, is this a zodiac tango case?" She pointed to Liliana.

The false Alexander nodded authoritatively. "Yes, I believe it is."

"All right then. I know what to do." Zoe stepped up and took Liliana's other arm.

The petite spider kin tensed, moving her weight onto her toes. She didn't want to fight Zoe Giovanni or John Runningwolf. Zoe was Pete's friend and Alexander's loyal soldier. John Runningwolf was Alexander's Lieutenant and she thought he had started to become her friend. She didn't know what else to do. She tried one last time. "I'm telling you that is not Alexander. I can see."

Zoe Giovanni's voice was gentle as she patted Liliana's back. "You're right, of course. We all know you can see things that we can't."

The words were said as if she were humoring Liliana, but they were exactly accurate as spoken. If she took the words literally, they were true. And the Sergeant knew that the spider seer always took everything literally. She looked at Zoe Giovanni's face, startled.

Zoe looked back at her, meeting her eyes for less than a second, then turning to John. "I've got her Lieutenant. Come on Anna Sees All."

For the barest moment, John Runningwolf's grip on Liliana's arm loosened.

The agile spider seer twisted out of his loose grip. Zoe released her immediately. She leapt towards the false Alexander, knowing Zoe would back her.

Zoe stepped in front of the were-badger, interfering with John's attempt to move forward, slowing him down for a crucial second.

Liliana popped out her arm blade as she jumped. She sliced across the chest of the thing with Alexander's face.

A loud popping sound and fiery pain in her calf occurred at the same time.

There was no blood, even though Liliana's arm blade pierced deep, slashing the thing from right collar bone to left hip. It looked like Alexander stood there for a moment. Staring down at his chest in disgust. "Such a nice shirt."

Liliana stumbled to one knee as her leg failed.

Then the thing pretending to be Alexander exploded in a cloud of sawdust and odd-smelling leaves and twigs. The clothes collapsed to the ground in an empty pile.

John shoved Zoe aside, swung his gun toward Liliana, but froze as sawdust snowed down on them.

"Whoa, um ..." John looked at Liliana. "So, yeah. I guess that wasn't the Colonel after all."

Liliana glared at the insignia on his collar, not bothering to say, I told you so, but thinking it very loudly.

Zoe said it for her. "She told you it wasn't him. Pete says you can trust what she sees is accurate. I trust Pete, so ..." She shrugged.

John gave her a fast grin. "Welcome back, Sergeant."

Zoe's cheeks flushed a little. "I said some things, and..."

John gripped her shoulder. "What you do is so loud, I couldn't hear what you said."

"Damnit," Detective Jackson said. She dropped to her knees next to Liliana. She grabbed Alexander's slashed shirt off the floor, shook off the sawdust and pressed the white cloth against the spider seer's bleeding leg. "I'm an idiot."

Liliana felt an odd sort of mixed affection for the detective, despite the bullet wound in her calf. "You thought you were protecting Alexander, and you still did not shoot to kill."

"Yeah, well, I was wrong, and I'm an idiot." She wrapped the sleeves of the shirt around to press the wad of the shirt over the larger exit hole in her calf, putting pressure on the wound. It would stop the bleeding.

Liliana felt woozy for a moment from pain. "Thank you."

"Don't thank me," Detective Jackson said. "I'm the idiot who shot you. Did I mention that I'm an idiot?"

Liliana chuckled in spite of her panic for Alexander. "You did mention that."

John kicked the pile of sawdust, twigs and leaves. "What the hell?"

"It is a simulacrum," Liliana said. "Like the Fae who stole children used to leave in their place."

"What that is doesn't matter." Detective Jackson focused on Liliana. "The important question is, where is the real Colonel Bennett?"

CHAPTER 22

RIZKI

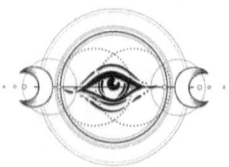

ZOE, JOHN, DETECTIVE JACKSON, AND THE OTHER soldiers who had rushed to the door all looked at Liliana.

Everyone was staring at her again. She hated that, but right now, she was far too worried about Alexander to care. "I do not know where Alexander is, but Officer West is hitting him. He is tied to a chair in a room like this, but with a window behind him with no glass."

"West?" Detective Jackson shook her head. "He was on protection detail with the rest of us, but I haven't seen him since before the fake Bennett and I were sealed in this room. Why would he turn against the Colonel?"

Why would Officer West hurt Alexander?

The big police officer who had tried to comfort Liliana when she shut down from so many people staring at her at the police station grabbed the blood-splattered shirt of her lover and yelled into his face, spittle flying from his lips. "Where is it? What did you do with the sword?"

Alexander smiled. There was blood on his teeth. "I ate it. I was feeling iron deficient."

A heavy fist hit his stomach, making him double over and gasp for breath.

Liliana flinched. "He seems to want information from Alexander." She didn't mention the sword since that was a secret. "But Officer West isn't acting like ... like Officer West."

Detective Jackson pressed her lips together. "So, I was guarding the wrong body. And I shot the one person who can tell who is really who."

"Charlie Foxtrot without doubt." John brushed his hand across his short black hair, scattering sawdust. "Are the rest of us actually us?"

Liliana looked around the room with her third eyes. Everyone's aura was the normal myriad vibrant colors of Fae or beast-kin with the exception of Zoe and Detective Jackson who had the slightly less bright souls of Normals. "Yes, the rest of you are who you appear to be."

Detective Jackson used the long sleeves wrapped around the bulk of the shirt to tie off the makeshift bandage and sat back. "But the person you're seeing isn't West, though?"

Liliana shrugged and shook her head at the same time. "My fourth eyes can only see what appears to be. They cannot pierce the surface of things like my third eyes, but the person who looks like Officer West is not acting like Officer West."

She watched with her fourth eyes as Alexander caught his breath.

Officer West pulled his head back by the hair and asked. "You stole the sword from the red wolf. I already know that. Where did you hide it?"

Alexander flashed teeth in a smile that was more angry than happy. "Aurore's information is faulty. She's sent you on a wild goose chase."

The man laughed. It sounded eerily familiar to Liliana, but it wasn't Officer West's laugh. "Do you think your sister is the only one in the world who wants Fraegerthach?"

Liliana frowned at that. If Princess Aurore did not send the man, who did?

Detective Jackson's brows scrunched, thinking about an

entirely different, and far more immediate problem. "If the person with Bennett isn't West, then where the heck is West?"

Where is the real Officer West?

Liliana's fourth eyes shifted focus to a vision of the police officer lying unconscious in his underwear somewhere dark with a deep cut in his short hair that bled profusely. His hands and feet were bound. "The one hurting Alexander is definitely not Officer West any more than that thing was Alexander." She pointed to the pile of sawdust, twigs, and clothes. "Officer West is injured and unconscious somewhere. We must find him soon or he could die."

John said, "Sergeant, you and the detective, look for the missing cop. I'll focus on finding the Colonel."

Giovanni nodded and Detective Jackson stood.

Liliana spoke to Zoe. "Officer West is in the dark, bound, gagged, and hurt, probably somewhere nearby. I saw cinderblock like the walls here, and wooden boxes around him."

Zoe nodded. She ran out of the room. Detective Jackson went with her. "Lopez, Delgado, you're with me. Search every shed, room, or hidey hole. We've got a man down. Start here, circle and push out."

John squatted beside Liliana. "You said the Colonel is in a room like this, but with a window, right? With no glass?"

Liliana nodded.

"There's someone stationed at every window on the first four floors. The next two floors, the windows are bricked over. Only the top floor of the fire tower has open windows. We built a cinder block wall across the stairs last spring to make it harder to get up there for drills. The only way is to drop down from the roof or climb the building."

Liliana looked at the outside of the building with her fourth eyes. There were ledges here and there where windows had been bricked over, and places where the mortar had crumbled exposing the steel building understructure. When they called this building a fire tower, it looked like they meant that they had set it on fire a few times, and possibly fired small artillery at it. "I can climb this building."

John looked down at her leg, wrapped in a thick, bloody shirt serving as a bandage. "I can radio a helicopter. Get it here in fifteen minutes."

Liliana looked again. She flinched as a huge fist impacted Alexander's temple. His face went slack. He lost consciousness and a big gash streamed blood where a ring on the big man's finger ripped the skin. With a sharp inhale, she recognized that ring.

"I do not think Alexander has fifteen minutes."

John extended a hand.

Liliana got to her feet, or rather foot. Gingerly, she tested her weight on the other side. Pain flooded her when she did, making her dizzy, but the leg held. Alexander was bound and unable to fight, in a room with a professional assassin. "I will climb."

John looped her arm over his shoulder. He put his arm around her waist, supporting half her weight. They stumble ran out of the building and around. He pointed with his free hand. "There are windows on the eighth floor there. Any other information you can give me to narrow it down?"

Liliana focused on Alexander, unconscious in the chair, bloody drool dripping from his slack mouth. She tried to see beyond him. It was always so hard to see beyond something so emotionally charged. The room looked the same, plain gray concrete with an empty window frame casting light on the back and one side of Alexander's bloody face.

She looked at the sky with her human eyes, considering the slant of the light. "He is in a room on that side of the building."

John nodded. To Liliana's surprise, with apologies, he lifted her off her feet with one arm and ran up several flights of stairs until a solid cinderblock wall blocked their path. He went into an empty room on the side of the building she'd indicated. He led her over to a window sealed in with plain brick and mortar, only a few inches thick. Cinderblock wider than her hand outspread made up the rest of the building.

John let go of her. He left Liliana leaning on the wall as his body changed. His nose elongated to something pointy with a dark nose and a lot of teeth. His dark hair was split by a stripe of white that ran down his long nose as tawny fur spilled over his skin. Impressive six-inch claws extended from his fingers. His shoulders bulked well beyond their normal, already sturdy form while his arms became shorter and thicker. Unlike nearly every other shifter she knew, the badger-kin didn't become any taller. If anything, he shrank slightly, gaining in width and bulk, but losing inches in his legs.

He hunched in tight and clenched his clawed hands, then focused all that compact power, starting at his hips and flowing into a punch into the center of the brick filling the window frame. The mortar cracked and the bricks moved where his fist hit. A spot of red was left behind when he drew his hand back. He struck with the other hand.

"Your hands!" Liliana said.

John shrugged his over three-foot-wide shoulders. "I'll heal," he growled.

He struck again with each hand, the bricks breaking, sliding, and crumbling, leaving the bloody imprints of his knuckles in the indentations. Finally, he bared his sharp teeth and growled as he struck. Bones crunched as the blocks ground together and fell out of the window. John cradled that hand to his chest. When the blocks stopped falling, a two-foot-wide hole let in the fresh air. It had taken less than half a minute.

He hit the blocks on either side with his shoulders, toppling them to the ground to make the hole big enough for Liliana's slight form.

John helped her through the hole and extended his unbroken hand through it, palm up like a step. She pulled a safety line from the spinneret in her wrist and looped the end around John Runningwolf. He seemed to be the sturdiest thing in the area.

"Go, go!"

Liliana went. She put the majority of her weight on the leg that didn't have a hole in it and a bulky bloody bandage tied to it. She hooked her arm blades into ragged cracks in the mortar, stuck her silk to anything that looked sturdy enough to hold her weight. She went up nearly as fast as an insect. When she had to put her weight on the bad leg, she just gritted her teeth like John punching the bricks with the crunch of broken bone.

Her leg would heal, too.

It made her dizzy when she pushed with too much of her weight on that leg. She really needed not to pass out right now. The drop was seven stories at this point. She probably wouldn't go splat at the bottom, but she couldn't save Alexander if she was dangling unconscious from a safety line.

She checked on him with her fourth eyes.

The man who looked like Officer West poured water from a bottle over the unconscious man's head, then tossed the water bottle aside.

Alexander blinked blearily to wakefulness, water dripping from his face and hair.

He lived, for now. But looking forward in time, she still saw him on the ground, unbound from the chair. Zoe Giovanni put two fingers on his throat for a long moment, and with despair in her voice, said, "He's dead."

No matter what Liliana did, she couldn't save him.

Blinking tears, she climbed in through the window. It didn't matter how long he would live, she would fight for this man until he drew his last breath.

Alexander looked over his shoulder and the assassin who had a fist cocked back to hit him again, stopped and looked up.

"I thought maybe you decided not to come after all," Alexander said.

She stood to her full height once inside. "Sorry I'm late. I had a very bad day." She limped a few steps, the bloody sleeves of the makeshift bandage dragging.

Alexander spat blood onto the floor, then wiped his mouth on his t-shirt. "Mine hasn't exactly been roses and sunshine either."

"I suppose I should have expected you," the man with Officer West's face said.

"Hello, Rizki," Liliana said. "Everyone already knows you are not Officer West."

"Hah!" he laughed. "You have cost me my scapegoat, Spiderling. I should be mad, but I am glad to see that you grew up so smart."

"I'm not a child anymore."

"You two know each other?" Alexander asked blearily.

"This is my sister's husband," she told Alexander. "Let him be, Rizki." Liliana limped another step closer until she stood next to the chair Alexander was tied to. "He is mine to protect. You cannot have his life."

The big man shrugged. He touched his belt buckle with three fingers. His face and body melted like hot wax when the candle flame is lit. He changed to someone smaller, only a few inches taller than Liliana, his hair dark and his eyes almond, but the belt buckle stayed the same. He stretched as if wearing another man's body and face had been confining. The handsome Asian features and the sparkle in his eye were all too familiar. "Ah, Spiderling, I am sorry, but I have a contract." Even his voice shifted, from Officer West's baritone to a lightly accented tenor. "I have already accepted the money." He shrugged as if in apology, his voice expressing mild regret. "You know my honor will not allow him to live now."

In one motion, he drew a short, straight sword from a sheath on his back and brought it down.

Liliana's arm blade blocked it just above Alexander's stoic face.

He barely flinched.

She suspected Rizki meant to make Alexander's death a fait accompli so he could avoid having to fight her. He would win. Rizki was an expert swordsman before Liliana was born. Plus, she wasn't exactly in top fighting form with the bullet hole in her leg.

If she fought him, she would die, but she knew Rizki didn't want to kill her. No one had paid him for her life. He hated to work for free.

"Your client doesn't want his death," she said. "Your client wants the sword."

"Ha! Actually, both." Rizki grinned at her, pulling his sword back into a ready position. "Are you offering to give me a legendary Fae sword to save his life? Who is this man to you?"

"I can tell you where it is now. You will have to go get it yourself." She ignored the other question. It was none of his business.

"Maybe I will just slit his throat before I go, huh?" Rizki was still grinning.

"If he dies, the deal is off." Liliana lifted her chin. "You will never find Fragarthach. I will make sure of it."

"Ah, you drive such a hard bargain." Rizki slowly raised his sword and his other hand in a gesture of surrender. "Bargain is done, then. The man lives." He pointed his sword at her. "You are right that the client wants the sword more than his life and will accept it alone as fulfillment of my contract." He sheathed his short sword.

Liliana could hear the sound of a helicopter coming to land on the roof above and metallic pounding on the thick cinderblocks below that blocked the stairs. The assassin didn't look nervous in the least. She had no doubt that Rizki would find a way out. He'd probably take on the form of one of the other soldiers, then slip out among them. Whatever artifact he had in his belt buckle, it had mimicked Officer West perfectly, even his voice and North Carolina accent.

"Now, you must uphold your end of the bargain, little sister." Rizki's voice was warm, but his eyes were as cold as they always were. "Where is this legendary sword that no one has seen for millennia that they tell me is now in this podunk town?"

"Who told you it was in Fayetteville?"

Rizki grinned again, a dazzlingly bright, but empty smile. Her third eyes showed Liliana the cold calculation behind it. "Ah, ah, ah. That was not information you bargained for." He shook his finger at her.

She gave Rizki Pete's address. Her brother-in-law knew that she never lied, couldn't lie. As he turned to leave, she said, "Rizki, many of the people here are my friends. Try not to kill anyone on the way out."

Rizki flashed his bright grin at her. "You ask a lot, Spiderling, but for you? Ah, for you, I will do my best. No promises, though." He left her alone with Alexander.

Liliana dropped to her knees in front of the chair. She cut the ropes on his hands and feet, freeing him from the chair.

"Why did you give that bastard Pete's address?" Alexander was looking at her oddly, his head turned slightly.

"Pete has his sword. His Normal beloved is not home. Doctor Nudd and Siobhan are with him. Rizki will be in jail before the sun sets."

Alexander chuckled, then stopped like it hurt. "That's my Little Spider."

A heavy iron bracelet encircled one of his wrists. She couldn't figure out how to get it off him.

"Time locked," he said. "The spell will break and it will unlock by itself in forty-eight hours. In the meantime, I'm cut off from the land and my power." His other hand came up to cup her face. "Thank you for saving my life."

Liliana rubbed her face against his warm palm. "I have not saved you. You are dying." She looked closely at him with all her eyes, trying to figure out why he would die. With her second eyes, she saw heat blossoming on one side of his head where he'd taken the hard blow that knocked him out. Her human vision told her the pupil on one eye was blown, but not the other. "Are you blind in one eye?" she asked.

He nodded, a bare movement. "Is that bad?"

"I think your brain is bleeding. It will kill you in minutes."

"It's not that serious, I don't think." He wiped some of the blood off his face and tried to stand. His knees buckled.

Liliana tried to catch him, but her bad leg gave under her. Alexander fell with her underneath. She managed to turn his body a little as they fell. They ended up lying together on the ground. "You must let me bite you, my prince."

"I told you I wouldn't allow that."

"My venom can heal you." She knew that wouldn't be enough for him. "Alexander, I love you."

He smiled, a soft, half-asleep expression of genuine pleasure. His hand stroked her hair. He blinked slowly. "I'm not sure I deserve that."

"Please, Alexander. I give you my word I will not tell you to do anything you don't want to." Tears filled her eyes. "Don't make me watch you die."

He pulled her in close and whispered in her ear. "I trust you." His hand guided her head to his neck.

For this man, his trust was perhaps a more difficult thing to gain than his heart. "I do not have time to make it not hurt." She bit the band of muscle where it met his shoulder, pushing hard to give him enough venom, she hoped, to heal his injury before it killed him.

He grunted softly in her ear.

She pulled back and looked at his face.

The pained tension vanished. His soul washed clean of pain. At least, he no longer hurt. His aura shifted to a warm, contented sunflower yellow.

Alexander's calm face regarded her from his one functioning eye where they lay. "Were you in time?" His thumb stroked her cheek.

"I am not certain."

"Kiss me, then. If I'm going to die in minutes, that's how I want to spend the time."

Liliana kissed him.

He kissed her right back. His lips and tongue tasted of blood, but he was warm. His mouth covered hers to claim her like he wanted to mark her as his forever. His hand in her hair angled her head just right so he could kiss her more deeply, the blocky bracelet bumped heavy and cold against her throat.

She watched his contentment flood with red passion that flared white at the center for a moment, like the rose he gave her.

His hand fell lax from her hair. The colors of his soul faded to dim flickers.

She sat up and looked down on him with her second eyes. Heat still shone in a nameless color that wasn't red on one side of his head. She didn't know if she'd saved him or not.

She carefully kept her fourth eyes closed. She didn't want to know. She didn't want to see.

She scooted back on her arms and one leg into the corner then wrapped her arms around her knees. She put her face down. There was no more she could do. She let herself shut down. Time went away. Fear, pain. For a while at least, all of it went away.

CHAPTER 23

LOVE AND TRUST

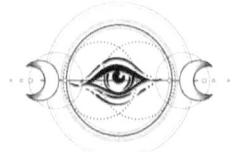

WHEN SHE CAME BACK TO HERSELF, THE ROOM WAS FULL of people.

Zoe was on her knees, two fingers on Alexander's throat. She paused there for a long moment. Everyone in the room fell silent.

Liliana had seen this. Her eyes felt hot. She knew what came next.

"He's alive," Zoe said.

Liliana blinked and the hot tears that had been welling in her eyes rolled down her cheeks. "Wait." She blinked again, hope blooming like a painful warmth in the ice of her chest. "What did you say?" Her trembling voice was so tiny, she wasn't sure Zoe would hear her.

The sergeant looked at her in the corner. "He's alive," she repeated firmly. "Pulse is strong. He should be coming around any minute."

"He's alive." Liliana repeated it softly to herself. She'd been in time. Her venom healed him. "Officer West?"

"We found him," Zoe said. "Detective Jackson took him straight to Womack Medical."

Liliana closed her eyes again, a feeling of relief flooding through her. "My leg hurts."

Zoe chuckled. "I'll call Nudd."

An hour or more of too many people in the small room later, Liliana sat on the ledge outside the glassless window, hiding from the bustle.

Alexander woke in the midst of a pair of military EMT's and a cluster of soldiers, all worried about him. He started issuing orders within seconds of regaining consciousness.

Without leaving her perch, Liliana used her fourth eyes to watch that one part of all the bustling that mattered to her.

Zoe Giovanni saluted Alexander when the EMT's stopped fussing. They kept telling him how lucky he was that his head injury wasn't more than a mild concussion and urging him to go to Womack Medical Center to get checked. He nodded to them politely and ignored their advice.

"Sergeant," Alexander said solemnly when he saw Zoe. "I thought you were heading out on leave."

"Yes, sir. I was, but Anna needed to get to you as fast as possible. My car was closest."

"You probably saved my life," he said softly. "If Liliana arrived even a few minutes later, I'd have been a dead man."

"She saved your life. I just got her here so she could." She took a deep breath and let it out. "Sir, I've been an ass, and I owe you, Pete, and most of your unit an apology."

"Yes, you do." He looked up at the remaining EMT's and said, "Give me the room, please. I need to discuss something you don't have clearance for."

The emergency medical people left with a few final admonishments to get a follow-up from one of the doctors at Womack. Alexander assured them that he would have Doctor Nudd give him a thorough check-up.

His own people continued as if he hadn't spoken.

When the EMTs were gone, Zoe cleared her throat. "I kept thinking Others had to be different in the head because they were different in other ways. Kept saying it, even, to my best friend, Pete. He never said anything except that I was wrong. I realized some of your people were Others, but I figured you had them on a short leash."

Alexander snorted.

"Yeah." She made a wry expression. "I get how stupid that was. But I've been following where you lead for years. When you turned out to be Other, and Pete, too, it was like you'd both lied straight to my face. I felt betrayed. I made it all about me, like you and Pete somehow became Others just to mock me...I kind of lost it."

Alexander held a hand up to stop her. "Do you still want a transfer?"

"No, sir. I'll understand if you put it through anyway, but...no, sir. I don't want it."

He nodded. "I'll take care of it. Get back to work, Sergeant. Your leave is cancelled."

Zoe grinned and saluted. "Yes, sir."

Liliana smiled where she sat on the window ledge, a fresh breeze on her face. Her injured leg was tucked against her chest, the other leg dangling over eight stories of air. Her safety line was firmly attached to the concrete wall beside her. Her first mother nodded approval in her fourth vision. *I won't forget Mut. I promise.*

The eighth-floor perch felt oddly comfortable. She was practically raised on a trapeze. Her second mother loved to nap on the high branches of trees, sometimes with Liliana right beside her. Her father had been their anchor, the one whose strong hands always caught Liliana when she flew.

Liliana swallowed a lump in her throat.

I have fallen in love, Mut, Mamae, Pater. I wish you could meet him.

She hadn't known how completely Alexander owned her heart until she almost lost him. Now that she loved him and knew it, she was in a vulnerable position. Alexander did not love her back. His trust touched her, but it was not what she wanted from him.

Pete's advice to her had been to give the relationship time and have patience.

She wrinkled her nose. She loved Alexander now. Her patience was not infinite, and they had almost abruptly run out of time today.

Nudd showed up at some point. He reported to Alexander that Rizki was in custody and switched out the wadded shirt on Liliana's leg for a clean bandage.

Slowly, the chaos in the room died down to a single guard on the door.

Alexander ordered the last of the many people to get back to their regular jobs. He no longer needed any more medical attention or an extra protection detail. He even sent away Lieutenant Runningwolf to get some rest. His broken fingers were splinted thanks to Doctor Nudd so the bones would knit correctly.

When the only one remaining was Alexander, he came to the window. Liliana realized that even from this height at the edge of Fort Liberty looking out, every bit of land she saw was his. The Fae prince's influence had been spreading more and more. Soon, all of Fayetteville and much of the Fae of central North Carolina would owe allegiance to the man she loved. "That land is all yours."

His strong hand brushed her hair back, exposing one of her open second eyes. "You didn't give a damn about that when you climbed up here to fight an assassin for me with a bullet hole in your leg."

"I didn't want you to die."

Alexander's arm went around her back. His other arm, with the heavy iron bracelet scooped under her knees. "Let's go home."

"I would like to go to my home." She snuggled comfortably in his arms, savoring the warm, strong, very much alive man with his turned earth and gun oil scent.

"Then that's where we'll go."

"You seem to be carrying me a lot lately." She rubbed her cheek against his chest muscle, covered only by a thin t-shirt spattered with spots of his blood. "I like it."

"So do I." A small smile played at the corners of his lips. That warm yellow contentment he'd had when her venom took away his pain shaded his aura.

He carried her down eight flights of steps, stepping over a thick shattered cinderblock wall at some point. His steps were steady. He didn't show any sign of strain.

"You let me bite you." Satisfaction flooded her as she saw on his face the clear signs of her healing venom. The cut over his eye had been pulled together with butterfly tape, but the injury looked days old already.

He smiled, that subtle quirk of lips on the corners that she loved to see. "I did. And you didn't order me to do anything, even when you could have."

"You ordered me to kiss you. Even under the influence of venom, you are very bossy."

He chuckled low. "Everyone I know would likely confirm that."

"Can I bite you again when we get to my house?"

He stopped for a moment as they reached his car. He set her on her one fully functional foot, letting her lean against the big vehicle while he opened the door. His hands on her hips lifted her onto the high seat, bringing them face to face.

"I trust you," he said. His voice was hoarse. That was not a statement he made very often, and he'd said it twice to her today.

Liliana kissed him very thoroughly. "Let's go to my house and have a lot of sex."

He chuckled and kissed her hand, that mischievous sparkle in his eyes that she adored. "I'm glad you live close by."

It only took a few minutes to drive back across the base to the same gate she'd come in through.

As they went, Liliana considered that the killer she'd first foreseen changed soon after she'd warned Alexander. He had apparently decided to change his future path without telling her. That killer was probably even now at his house, wondering why the target didn't come home. Liliana would make sure her prince did not go to his house tonight. By morning, that female killer would be somewhere else. But that was a problem for tomorrow.

The other big question was Rizki. Why was he here? Who hired him?

Alexander glanced at her face, scrunched into an unhappy frown. "What are you thinking?"

"I am wondering who hired Rizki. He makes his living as an assassin. He would not cross the ocean to kill you unless someone paid him. Clearly, that was someone who wanted Pete's sword."

"I don't think it was Aurore."

Liliana nodded her agreement. "But that means that more people know about Fraegarthach now than just Princess Aurore. Word of its location have gotten out. Every royal Sidhe in the world dreams of wielding that sword."

"Doesn't narrow down the suspect list much."

As they pulled up to the gate, Liliana hunched over and let her hair fall over her face. So many cameras and scanners. Alexander gave his word that her earlier appearance on those cameras would be erased, but she doubted he could do that for her every time.

"You hate going through the gates, don't you?"

She could only nod.

"How did you get on base that first time you visited me?"

"I came through but avoided the cameras and guards. That was better. It took longer, though. I couldn't do that when I needed to get to you fast."

Alexander grinned slightly. That light of mischief sparkled in his aura like purple fireworks. "Next time you want to come in, do that again. I'll put you down as a security consultant. If anyone spots you coming in, they're not to stop you, just note it in the log. If they spot you, that will reflect well on them. If not, I can dress them down for missing you coming in. That should put them on their toes."

Liliana smiled. "I will not have to use the card and let myself be photographed by the cameras again. But I will be able to enter the base any time I wish without getting shot at if someone sees me."

Alexander nodded. "Exactly." He waved at a guard. They let him pass through. He was well known and the scrutiny of someone leaving the military base was far less than someone entering it.

It was a good solution. One that made Liliana's shoulders droop in relief. It also gave Alexander an advantage of increased alertness in the base guards. Her prince rarely did anything for only one reason.

She remembered his rejection of William Eliot, how angry and hurt the wizard had looked. The wizard had a huge old house and land. He might be able to afford to pay an assassin's price. "Do you think William Eliot hired Rizki?"

Alexander shook his head as he drove his big, camouflaged car the few blocks to her place. "If William sent him, he would have been less concerned with completing the mission and more focused on doing something cruel and spiteful."

Liliana looked up at him suddenly. "You knew what kind of man Eliot was, yet you still had a relationship with him."

"He was useful." He shrugged.

Liliana swallowed. That was how her prince defined a desirable partner, someone who was useful. She could be useful. "I am good at getting past guards. When I go in and out, I will advise the base guards what they are doing wrong that allows me to pass. It will help tighten base security."

He studied her for a moment. His expression blanked, his default for when strong emotion hit him. He parked in the driveway behind her house. Her garage had gym mats on the floor and trapeze swings in the rafters. It was not really a good place for cars.

Liliana opened the car door, trying to think of other ways she could be useful to Alexander.

He put a hand on her arm, stopping her from getting out. "You're not useful, Liliana."

The words hit like a blow. She blinked hard. Did he want to end their relationship? Had she done something wrong like Eliot did? "I just saved your life."

"That's not..." Alexander rubbed his face with his hand and winced when he hit the big iron bracelet against his chin. "I mean..." He took a deep breath. "You're not just useful."

Liliana looked at him with all her eyes since he no longer seemed to mind. She really needed to understand. His complex soul showed a variety of shades of embarrassment, confusion, the red of undimmed desire, some of that creamy white. It looked like love, but was so fleeting, she wasn't sure. A surge of warmth soothed her hurt. He was having trouble expressing his feelings, something he didn't often do. "You know, a prince is supposed to be good with words. You should probably work on that."

"Are you teasing me?" He asked, a hint of a smile, with some disbelief.

As intimidated by him as most people are, I bet no one teases him. "Someone should. You don't laugh enough."

Alexander shook his head and got out of the car, that amused little smile broader than she had ever seen it. His eyes crinkled with suppressed laughter that sparkled bright in his aura.

She got out of the car by balancing on one foot, but didn't get a chance to wonder how she would get into her house.

He scooped her up and carried her in like she weighed nothing.

Liliana ripped off his t-shirt when he'd barely got her inside. It was torn and blood splattered anyway. She'd almost lost him. She'd seen him die a hundred times. She needed to feel him warm and alive.

He gave her a flash of an amused smile big enough to show teeth, then leaned in to kiss her.

Liliana put her hand in front of his mouth to stop him. "No, I get to kiss your chest this time."

Alexander laughed and sat down on the bed with her in his lap. He spread his arms wide. "I am yours."

Finally, she got to touch him, swirl her tongue around his nipples, taste his washboard belly. "Hold the headboard," she ordered.

"Now, who's bossy?" he teased her, but he laid back. He put his hands up to either side of her narrow bed, holding the support posts. Her bed was never meant for two, especially if one was as big as her prince.

His smile vanished in a gasp as she straddled him and unbuttoned his pants. She got to taste all of him. She didn't stop until he was moaning and squirming under her.

He let go of the headboard at last. His fingers tangled in her hair as he pulled her up for a desperate, gasping kiss.

He helped her shed her clothes in moments.

With him on his back, she mounted and rode him, his body buried in hers. As his big hand ran down her back, making her shiver, she blurted out, "May I bite you again now?"

"I don't need healing," he said. "I feel better than fine." He rocked his hips and gifted her with that hungry shark smile that was broad and real and full of desire as he heard her moan.

Liliana could barely think with her own desire, a kind of impatient need. "Not for healing. To share venom." She rocked her own hips as she leaned down to lick his tight nipple. "Because it will be good."

His hand stroked her hair, fingers deliberately entangling in the thick tresses. "You want to lay a deeper claim to me," he said, a smile still in his voice.

"Yes," she said very seriously. "Please. I almost lost you."

His hand behind her head pulled her to him. "I'm here, Little Spider. I trust you."

The words still made her stomach flutter the third time he'd said them to her. With care she hadn't had time for before, she nibbled the thick slab of pectoral muscle, barely piercing the surface with a fang. She rocked her hips at the same time so his groan was far more of pleasure than of pain.

The drop of venom would make the area impervious to pain. Once it had a moment to do its work, she bit again, deeper, giving her lover the gift that was hers alone to give. She licked the tiny trickle of blood from the puncture marks he never even felt, and sat up again, enjoying the shift of angle of him inside her.

All eight of her eyes watched as his pleasure increased. She rode him hard, driving that pleasure forward.

He threw his head back, face lost in ecstasy.

When he reached the peak, she went over with him, shuddering and shouting until her throat hurt.

She collapsed on his chest.

He cradled her in strong arms. *"Je t'aime ma petite araignée,"* he murmured, his diction slurred with venom and a gloriously relaxed warmth that dragged him straight into sleep.

Liliana froze for a moment, watching as the brilliant colors of his soul calmed into the peace of sleep.

He'd said he loved her. In French.

Men often said things they didn't mean in the throes of orgasm, and under the influence of venom. Both applied here.

Alexander didn't mean that.

His heart was too well-guarded to be hers already.

Liliana smiled to herself as she drifted to sleep in the cradle of his arms. She was good at getting past guards.

In the vase on her dresser, the rose he'd given her opened fully, creamy white heart surrounded by scarlet petals. The scent perfumed her dreams.

Thank you for reading! Did you enjoy? Please add your review because nothing helps an author more and encourages readers to take a chance on a book than a review.

And don't miss the next book, SPIDER'S PRIDE, coming soon from Paige E. Ewing at www.paigeewing.com

Until then, read HOW TO DATE A FURY by City Owl Author, Luna Joya. Turn the page for a sneak peek!

Also be sure to sign up for the City Owl Press newsletter to receive notice of all book releases!

Sneak Peek of How to Date a Fury

By Luna Joya

Momma always warned me that coming to Syn City would be the death of me, but taking my first step into The Rink tonight, I've never felt so alive.

A massive indoor coliseum with seats stretching to the tippy top, the place vibrates with excitement. Thrumming bass pours through the speakers. The cold air conditioning blasts my sweaty skin, chasing away the hot, sticky humidity of the summer night. I'm a grown woman who had to sneak past her mother to make it here, but like a kid in a sweet shop, I gape at the oval-shaped skating track below that's the center stage.

A woman struts to the middle of the rink. "Welcome beloved humans," she booms into a bedazzled microphone. "You've come to see the seven Houses, yes?" The way she asks the question invites only one answer. Piercing whistles, thundering applause, and rowdy yells echo from every direction.

Shuffling forward with the other humans in line, I'm on sensory overload, trying to memorize the sights, sounds, and smells so I can tell Connie every detail when a woman wearing a neon shirt that says *Naughty* waves me forward. Her hair shimmers iridescent blue streaked with green. Those sparkling strands could be a trick of the light, but I'm guessing they mark her as supernatural.

"Your ticket?" she asks.

My cheeks heat, and my heart bangs a *here-stands-a-newb* gong beat. "I showed it at the door. Didn't know I'd need it again." My voice comes out too high. *Great.* Now, everyone knows I'm a Rink virgin. Shoving my hand into my pocket, I fish for the wadded mess.

"You'll want to find your seat before the show starts unless you scored pit passes." She tips her head toward where the announcer stands.

"No. I'm not in the pit tonight." As if I could ever be. Anyone with an eye or two or three could tell that I can't afford to buy my way into the pit and don't have the gods-loved luck to win my way in. My cousin Connie teases I was born with enormous luck, all of it bad. Fifteen to my ancient twenty-four, Connie knows everything. Just ask her.

"All right then." The woman's sugar-sweet voice coats the innocent statement with raw sexual insinuation that has me blushing again. She must be a Nymph. I should've known which of the seven Houses she came from with her perfect hair, figure, and face. "Let's see what seat you've picked."

I pull out the wadded ticket and try to smooth it. My efforts do nothing except smear the ink. "Sorry."

The Nymph glances at the wrinkled mess. "Ah, the nosebleed section. You're wanting the highest viewpoint for your first trip?"

"Yes." That explanation sounds much better than I counted my coins ten times when figuring out how much the ticket and trip would cost. I didn't have the money to take the air-conditioned hover ferry that brought most people here. No, I'd ridden the hot and cramped bus across the bridge that spans the massive lake inhabited by sea hags and water creatures waiting to snatch crash victims into the depths. But I'm not discussing my sad cleaning lady pay with the daughter of a goddess. "I've always wanted to see the show." It's the truth, something I don't get to say at home.

"Of course, who doesn't? It's the grandest event in the world. Your name?" A musical lilt to her voice draws me in.

I shouldn't give her my true name, shouldn't give anyone here any information about me according to the horror stories my momma has spun. But tonight's about taking chances, going on new adventures before I'm permanently stuck in my tiny hometown. "Dottie."

"Dorothy?" she asks.

"Nope, just plain Dottie." Because momma said I was a plain-looking baby from the start. No way I'd be sharing that pitiful detail with the Nymph, hypnotic voice or not. Even my cousin Connie can claim Constance with a long list of middle names, but then she might rather have a living mother, I suppose.

"Okay, not-at-all plain Dottie, this way." The Nymph strolls through the crowds toward the far side of the coliseum, waving her hand at the booths set up along the back wall at this level. "So you don't miss a moment once the show starts, we have the concessions, merchandise, and signing booths here on the mezzanine." The longest line snakes from where one of the players chats prettily and signs photos, caps, and body parts.

"A Muse?" I ask. Definitely not a Gorgon with those striking looks, and probably not a Styx since the woman signing doesn't give off an undead vibe and she's unmasked, but she could be a Huntress maybe. Or a Mad Mae. She smiles too much to be a Fury. I wouldn't remember all seven Houses except their banners stand like silent soldiers surrounding the rink. "Or a Nymph?" She doesn't have my guide's blue hair and sparkle, but she'd lure enough suitors to her table to keep her busy for hours.

"Ugh, no way she'd be a member of my House." The Nymph sounds annoyed I might've considered such a notion. "Fancy-ass Muses might have talent, but they don't have our skills in the sack."

All right, lesson learned. Don't confuse the Houses. Most certainly don't mix up Muses with Nymphs. Probably best to skip the guessing in the future. "What else is on this level?"

"The magical makeup booths, although they're not really magic, you know, just tech. And the most important place in The Rink besides the rink itself—our bar."

Glancing at the ginormous bar with bright-colored liquor bottles lining the high shelves, I do a double take at the bartender with dark blond hair and tanned skin, prowling from customer to customer with a grace no man that size should possess. Seeing him sends me back to my fifteenth birthday. Not some happy party full of cake and candles and wishes coming true, but me waiting alone at the bus stop in the cold rain for a boy who never showed. Shaking off the memory, I hurry to catch the Nymph. No way would I let Chase Malone ruin another night for me. Not ever again.

The lights lower, and a hush falls over the crowd. Scents of popcorn and sugary treats waft from the concessions, and my belly grumbles, loud and obnoxious.

"Maybe you should stop for snacks before you climb to your seat," the Nymph suggests with a provocative giggle that softens the insult. Something tells me she takes little in life all that seriously, and I envy her for that.

"I skipped dinner. Excitement," I lie. Lack of cash is more like it.

"Don't pass out from hunger on us. The seven Houses guarantee safety here to our human visitors. You already look damaged enough." She glances at the scrapes on my legs and arms.

Oops, maybe my shorts and tank top show too much bruised skin, but it's roasting outside. Swamp and summer mean sweat. Being klutzy and a professional cleaner mean a rainbow of nicks and bangs color my skin. "It's nothing."

"Uh huh." Obviously not believing me, she points toward the highest seats to our right. "You're up there at the top, halfway in. Grab something to eat, don't fall out on your way up, and enjoy the show. Word of advice: you can be *anything* in Syn City so decide what it is you really want or maybe *who* you will become while you're here. See you around, Dottie doll." With the goodbye, she spins, beautiful blue hair waving around her as if submerged in a storybook drawing, and leaves me by myself in this strange, supernatural city.

Doing the math, if I splurge on popcorn and a soda, I'll need to take the latest bus home. My stomach growls again as if deciding for me. I buy both, knowing I'll regret the wait later at the bus stop long after the crowds have gone home. Memories of that night waiting for Chase to show haunt me again, and I stomp up the stairs, leaving the ugly past behind one sticky step at a time.

"The seven Houses welcome you as our guests," the announcer booms. "You know the history, but we're here to remind you."

Beams of red illuminate the dark ceiling. Acrobats drop from the rafters on invisible strings with their glittery hoops and fluttering ribbons. They pause, hanging in suspended stillness and waiting for the story to continue as if actors in an aerial play.

The announcer raises her microphone, demanding the audience's full attention again. "Decades ago, the Witching Wars pitted neighbor against neighbor in the attempted genocide of those deemed *different*. The violence first erupted in that now great witch sanctuary, the City of Angels."

Women with elaborate black and silver wings dive fast and low from the ceiling. My breath catches, and my still starving belly swoops and slides into snarled knots, suddenly silent. Gasps and whispers come from below. *The Furies.* Connie had told me the rumors that some of them had real wings, but I'd thought it gossip spun to sell tickets. Seeing them fly in person? *Incredible.*

The announcer glances upward, cocking her hip to one side as if annoyed that the women above stole her spotlight. "The humans burned witches and attempted to wipe out the supernaturals. For years, the two sides clashed in epic, awful battles."

Harlequin-masked dancers drop from the shadows, spreading ribbons that unfurl in red, yellow, and orange like flames. The Mad Maes, they had to be. If the silly masks weren't proof enough, those toy guns shooting "pow" signs would be. Their maniacal laughter sends shivers racing over my skin. Legends say those women could drive anyone insane. Of course, the tabloid Connie reads could've been lying, but who would want to test the theory? Not me. That's for sure. I have enough problems without pissing off some booze god's psycho daughters.

"Death reigned." This time the announcer pauses for undead beauties rising from the floor inside the pit. My heart *bump-da-dumps* faster in my chest, fear wrapping around the poor battered thing and squeezing. I walk into hazmat situations nightly with gross and disturbing discoveries, but the Styx weave dread through the room like a coven's super spell. I'd read descriptions of the women who wore faceless masks and were rumored to come from their namesake's river, but I hadn't believed the hype. Now I do.

The Rink's audience goes deathly silent, no pun intended. No one dares speak or whisper or even crunch on snacks. The announcer thumping the mic has me and others jumping in our seats. "When magic returned to the public realm, when humans realized that the powers were real, the old gods woke. They brought forth their mortal deity daughters, made in their divine essence." Running a hand along her curves, she shimmies and shakes to whistles and catcalls. "So now, you luckies have the seven Houses, their Syndicate, and Syn City, where everyone who's anyone comes to parrrrty." Her prolonged rebellious yell breaks the tension that has my shoulders creeping toward my ears.

She only told basic history. Everyone knows it, although seeing the major milestones acted out so vividly makes me wonder if parts hadn't been left out of our human history books. But I don't think on the possibility long with the sudden glitz and glamour exploding throughout The Rink. Fireworks bang, and smoke fills the air, stinging my nose and eyes. Relief comes when waves of spice and sage roll through, clearing the path.

The Furies zoom to the rafters, cloaked in darkness, and a show begins that's part burlesque, part circus, part rock concert—all mixed and spun in a spectacular extravaganza. No holograms here. It's loud and live and all-consuming.

Singers and dancers transform the stage into oceans, clouds, and space in a frenzied, fever dream of flashing lights and thumping music. At some invisible signal, the performers stop, freezing in place. Our applause comes in a deafening cacophony of clapping hands and stomping feet. I'm swept into the excitement with everyone else. For a glorious moment, I'm part of a bigger, better whole.

Muses and Nymphs rush off stage with winks and blown kisses that project a thousand times larger than their already bigger-than-life presences on the holo-screens, covering the house banners with beautiful faces and graceful strength. I spot my earlier usher with her *Naughty* shirt in the prism of mermaid and unicorn-colored hair.

A spotlight pierces the sudden darkness, focusing on the announcer who has changed into a jewel-encrusted bodysuit. Rubies, sapphires, and diamonds wink when she raises the microphone. Real gems? Maybe. It's The Rink. Anything goes.

"Who enjoyed the pre-show?" she asks, pausing for us to lose our collective minds. "Ready for the real show?" Another pause, another surge of applause. "We have a roller derby bout—that's a game or match for our first-time visitors—for you tonight between last year's champions, the Huntresses, and their closest contender, the Furies." Cheers for both houses go up from the crowd. "You may have heard the rumor that the best player for the Furies has retired from the league?" She drawls out the last with fake sympathy, putting her manicured hand over her glittering chest. "It's true."

A collective groan comes from my right along with heckles from lower down the stands.

Like a giant middle finger to the announcer, or maybe the crowd, the Furies zip onto the rink, speeding along the flat track on tricked-out roller skates. With names like Slaya and Killa, the mortal daughters of vengeance deities dominate through punk rock badassery.

The holo-screens pick up tiny details of their uniforms that I otherwise couldn't see from so far away—fishnet tights, skull-printed laces, and wings on the backs of their jerseys. The Huntresses swarm the rink, but I can't take my eyes off the Furies. Their *look-at-us* ferocity doesn't have the same brutality as the Gorgons or the creep factor of the Styx, but it's amazing. So amazing that I feel bad for them when they lose, and I stay until the last Fury rolls off the rink.

I linger in the stands as long as I dare. Floodlights blare like sunlight blazing on the track, exposing some of its secrets. I can make out trap door seams along with a massive sunken section of the pit floor that must raise and lower, a giant platform to cast the illusion of performers appearing out of thin air.

At the bar, a grey-haired man scrubs and scours to loud rock music. I haven't cleaned restaurants and bars in years, other than crime scene cleanups. My gigs come from human law agencies or from the marshals who serve the shifters. Maybe Syn City doesn't have to sanitize as much since the belief you could catch lycanthropy from drinking after a shifter seems to be a thing of the past except in my puny hometown of Petunia. There's no sign of the handsome hottie who'd made me remember Chase.

My high school dream guy, Chase had gorgeous green eyes that seemed to take in everything except my galaxy-sized crush on him. Tall with broad shoulders and lean muscles, he'd been as coordinated as I am clumsy. The guy could literally drop off a ladder from defacing homecoming banners and land on his feet. I'd trip just looking at the same ladder. The cheerleaders had made fun of me for wearing hand-me-down threads, and Chase had wanted revenge on my behalf. It seems so petty now, but then? His standing up for me had meant everything. Until he actually stood me up.

Ugh, I shove aside the memory again. I haven't thought of him so much in years. Okay, okay, so I worried about what'd happened to him since his whole family had disappeared with him, and I wondered how things might've played out if that night had gone differently. Would I still be in Petunia, the small town full of big mouths? Would I be single? Would he mind the lingering scent of ammonia in my hair or the clunky, steel-toed boots required for my job? But his green eyes and lazy smile only came to mind once a day now instead of once an hour.

A man slams into me, or maybe I slam into him. The quick contact knocks me back to reality. "Oof." My breath rushes out, and I trip over my heavy boots, dreading the drop to the concrete floor.

He grabs for me, losing his grip on a big cardboard box that sends glittering balls bouncing in all directions with a perky *ping-ping-ping*. "Are you okay?"

I did that. My daydreaming about stuff best forgotten did that. "I am sooo sorry." Scrambling to my knees, I chase one ball, then another as the first slips from my fingers. "I should've been paying more attention to where I was going."

"No worries as long as you're all right." He crouches next to me, a skinny, baby-faced guy in his thirties in a long-sleeved shirt with *The Rink* printed across the front. "I didn't realize any guests were around, or I would've ducked through an inner corridor." He joins me in corralling the runaway balls.

The casual way he mentions my loitering has me cringing. "I'm on my way out to catch the late bus."

What I said has him snapping his head up, his gaze meeting mine. "Alone? Everyone has either caught the ferry or headed to the pleasure district. The bus stop will be deserted."

Anxiety crawls up my spine, but I push it away. Or I do a right fine job of ignoring it, at least. I'm too poor to afford worrying about stuff I can't change. "I'll be okay."

He looks unsure, then nods in a bobblehead bounce that reminds me of a bumbling imitation of the glitter balls around us. "Overthinking things is part of my job."

I catch myself grinning. It's nice to hear someone else second-guesses everything. "How so?"

"I'm the props manager here."

"For that pre-show?" Excitement bubbles through me like fizzy soap suds. "The flying Furies, the streamers and swords for the Mad Maes, the dancers and everything else? So amazing."

"Thanks. I do my best. Can you imagine if I misplaced a Styx's ceremonial cape or swapped out a Muse's microphone for a plain one without the sparkles?" He chuckles as if either might be a fate worse than death. "You human?"

"Yeah, is it so obvious?"

"Humans keep Syn City going. If visitors like you didn't bring in the money, the Houses couldn't afford the many useless toys I keep track of, such as hundreds of bouncing balls to amuse the Mad Maes." He stands at the same time I do, brushing his fingers against mine when he takes the last glittery ball from me. His touch is shy and sweet in an old-fashioned kind of way with no hint of a spark.

I'm only attracted to blond-haired, green-eyed bad boys. Maybe it's a chronic affliction with a magical cure.

I clear my throat. "I'm afraid I don't bring in much cash for new toys, or I wouldn't be taking the late bus. I've always heard Syn City was completely safe, but I'll admit you've freaked me out a bit about the abandoned bus stop."

"No, no, the town's safe. Sorry about that. Want me to walk you out now that I've spooked you? I need to finish up here, but I should be done in time. Or I could ask security if you don't mind shifters."

Something about the last weirds me out. I've been cleaning up supernatural messes for years. Walking to a bus stop should be no big deal, and frankly, this guy looks no stronger than me. His arms and legs could double as twigs. In fact, I'm probably tougher after years of putting up with bullies and shoveling toxic dumps in Petunia. "I'll be fine, but thanks for the offer."

"No worries. Maybe see you around again?"

"Hopefully." My empty bank account disagrees.

"My name's Marty. Ask for me so I can get you a ticket discount."

"I'm Dottie, and thanks." What a nice guy.

"Least I can do to make up for running over you. Hope to see you again soon." He struggles to lift the box as though it weighs a million pounds and staggers away under the load. I'm glad I refused his gallant offer to walk me to the bus stop. The gear I heft on my cleaning jobs would outweigh his jumbo collection of bouncy glitter balls a hundred times over.

Sticky heat smacks me in the face as I step out of The Rink, clinging to my skin as though I'd somehow dared to betray the weather spirits by hiding in an air-conditioned oasis. Sweat droplets roll down my back, and my hair sticks to my cheeks. Summer nights don't get much cooler than the days here.

Along the path to the bus stop, vines and moss blanket the trees and bushes. The smell of swamp stench comes at me in violent waves as though the marsh might be reclaiming this city one inch at a time. Crickets and bullfrogs serenade me with their chirps and bellows. Water sloshes from not so far away. Thank the tech gods for the flickering lights that hover above, casting a blue and gold glow between the swallowing shadows.

I'm alone out here, far from the pounding music of the pleasure district's clubs and bars and whatever else. A tingling sensation wriggles down my neck, more than just another sweat bead spilling. The prickling has shivers dancing along my arms, more menacing than the Mad Maes. My heart kicks into overdrive, bumping harder than those distant beats.

Resisting the urge to run, I sneak a glance over my shoulder. Nothing there. *Stupid.* Except a rustling comes from somewhere nearby that's louder than the pounding pulse in my ears. Terror steals my breath, and I tear down the path, gravel sliding beneath my heavy boots. Years of running from bullies means I'm fast.

The sweat slicking my skin turns clammy. Fear flows like iced tea through my veins, and my throat closes thicker than molasses in January. I slip and stagger and screech louder than a barn owl.

Syn City's a safe zone, protected by the Syndicate. The thinking part of my brain fires the message on repeat, but the primal part—the instinct that knows monsters under the bed can be real—screams to run *faster*.

A crunch of gravel behind me has me spinning, fists clenched and feet ready to deliver an ass kicking in these boots. Not that I know how, but I'll face down whoever or whatever is coming for me. Momma might've raised me to smile through whatever nasty comes my way, but she didn't raise a coward. With a fighting yell, I glimpse a figure taller than me, a hooded sweatshirt, and a massive hammer coming at my head.

I hear the whir of speeding air.

Then...nothing.

* * *

Don't stop now. Keep reading with your copy of HOW TO DATE A FURY

Don't miss the next book, Spider's Pride, coming soon, and find more from Paige E. Ewing at www.paigeewing.com

Until then, discover HOW TO DATE A FURY by City Owl Author, Luna Joya!

Who knew dying would be the easy part of my day?

It all started the night Chase, my mountain lion shifter ex, reappeared. We'd had a whole good girl/bad boy romance going until he abandoned me a decade ago. I'd gone to Syn City for a little fun before being trapped in my hometown forever.

Then I was murdered by a maniac and my night really fell apart.

But somehow, Chase managed to strike a deal on a blood oath and bring me back as a Fury. He wants a second chance at romance, claiming we're fated mates.

Now, I have to deal with the guy I thought I'd never see again, find and punish my murderer, and participate in a giant supernatural roller derby (long story)—all while trying to earn my wings.

And if I fail? I'll end up dead. Again...only this time, it'll be permanent.

All I can say is that it's a good thing hell hath no fury like, well, an actual Fury.

Please sign up for the City Owl Press newsletter for chances to win special subscriber-only contests and giveaways as well as receiving information on upcoming releases and special excerpts.

All reviews are **welcome** and **appreciated**. Please consider leaving one on your favorite social media and book buying sites.

For books in the world of romance and speculative fiction that embody Innovation, Creativity, and Affordability, check out City Owl Press at www.cityowlpress.com.

ACKNOWLEDGMENTS

A big thank you to Michelle Hauck of Storm Literary Agency who believed in my work. And another big thanks to Lisa Green, my City Owl editor, who has never failed to find ways to make manuscripts I thought were done into even better books.

ABOUT THE AUTHOR

PAIGE E. EWING writes about superheroes and sentient cities, were-spiders and gun-loving fairies, werewolves and fighter pilots. For her day job, she gives speeches and writes about big data analysis and data architectures, a subject which also doubles as a sleep aid for many.

For fun, she shoots arrows, and throws axes. She lives in the middle of nowhere, Texas, and will show you far too many pictures of her garden if you let her. She once invented a way to grow food on Mars that NASA liked, and has a cute trophy to show for it. Her dogs and horses are unimpressed.

www.paigeewing.com

✕ x.com/PaigeEwing
 mastodon.social/@PaigeEwing
 instagram.com/paigeewing_author

ABOUT THE PUBLISHER

City Owl Press is a cutting edge indie publishing company, bringing the world of romance and speculative fiction to discerning readers.

Escape Your World. Get Lost in Ours!

www.cityowlpress.com